P9-ASJ-255

"A MYSTERY LOVER'S FEAST."
—Los Angeles Herald Examiner

"The writing is realistic in the best sense of the word. There are no artificial heroics, forced lines of dialogue or false moves."

—New York Times

"An extremely well-told tale of cross, double-cross, and murder most foul."

—Associated Press

"Block is an accomplished storyteller and Matt Scudder is a fine example of hero as human being."
—Publishers Weekly

"Lawrence Block's latest Matt Scudder mystery runs fast and furious . . . The ex-detective is at his bar-hopping best."

—UPI

—MORE—

"A CHILLING FINISH."
—*Washington Post*

"Block captures the grittiness of New York's mean streets."

—*Providence Sunday Journal*

"One of the best of the tough private eyes in fiction."

—*Savannah News Press*

"Snappily written, with Block's great styling . . . detective work at its best, in the hard-boiled manner of all the greats."

—*Ocala Star-Banner*

"Block's characters, the bar-flies and the cops are as much flesh and blood as any mystery writer's working today."

—*Greensboro News and Record*

"Its dialogue is sharp and its characters interesting. The plot is well-developed and the story moves fast. And oh yes, the mystery is intriguing. What more can you say of a book? Reading this book is as satisfying as finding that last piece of a good jigsaw."

—*Winston-Salem Journal*

LAWRENCE BLOCK

WHEN THE SACRED GINMILL CLOSES

JOVE BOOKS, NEW YORK

The author gratefully acknowledges permission to include excerpted lyrics from the song "Last Call," by Dave Van Ronk. Copyright © 1973 by Folklore Music ASCAP. Used by permission.

This Jove book contains the complete
text of the original hardcover edition.
It has been completely reset in a typeface
designed for easy reading and was printed
from new film.

WHEN THE SACRED GINMILL CLOSES

A Jove Book / published by arrangement with
Arbor House Publishing Company

PRINTING HISTORY
Arbor House edition / May 1986
Charter edition / October 1987
Jove edition / February 1990

Jove Books are published by The Berkley Publishing Group,
200 Madison Avenue, New York, New York 10016.
The name "JOVE" and the "J" logo
are trademarks belonging to Jove Publications, Inc.

For Kenneth Reichel

And so we've had another night
Of poetry and poses
And each man knows he'll be alone
When the sacred ginmill closes

—DAVE VAN RONK

1

The windows at Morrissey's were painted black. The blast was loud enough and close enough to rattle them. It chopped off conversation in midsyllable, froze a waiter in midstride, making of him a statue with a tray of drinks on his shoulder and one foot in the air. The great round noise died out like dust settling, and for a long moment afterward the room remained hushed, as if with respect.

Someone said, "Jesus Christ," and a lot of people let out the breath they'd been holding. At our table, Bobby Ruslander reached for a cigarette and said, "Sounded like a bomb."

Skip Devoe said, "Cherry bomb."

"Is that all?"

"It's enough," Skip said. "Cherry bomb's major ordnance. Same charge had a metal casing instead of a paper wrapper, you'd have a weapon instead of a toy. You light one of those little mothers and forget to let go of it, you're gonna have to learn to do a lot of basic things left-handed."

"Sounded like more than a firecracker," Bobby insisted. "Like dynamite or a grenade or something. Sounded like fucking World War Three, if you want to know."

1

"Get the actor," Skip said affectionately. "Don't you love this guy? Fighting it out in the trenches, storming the windswept hills, slogging through the mud. Bobby Ruslander, battle-scarred veteran of a thousand campaigns."

"You mean *bottle*-scarred," somebody said.

"Fucking actor," Skip said, reaching to rumple Bobby's hair. " 'Hark I hear the cannon's roar.' You know that joke?"

"I told *you* the joke."

" 'Hark I hear the cannon's roar.' When'd you ever hear a shot fired in anger? Last time they had a war," he said, "Bobby brought a note from his shrink. 'Dear Uncle Sam, Please excuse Bobby's absence, bullets make him crazy.' "

"My old man's idea," Bobby said.

"But you tried to talk him out of it. 'Gimmie a gun,' you said. 'I wanna serve my country.' "

Bobby laughed. He had one arm around his girl and picked up his drink with his free hand. He said, "All I said was it sounded like dynamite to me."

Skip shook his head. "Dynamite's different. They're all different, different kinds of a bang. Dynamite's like one loud note, and a flatter sound than a cherry bomb. They all make a different sound. Grenade's completely different, it's like a chord."

"The lost chord," somebody said, and somebody else said, "Listen to this, it's poetry."

"I was going to call my joint Horseshoes & Hand Grenades," Skip said. "You know what they say, coming close don't count outside of horseshoes and hand grenades."

"It's a good name," Billie Keegan said.

"My partner hated it," Skip said. "Fucking Kasabian, he said it didn't sound like a saloon, sounded like some kind of candy-ass boutique, some store in SoHo sells toys for private-school kids. I don't know, though. Horseshoes & Hand Grenades, I still like the sound of it."

"Horseshit and Hand Jobs," somebody said.

"Maybe Kasabian was right, if that's what everybody woulda wound up calling it." To Bobby he said, "You want to talk about the different sounds they make, you should hear a mortar. Someday get Kasabian to tell you about the mortar. It's a hell of a story."

"I'll do that."

"Horseshoes & Hand Grenades," Skip said. "That's what we shoulda called the joint."

Instead he and his partner had called their place Miss Kitty's. Most people assumed a reference to "Gunsmoke," but their inspiration had been a whorehouse in Saigon. I did most of my own drinking at Jimmy Armstrong's, on Ninth Avenue between Fifty-seventh and Fifty-eighth. Miss Kitty's was on Ninth just below Fifty-sixth, and it was a little larger and more boisterous than I liked. I stayed away from it on the weekends, but late on a weekday night when the crowd thinned down and the noise level dropped, it wasn't a bad place to be.

I'd been in there earlier that night. I had gone first to Armstrong's, and around two-thirty there were only four of us left—Billie Keegan behind the bar and I in front of it and a couple of nurses who were pretty far gone on Black Russians. Billie locked up and the nurses staggered off into the night and the two of us went down to Miss Kitty's, and a little before four Skip closed up, too, and a handful of us went on down to Morrissey's.

Morrissey's wouldn't close until nine or ten in the morning. The legal closing hour for bars in the city of New York is 4:00 A.M., an hour earlier on Saturday nights, but Morrissey's was an illegal establishment and was thus not bound by regulations of that sort. It was one flight up from street level in one of a block of four-story brick houses on Fifty-first Street between Eleventh and Twelfth Avenues. About a third of the houses on the block were abandoned, their windows boarded up or broken, some of their entrances closed off with concrete block.

The Morrissey brothers owned their building. It couldn't have cost them much. They lived in the upper two stories, let out the ground floor to an Irish amateur theater group, and sold beer and whiskey after hours on the second floor. They had removed all of the interior walls on the second floor to create a large open space. They'd stripped one wall to the brick, scraped and sanded and urethaned the wide pine floors, installed some soft lighting and decorated the walls with some framed Aer Lingus posters and a copy of Pearse's 1916 proclamation of the Irish Republic ("Irishmen and Irishwomen, in the name of God and of the dead generations . . ."). There was a small service bar along one wall, and there were twenty or thirty square tables with butcher-block tops.

We sat at two tables pushed together. Skip Devoe was there, and Billie Keegan, the night bartender at Armstrong's. And Bobby Ruslander, and Bobby's girl for the evening, a sleepy-eyed redhead named Helen. And a fellow named Eddie Grillo who tended bar at an Italian restaurant in the West Forties, and another fellow named Vince who was a sound technician or something like that at CBS Television.

I was drinking bourbon, and it must have been either Jack Daniel's or Early Times, as those were the only brands the Morrisseys stocked. They also carried three or four scotches, Canadian Club, and one brand each of gin and vodka. Two beers, Bud and Heineken. A Cognac and a couple of odd cordials. Kahlúa, I suppose, because a lot of people were drinking Black Russians that year. Three brands of Irish whiskey, Bushmill's and Jameson and one called Power's, which nobody ever seemed to order but to which the Morrissey brothers were partial. You'd have thought they'd carry Irish beer, Guinness at least, but Tim

Pat Morrissey had told me once that he didn't fancy the bottled Guinness, that it was awful stuff, that he only liked the draft stout and only on the other side of the Atlantic.

They were big men, the Morrisseys, with broad high foreheads and full rust-colored beards. They wore black trousers and highly polished black brogans and white shirts with the sleeves rolled to the elbow, and they wore white butcher's aprons that covered them to their knees. The waiter, a slim, clean-shaven youth, wore the same outfit, but on him it looked like a costume. I think he may have been a cousin. I think he'd have had to have been some sort of blood kin to work there.

They were open seven days a week, from around 2:00 A.M. to nine or ten. They charged three dollars for a drink, which was higher than the bars but reasonable compared to most after-hour joints, and they poured a good drink. Beer was two dollars. They would mix most of the common drinks, but it was no place to order a pousse-café.

I don't think the police ever gave the Morrisseys a hard time. While there was no neon sign out front, the place wasn't the best-kept secret in the neighborhood. The cops knew it was there, and that particular evening I noticed a couple of patrolmen from Midtown North and a detective I'd known years back in Brooklyn. There were two black men in the room and I recognized both of them; one I'd seen at ringside at a lot of fights, while his companion was a state sentator. I'm sure the Morrissey brothers paid money to stay open, but they had some strong connections beyond the money they paid, ties to the local political clubhouse.

They didn't water the booze and they poured a good drink. Wasn't that as much of a character reference as any man needed?

Outside, another cherry bomb exploded. It was farther off, a block or two away, and it didn't slam the door shut on any conversations. At our table, the CBS guy complained that they were rushing the season. He said, "The Fourth isn't until Friday, right? Today's what, the first?"

"It's been the second for the past two hours."

"So that's still two days. What's the hurry?"

"They get these fucking fireworks and they get the itch," Bobby Ruslander said. "You know who's the worst? The fucking chinks. For a while there I was seein' this girl, she lived down near Chinatown. You'd get Roman candles in the middle of the night, you'd get cherry bombs, anything. Not just July, any time of the year. Comes to firecrackers, they're all little kids down there."

"My partner wanted to call the joint Little Saigon," Skip said. "I told him, John, for Christ's sake, people're gonna think it's a Chinese restaurant, you're gonna get family groups from Rego Park ordering moo goo gai pan and two from Column B. He said what the hell's Chinese about Saigon? I told him, I said, John, you know that and I know that, but when it comes to the people from Rego Park, John, to them a slope is a slope and it all adds up to moo goo gai pan."

Billie said, "What about the people in Park Slope?"

"What about the people in Park Slope?" Skip frowned, thinking it over. "The people in Park Slope," he said. "*Fuck* the people in Park Slope."

Bobby Ruslander's girl Helen said, very seriously, that she had an aunt in Park Slope. Skip looked at her. I picked up my glass. It was empty, and I looked around for the beardless waiter or one of the brothers.

So I was looking at the door when it flew open. The brother who kept the door downstairs stumbled through it and careened into a table. Drinks spilled and a chair tipped over.

Two men burst into the room behind him. One was about five-nine, the other a couple inches shorter. Both were thin. Both wore blue jeans and tennis sneakers. The taller one had on a baseball jacket, the shorter one a royal-blue nylon windbreaker. Both had billed baseball caps on their heads and blood-red kerchiefs knotted around their faces, forming triangular wedges that hid their mouths and cheeks.

Each had a gun in his hand. One had a snub-nosed revolver, the other a long-barreled automatic. The one with the automatic raised it and fired two shots into the stamped-tin ceiling. It didn't sound like a cherry bomb or a hand grenade, either.

They got in and out in a hurry. One went behind the bar and emerged with the Garcia y Vega cigar box where Tim Pat kept the night's receipts. There was a glass jar on top of the bar with a hand-lettered sign soliciting contributions for the families of IRA men imprisoned in the North of Ireland, and he scooped the bills out of it, leaving the silver.

While he was doing this, the taller man held a gun on the Morrisseys and had them turn out their pockets. He took the cash from their wallets and a roll of bills from Tim Pat. The shorter man set down the cigar box for a moment and went to the back of the room, removing a framed Aer Lingus poster of the Cliffs of Moher from the wall to expose a locked cupboard. He shot the lock off and withdrew a metal strongbox, tucked it unopened under his arm, went back to pick up the cigar box again, and ducked out the door and raced down the stairs.

His partner continued to hold the Morrisseys at gunpoint until he'd left the building. He had the gun centered at Tim Pat's chest, and for a moment I thought he was going to shoot. His gun was the long-barreled automatic, he'd been the one who put two bullets in the tin ceiling, and if he shot Tim Pat, he seemed unlikely to miss.

There was nothing I could do about it.

Then the moment passed. The gunman breathed out through his mouth, the red kerchief billowing with his breath. He backed to the door and out, fled down the stairs.

No one moved.

Then Tim Pat held a brief whispered conference with one of his brothers, the one who'd been keeping the door downstairs. After a moment the brother nodded and walked to the gaping cupboard at the back of the room. He closed it and hung the Cliffs of Moher poster where it had been.

Tim Pat spoke to his other brother, then cleared his throat. "Gentlemen," he said, and smoothed his beard with his big right hand. "Gentlemen, if I may take a moment to explain the performance ye just witnessed. Two good friends of ours came in to ask for the loan of a couple of dollars, which we lent them with pleasure. None of us recognized them or took note of their appearance, and I'm sure no one in this room would know them should we by God's grace meet up with them again." His fingertips dabbed at his broad forehead, moved again to groom his beard. "Gentlemen," he said, "ye'd honor me and my brothers by havin' the next drink with us."

And the Morrisseys bought a round for the house. Bourbon for me. Jameson for Billie Keegan, scotch for Skip, brandy for Bobby, and a scotch sour for his date. A beer for the guy from CBS, a brandy for Eddie the bartender. Drinks all around—for the cops, for the black politicians, for a roomful of waiters and bartenders and night people. Nobody got up and left, not with the house buying a round, not with a couple of guys out there with masks and guns.

The clean-shaven cousin and two of the brothers served the drinks. Tim Pat stood at the side with his arms folded on his white apron and his face expressionless. After everyone had been served, one of his brothers whispered something to Tim Pat and showed him the glass jar, empty except for a handful of coins. Tim Pat's face darkened.

"Gentlemen," he said, and the room quieted down. "Gentlemen, in the moment of confusion there was money taken as was contributed to Norad, money for the relief of the misfortunate wives and children of political prisoners in the North. Our loss is our own, myself and my brothers, and we'll speak no more of it, but them in the North with no money for food . . ." He stopped for breath, continued in a lower voice. "We'll let the jar pass amongst ye," he said, "and if some of ye should care to contribute, the blessings of God on ye."

I probably stayed another half-hour, not much more than that. I drank the drink Tim Pat bought and one more besides, and that was enough. Billie and Skip left when I did. Bobby and his girl were going to stick around for a while, Vince had already left, and Eddie had joined another table and was trying to make points with a tall girl who waitressed at O'Neal's.

The sky was light, the streets empty still, silent with early dawn. Skip said, "Well, Norad made a couple of bucks, anyway. There couldn't have been a whole lot Frank and Jesse took out of the jar, and the crowd coughed up a fair amount to fill it up again."

"Frank and Jesse?"

"Well, those red hankies, for Christ's sake. You know, Frank and Jesse James. But that was ones and fives they took out of the jar, and it was all tens and twenties got put back into it, so the poor wives and wee childer in the North came out all right."

Billie said, "What do you figure the Morrisseys lost?"

"Jesus, I don't know. That strongbox could have been full of insurance policies and pictures of their sainted mither, but that would be a surprise all around, wouldn't it? I bet they walked with enough to send a lot of guns to the bold lads in Derry and Belfast."

"You think the robbers were IRA?"

"The hell," he said. He threw his cigarette into the gutter. "I think the Morrisseys are. I think that's where their money goes. I figure—"

"Hey, guys! Wait up, huh?"

We turned. A man named Tommy Tillary was hailing us from the stoop of the Morrisseys' house. He was a heavyset fellow, full in the cheeks and jowls, big in the chest, big in the belly, too. He was wearing a summer-weight burgundy blazer and a pair of white pants. He was wearing a tie, too. He almost always wore a tie.

The woman with him was short and slender, with light brown hair that showed red highlights. She was wearing tight faded jeans and a pink button-down shirt with the sleeves rolled up. She looked very tired, and a little drunk.

He said, "You guys know Carolyn? Course you do." We all said hello to her. He said, "I got a car parked around the corner, plenty of room for everybody. Drop you guys off."

"It's a nice morning," Billie said. "I think I'd as soon walk, Tommy."

"Oh, yeah?"

Skip and I said the same. "Walk off some of the booze," Skip said. "Wind down, get ready for bed."

"You sure? No trouble to run you home." We were sure. "Well, you mind walking as far as the car with us? That little demonstration back there, makes a person nervous."

"Sure thing, Tom."

"Nice morning, huh? Be a hot one today but it's beautiful right now. I swear I thought he was gonna shoot whatsisname, Tim Pat. You see the look on his face at the end there?"

"There was a moment," Billie said, "it could have gone either way."

"I was thinking, there's gonna be shooting, back and forth, I'm looking to see which table to dive under. Fucking little tables, there's not a lot of cover, you know?"

"Not too much."

"And I'm a big target, right? What are you smoking, Skip, Camels? Lemme try one of those if you don't mind. I smoke these filters and this time of night they got no taste left to them. Thanks. Was I imagining things or was there a couple of cops in the room?"

"There were a few, anyway."

"They got to carry their guns on or off duty, isn't that right?"

He'd asked the question of me, and I agreed that there was a regulation to that effect.

"You'd think one of 'em would have tried something."

"You mean draw down on the holdup men?"

"Something."

"It's a good way to get people killed," I said. "Throwing lead around a crowded room like that."

"I guess there'd be a danger of ricochets."

"Why'd you say that?"

He looked at me, surprised by the snap in my tone. "Why, the brick walls, I guess," he said. "Even shooting into the tin ceiling the way he did, a bullet could glance off, do some damage. Couldn't it?"

"I guess," I said. A cab cruised by, its off-duty light lit, a passenger sharing the front seat with the driver. I said. "On or off duty, a cop wouldn't start anything in a situation like that unless someone else had already started shooting. There were a couple of bulls in the room tonight who probably had their hands on their guns toward the end there. If that fellow'd shot Tim Pat, he'd probably have been dodging bullets on the way out the door. *If* anybody had a clear shot at him."

"And if they were sober enough to see straight," Skip put in.

"Makes sense," Tommy said. "Matt, didn't you break up a bar holdup a couple of years ago? Somebody was saying something about it."

"That was a little different," I said. "They'd already shot the bartender dead before I made a move. And I didn't spray bullets around inside, I went out into the street after them."

And I thought about that, and missed the next few sentences of the conversation. When I came back into focus Tommy was saying he'd expected to be held up.

"Lot of people in that room tonight," he said. "Night workers, people closed up their places and carrying cash on 'em. You'd think they would have passed the hat, wouldn't you?"

"I guess they were in a hurry."

"I only got a few hundred on me, but I'd rather keep it than give it to a guy with a hanky on his face. You feel relieved not to get robbed, you're real generous when they pass the jug for whatchacallit, Norad? I gave twenty bucks to the widows and orphans, didn't think twice."

"It's all staged," Billie Keegan suggested. "The guys with the handkerchiefs are friends of the family, they put on this little act every couple of weeks to boost the Norad take."

"Jesus," Tommy said, laughing at the idea. "Be something, wouldn't it? There's my car, the Riv. Big boat'll carry everybody easy, you want to change your mind and let me run you on home."

We all stayed with our decision to walk. His car was a maroon Buick Riviera with a white leather interior. He let Carolyn in, then walked around the car and unlocked his door, making a face at her failure to lean across the seat and unlock the door for him.

After they drove off, Billie said, "They were at Armstrong's until one, one-thirty. I didn't expect to see 'em again tonight. I hope he's not driving back to Brooklyn tonight."

"Is that where they live?"

"Where *he* lives," he told Skip. "She's here in the neighborhood. He's a married guy. Doesn't he wear a ring?"

"I never noticed."

"Caro-lyn from the Caro-line," Billie said. "That's how

he introduces her. She was sure shitfaced tonight, wasn't she? When he left earlier I thought for sure he was takin' her home—and come to think of it I guess he was. She was wearin' a dress earlier tonight, wasn't she, Matt?"

"I don't remember."

"I could swear she was. Office clothes, anyway, not jeans and a Brooks shirt like she had on now. Took her home, gave her a bounce, then they got thirsty and by that time the stores were closed, so off we go to the neighborhood after-hours, T. P. Morrissey, Prop. What do you think, Matt? Have I got the makings of a detective?"

"You're doing fine."

"He put on the same clothes but she changed. Now the question is will he go home to the wife or sleep over at Carolyn's and show up at the office tomorrow in the same outfit. The only problem is, who gives a shit?"

"I was just going to ask that," Skip said.

"Yeah. One thing *he* asked, I'll ask it myself. Why didn't they stick up the customers tonight? There must have been a lot of guys carryin' a few hundred each and a couple with more than that."

"Not worth it."

"That's a few grand we're talking about."

"I know," Skip said. "It's also another twenty minutes if you're gonna do it right, and that's in a room full of drunks with God knows how many of them carrying guns. I bet there were fifteen guns in that room."

"Are you serious?"

"I'm not only serious, I bet I'm guessing low. For openers you got three or four cops. You got Eddie Grillo, right at our table."

"Eddie carries a piece?"

"Eddie runs around with some pretty heavy guys, not even talking about who owns the joint where he works. There was a guy named Chuck, I don't really know him, works at Polly's Cage—"

"I know who you mean. He walks around with a gun on him?"

"Either that or he walks around with a permanent hardon and he's built funny. Believe me, there's a whole lot of guys walk around packing iron. You tell a whole roomful to reach for their wallets, some of them'll reach for their guns instead. Meanwhile they're in and out in what, five minutes tops? I don't think it was five minutes from the door flying open and the bullets in the ceiling until they're out the door and Tim Pat's standing there with his arms crossed and a scowl on his face."

"That's a point."

"And whatever they'd of got from people's wallets, that's small change."

"You figure the box was that heavy? What do you figure it held?"

Skip shrugged. "Twenty grand."

"Seriously?"

"Twenty grand, fifty grand, pick a number."

"IRA money, you were saying earlier."

"Well, what else do you figure they spend it on, Bill? I don't know what they take in but they do a nice business seven days a week and where's the overhead? They probably got the building for back taxes, and they live in half of it, so they got no rent to pay and no real payroll to come up with. I'm sure they don't report any income or pay any taxes, unless they pretend that playhouse on the ground floor shows a profit and pay a token tax on that. They have to be dragging ten or twenty grand a week out of that place and what do you think they spend it on?"

"They have to pay off to stay open," I put in.

"Payoffs and political contributions, of course, but not ten or twenty K a week's worth. And they don't drive big cars, and they never go out and spend a dollar in somebody else's joint. I don't see Tim Pat buying emeralds for some sweet young thing, or his brothers putting grams of coke up their Irish noses."

"Up your Irish nose," Billie Keegan said.

"I liked Tim Pat's little speech, and then buying a round. Far as I know, that's the first time the Morrisseys ever set 'em up for the house."

"Fucking Irish," Billie said.

"Jesus, Keegan, you're drunk again."

"Praise be to God, you're right."

"What do you think, Matt? Did Tim Pat recognize Frank and Jesse?"

I thought about it. "I don't know. What he was saying added up to 'Keep out of this and we'll settle it ourselves.' Maybe it was political."

"Fucking-A right," Billie said. "The Reform Democrats were behind it."

"Maybe Protestants," Skip said.

"Funny," Billie said. "They didn't look Protestant."

"Or some other IRA faction. There's different factions, aren't there?"

"Of course you rarely see Protestants with handkerchiefs over their faces," Billie said. "They usually tuck them in the breast pocks, the breast pockets—"

"Jesus, Keegan."

"Fucking Protestants," Billie said.

"Fucking Billie Keegan," Skip said. "Matt, we better walk this asshole home."

"Fucking guns," Billie said, back on that track suddenly. "Go out for a nightcap and you're surrounded by fucking guns. You carry a gun, Matt?"

"Not me, Billie."

"Really?" He put a hand on my shoulder for support. "But you're a cop."

"Used to be."

"Private cop now. Even the rent-a-cop, security guard in

a bookstore, guy tells you to check your briefcase on the way in, he's got a gun."

"They're generally just for show."

"You mean I won't get shot if I walk off with the Modern Library edition of *The Scarlet Letter?* You should of told me before I went and paid for it. You really don't carry a gun?"

"Another illusion shattered," Skip said.

"What about your buddy the actor?" Billie demanded of him. "Is little Bobby a gunslinger?"

"Who, Ruslander?"

"He'd shoot you in the back," Billie said.

"If Ruslander carried a gun," Skip said, "it'd be a stage prop. It'd shoot blanks."

"Shoot you in the back," Billie insisted. "Like whatsis-name, Bobby the Kid."

"You mean Billy the Kid."

"Who are you to tell me what I mean? Does he?"

"Does he what?"

"Pack a piece, for Christ's sake. Isn't that what we've been talking about?"

"Jesus, Keegan, don't ask *me* what we've been talking about."

"You mean you weren't paying attention either? *Jee-*zus."

Billie Keegan lived in a high-rise on Fifty-sixth near Eighth. He straightened up as we approached his building and appeared sober enough when he greeted the doorman. "Matt, Skip," he said. "See you guys."

"Keegan's all right," Skip told me.

"He's a good man."

"Not as drunk as he pretended, either. He was just riding it, enjoying himself."

"Sure."

"We keep a gun behind the bar at Miss Kitty's, you know. We got held up, the place I used to work before John and I opened up together. I was behind the stick in this place on Second Avenue in the Eighties, guy walked in, white guy, stuck a gun in my face and got the money from the register. Held up the customers, too. Only have five, six people in the joint at the time, but he took wallets off of them. I think he took their watches too, if I remember it right. Class operation."

"Sounds it."

"All the time I was being a hero in Nam, fucking Special Forces, I never had to stand and look at the wrong end of a gun. I didn't feel anything while it was going on, but later I felt angry, you know what I mean? I was in a rage. Went out, bought a gun, ever since then it's been with me when I been working. At that joint, and now in Miss Kitty's. I still think we should have called it Horseshoes and Hand Grenades."

"You got a permit for it?"

"The gun?" He shook his head. "It's not registered. You work saloons, you don't have too much trouble knowing where to go to buy a gun. I spent two days asking around and on the third day I was a hundred dollars poorer. We got robbed once since we opened the place. John was working, he left the gun right where it was and handed over whatever was in the till. He didn't rob the customers. John figured he was a junkie, said he didn't even think of the gun until the guy was out the door. Maybe, or maybe he thought of it and decided against it. I probably would have done the same thing, or maybe not. You don't really know until it happens, do you?"

"No."

"You really haven't had a piece since you quit the cops? They say after a guy gets in the habit he feels naked without it."

"Not me. I felt like I laid down a burden."

"Oh, lawdie, I'se gwine lay my burden down. Like you lightened up some, huh?"

"Something like that."

"Yeah. He didn't mean anything, incidentally. Talking about ricochets."

"Huh? Oh, Tommy."

"Tough Tommy Tillary. Something of an asshole, but not a bad guy. Tough Tommy, it's like calling a big guy Tiny. I'm sure he didn't mean anything."

"I'm sure you're' right."

"Tough Tommy. There's something else they call him."

"Telephone Tommy."

"Or Tommy Telephone, right. He sells shit over the phone. I didn't think grown men did that. I thought it was for housewives and they wind up making thirty-five cents an hour."

"I gather it can be lucrative."

"Evidently. You saw the car. We all saw the car. We didn't get to see her open the door for him, but we got to see the car. Matt, you want to come up and have one more before we call it a day? I got scotch and bourbon, I probably got some food in the fridge."

"I think I'll just get on home, Skip. But thanks."

"I don't blame you." He drew on his cigarette. He lived at the Parc Vendome, across the street and a few doors west of my hotel. He threw his cigarette away and we shook hands, and five or six shots sounded a block or so from us.

"Jesus," he said. "Was that gunfire or half a dozen little firecrackers? Could you say for sure?"

"No."

"Neither could I. Probably firecrackers, considering what day it is. Or the Morrisseys caught up with Frank and Jesse, or I don't know what. This is the second, right? July second?"

"I guess so."

"Gonna be some summer," he said.

2

All of this happened a long time ago.

It was the summer of '75, and in a larger context it seems in memory to have been a season in which nothing very important happened. Nixon's resignation had been a year earlier, and the coming year would bring the convention and the campaigns, the Olympics, the Bicentennial.

Meanwhile Ford was in the White House, his presence oddly comforting if not terribly convincing. A fellow named Abe Beame was in Gracie Mansion, although I never had the feeling he really believed he was mayor of New York, any more than Gerry Ford believed he was president of the United States of America.

Somewhere along the way Ford declined to help the city through a financial crisis, and the *News* headline read, *"Ford to City: Drop Dead!"*

I remember the headline but I don't recall whether it ran before, during or after that summer. I read that headline. I rarely missed the *News*, picking up an early edition on my way back to my hotel at night or scanning a later one over breakfast. I read the *Times* now and then as well, if there was a story I was following, and more often than not I'd pick up a *Post* during the afternoon. I never paid much attention to the international news or the political stuff, or anything much aside from sports and local crime, but I was at least peripherally aware of what was going on in the world, and it's funny how utterly it's all vanished.

What do I remember? Well, three months after the stickup at Morrissey's, Cincinnati would take a seven-game Series from the Red Sox. I remember that, and Fisk's home run in game six, and Pete Rose playing throughout as if all of human destiny rode on every pitch. Neither of the New York teams made the playoffs, but beyond that I couldn't tell you how they did, and I know I went to half a dozen games. I took my boys to Shea a couple of times, and I went a few times with friends. The Stadium was being renovated that year and both the Mets and Yanks were at Shea. Billie Keegan and I watched the Yankees play somebody, I remember, and they stopped the game because some idiots were throwing garbage onto the field.

Was Reggie Jackson with the Yankees that year? He was still in Oakland playing for Charlie Finley in '73, I remember the Series, the Mets losing badly. But when did Steinbrenner buy him for the Yankees?

What else? Boxing?

Did Ali fight that summer? I watched the second Norton fight on closed circuit, the one where Ali left the ring with a broken jaw and an unearned decision, but that was at least a year earlier, wasn't it? And then I'd seen Ali up close, ringside at the Garden. Earnie Shavers had fought Jimmy Ellis, knocking him out early in the first round. For God's sake, I remember the punch that took Ellis out, remember the look on his wife's face two rows away from me, but when was that?

Not in '75, I'm sure of that. I must have gone to the fights that summer. I wonder who I watched.

Does it matter? I don't suppose it does. If it did I could go to the library and check the *Times Index,* or just hunt up a *World Almanac* for the year. But I already remember everything I really need to remember.

Skip Devoe and Tommy Tillary. Theirs are the faces I see when I think of the summer of '75. Between them, they were the season.

Were they friends of mine?

They were, but with a qualification. They were saloon friends. I rarely saw them—or anyone else, in those days— other than in a room where strangers gathered to drink liquor. I was still drinking then, of course, and I was at a point where the booze did (or seemed to do) more for me than it did to me.

A couple of years previously, my world had narrowed as if with a will of its own until it encompassed only a few square blocks south and west of Columbus Circle. I had left my marriage after a dozen years and two children, moving from Syosset, which is on Long Island, to my hotel, which was on West Fifty-seventh Street between Eighth and Ninth Avenues. I had at about the same time left the New York Police Department, where I'd put in about as many years with about as much to show for it. I supported myself, and sent checks irregularly to Syosset, by doing things for people. I was not a private detective—private detectives are licensed and fill out reports and file tax returns. So I did favors for people, and they gave me money, and my rent always got paid and there was always money for booze, and intermittently I was able to put a check in the mail for Anita and the boys.

My world, as I said, had shrunk geographically, and within that area it confined itself largely to the room where I slept and the bars where I spent most of my waking hours. There was Morrissey's, but not all that often. I was off to bed more often than not by one or two, sometimes hung on until the bars closed, and only rarely went to an after-hours and made a full night of it.

There was Miss Kitty's, Skip Devoe's place. On the same block as my hotel, there was Polly's Cage, with its red-flocked bordello wallpaper and its crowd of after-work drinkers who thinned out by ten or ten-thirty; and McGovern's, a drab narrow room with unshielded overhead lights and customers who never said a word. I stopped in sometimes for a quick drink on a hard morning, and the bartender's hand shook when he poured it, as often as not.

On the same block there were two French restaurants, one next to the other. One of them, Mont-St.-Michel, was always three-quarters empty. I took women there for dinner a few times over the years, and stopped in alone once in a while for a drink at the bar. The establishment next door had a good reputation and did a better business, but I don't think I ever set foot inside it.

There was a place over on Tenth Avenue called the Slate; they got a lot of cops from Midtown North and John Jay College, and I went there when I was in the mood for that kind of crowd. The steaks were good there, and the surroundings comfortable. There was a Martin's Bar on Broadway and Sixtieth with low-priced drinks and good corned beef and ham on the steam table; they had a big color set over the bar, and it wasn't a bad place to watch a ball game.

There was O'Neal's Baloon across from Lincoln Center—an old law still on the books that year prohibited calling a place a saloon, and they didn't know that when they ordered the sign, so they changed the first letter and said the hell with it. I'd stop in once in a while during the afternoon, but it was too trendy and upbeat at night. There was Antares and Spiro's, a Greek place at the corner of Ninth and Fifty-seventh. Not really my kind of place, a lot of guys with bushy moustaches drinking ouzo, but I passed it every night on the way home and sometimes I'd stop in for a quick one.

There was the all-night newsstand at the corner of Fifty-seventh and Eighth. I generally bought the paper there, unless I bought it from the shopping-bag lady who hawked them on the sidewalk in front of the 400 Deli. She bought them for a quarter each from the newsstand—I think they were all a quarter that year, or maybe the *News* was twenty cents—and she sold them for the same price, which is a tough way to make a living. Sometimes I'd give her a buck and tell her to keep the change. Her name was Mary Alice Redfield, but I never knew that until a couple of years later, when someone stabbed her to death.

There was a coffee shop called the Red Flame and there was the 400 Deli. There were a couple of okay pizza stands, and there was a place that sold cheese steaks that nobody ever went to twice.

There was a spaghetti joint called Ralph's and a couple of Chinese restaurants. There was a Thai place that Skip Devoe was crazy about. There was Joey Farrell's on Fifty-eighth Street—they'd just opened the past winter. There was, hell, there were a lot of joints.

Mostly there was Armstrong's.

Christ, I lived there. I had my room to sleep in and I had other bars and restaurants to go to, but for a few years there, Jimmy Armstrong's was home to me. People who were looking for me knew to check for me there, and sometimes they called Armstrong's before they called the hotel. The place opened up around eleven, with a Filipino kid named Dennis behind the stick days. Billie Keegan took over around seven and closed at two or three or four, depending on the crowd and how he was feeling. (That was the weekday routine. There were different day and night bartenders on weekends, and the turnover among them was high.)

Waitresses came and went. They got acting jobs or broke up with their boyfriends or got new boyfriends or moved to Los Angeles or went home to Sioux Falls or had a fight with the Dominican kid in the kitchen or got fired for stealing or quit or got pregnant. Jimmy himself wasn't around much that summer. I think that was the year he was looking to buy land in North Carolina.

What can I say about the place? A long bar on the right hand side as you came in, tables on the left. Blue-checkered cloths on them. Dark wood-paneled walls. Pictures on the walls, and framed advertisements from old magazines. A deer's head was mounted incongruously on the back wall; my favorite table was right under the thing, so I didn't have to look at it.

The crowd was a mixed bag. Doctors and nurses from Roosevelt Hospital across the street. Professors and students from Fordham. People from the television studios— CBS was a block away, and ABC a short walk. And people who lived nearby, or kept shops in the neighborhood. A couple of classical musicians. A writer. Two Lebanese brothers who had just opened a shoe store.

Not many kids. When I first moved into the neighborhood Armstrong's had a jukebox with a nice selection of jazz and country blues, but Jimmy took it out early on and replaced it with a stereo system and classical music on tape. That kept the younger crowd out, to the delight of the waitresses who hated the kids for staying late, ordering little, and tipping hardly at all. It also kept the noise level down and made the room more suitable for long-haul maintenance drinking.

Which was what I was there for. I wanted to keep an edge on but I didn't want to get drunk, except once in a while. I mostly mixed my bourbon with coffee, moving to straight booze toward the end of an evening. I could read a paper there, and have a hamburger or a full meal, and as much or as little conversation as I was in the mood for. I wasn't always there all day and night, but it was a rare day that I didn't get in the door at least once, and some days I got there a few minutes after Dennis opened up and was still there when Billie was ready to close. Everybody's got to be someplace.

Saloon friends.

I got to know Tommy Tillary in Armstrong's. He was a regular, apt to turn up three or four nights out of seven. I don't recall the first time I was aware of him, but it was hard to be in a room with him and not notice him. He was a big fellow and his voice tended to carry. He wasn't raucous, but after a few drinks his voice filled a room.

He ate a lot of beef and drank a lot of Chivas Regal, and they both showed in his face. He must have been close to forty-five. He was getting jowly, and his cheeks were blooming with a tracery of broken capillaries.

I never knew why they called him Tough Tommy. Perhaps Skip was right, perhaps the name's intent was ironic. They called him Tommy Telephone because of his job. He worked in telephone sales, peddling investments over the phone from a bucket shop in the Wall Street area. I understand people change jobs a lot in that line of work. The ability to coax investment dollars out of strangers over a telephone line is a rather special talent, and its possessors can get work readily, moving from one employer to another at will.

That summer, Tommy was working for an outfit called Tannahill & Company, selling limited partnerships in real-estate syndications. There were tax advantages, I gather, and the prospect of capital gains. I picked this up inferentially, because Tommy never pitched anything, to me or anyone else at the bar. I was there one time when an obstetrics resident from Roosevelt tried to ask him about his offerings. Tommy brushed him off with a joke.

"No, I'm serious," the doctor insisted. "I'm finally making a buck, I ought to start thinking about things like that."

Tommy shrugged. "You got a card?" The doctor didn't. "Then write your phone on this and a good time to call you. You want a pitch, I'll call you and give you the full treatment. But I got to warn you, I'm irresistible over the phone."

A couple of weeks later they ran into each other and the resident complained that Tommy hadn't called him.

"Jesus, I been meaning to," Tommy said. "First thing, I'll make a note of it now."

He was acceptable company. He told dialect jokes and he told them reasonably well, and I laughed at my share of them. I suppose some of them were offensive, but they weren't often mean-spirited. If I was in a mood to reminisce about my days on the force, he was a good enough listener, and if the story I told was a funny one his laugh was as loud as anybody's.

He was, on balance, a little too loud and a little too cheery. He talked a little too much and he could get on your nerves. As I said, he'd turn up at Armstrong's three or four nights a week, and about half the time she was with him. Carolyn Cheatham, Carolyn from the Caro-line, with a soft you-all accent that, like certain culinary herbs, became stronger when you steeped it in alcohol. Sometimes she came in on his arm. Other times he'd get there first and she'd join him. She lived in the neighborhood and she and Tommy worked in the same office, and I figured—if I bothered to think about it—that the office romance had served to introduce Tommy to Armstrong's.

He followed sports. He bet with a bookie—mostly ball games, sometimes horses—and he let you know when he won. He was a little too friendly, a little too indiscriminately friendly, and sometimes there was a chill in his eyes that belied the friendship in his voice. He had cold little eyes, and there was a softening around his mouth, a weakness there, but none of that got into his voice.

You could see how he'd be good over the phone.

Skip Devoe's first name was Arthur, but Bobby Ruslander was the only person I ever heard call him that. Bobby could get away with it. They'd been friends since fourth grade, they grew up on the same block in Jackson Heights. Skip had been christened Arthur Jr., and he'd acquired the nickname early on. "Because he used to skip school all the time," Bobby said, but Skip had another explanation.

"I had this uncle was in the navy and never got over it," he told me once. "My mother's brother. Bought me sailor suits, toy boats. I had this whole fleet and he called me Skipper, and pretty soon so did everybody else. Coulda been worse. There was a guy in our class everybody called Worm. Don't ask me why. Imagine if they still call him that. He's in bed with his wife: 'Oh, Wormy, put it in deeper.'"

He was around thirty-four, thirty-five, about my height but lean and muscular. The veins showed on his forearms and the backs of his hands. There was no spare flesh on his face, and the skin followed the curve of the bone, giving him deeply sculpted cheeks. He had a hawk nose and piercing blue eyes that showed a little green under the right lighting. All of this combined with assurance and an easy manner to make him quite attractive to women, and he rarely had trouble finding a girl to go home with when he wanted one. But he was living alone and not keeping steady company with anyone, and seemed to prefer the regular company of other men. He had either lived with or been married to someone and it had ended a few years ago, and he seemed disinclined to get involved with anyone else.

Tommy Tillary got called Tough Tommy, and had a certain tough-guy quality to his manner. Skip Devoe actually *was* tough, but you had to sense it underneath the surface. It wasn't on display.

He'd been in the service, not the navy you'd have thought his uncle would have preconditioned him for but the army's Special Forces, the Green Berets. He enlisted fresh out of high school and got sent to Southeast Asia during the Kennedy years. He got out sometime in the late Sixties, tried college and dropped out, then broke in behind the stick at an Upper East Side singles' bar. After a couple of years he and John Kasabian pooled their savings, signed a long lease on an out-of-business hardware store, spent what they had to remodeling it, and opened up Miss Kitty's.

I saw him occasionally at his own place, but more often at Armstrong's, where he'd drop in frequently when he wasn't working. He was pleasant company, easy to be with, and not much rattled him.

There was something about him, though, and I think what it may have been was an air of cool competence. You sensed that he'd be able to handle just about anything that came along, and without working up a sweat. He came across as a man who could do things, one too who could make quick decisions in midaction. Maybe he acquired that quality wearing a green hat in Vietnam, or maybe I endowed him with it because I knew he'd been over there.

I'd met that quality most often in criminals. I have known several heavy heist men who had it, guys who took off banks and armored cars. And there was a long-haul driver for a moving company who was like that. I got to know him after he'd come back from the Coast ahead of schedule, found his wife in bed with a lover, and killed them both with his hands.

3

There was nothing in the papers about the robbery at Morrissey's, but for the next few days you heard a lot of talk about it around the neighborhood. The rumored loss Tim Pat and his brothers had sustained kept escalating. The numbers I heard ranged from ten thousand to a hundred thousand. Since only the Morrisseys and the gunmen would know, and neither were terribly likely to talk, one number seemed as good as the next.

"I think they got around fifty," Billie Keegan told me the night of the Fourth. "That's the number keeps coming up. Of course everybody and his brother was there and saw it."

"What do you mean?"

"I mean so far there's been at least three guys assured me they were there when it happened, and I *was* there and can swear for a fact that they weren't. And they can supply bits of color that somehow slipped by me. Did you know that one of the gunmen slapped a woman around?"

"Really."

"So I'm told. Oh, and one of the Morrissey brothers was shot, but it was only a flesh wound. I thought it was exciting

29

enough the way it went down, but I guess it's a lot more dramatic when you're not there. Well, ten years after the 1916 Rising they say it was hard to find a man in Dublin who hadn't been part of it. That glorious Monday morning, when thirty brave men marched into the post office and ten thousand heroes marched out. What do you think, Matt? Fifty grand sound about right to you?"

Tommy Tillary had been there, and I figured he'd dine out on it. Maybe he did. I didn't see him for a couple of days, and when I did he never even mentioned the robbery. He'd discovered the secret of betting baseball, he told everybody around. You just bet against the Mets and the Yankees and they'd always come through for you.

Early the next week, Skip came by Armstrong's in midafternoon and found me at my table in the back. He'd picked up a dark beer at the bar and brought it with him. He sat down across from me and said he'd been at Morrissey's the night before.

"I haven't been there since I was there with you," I told him.

"Well, last night was my first time since then. They got the ceiling fixed. Tim Pat was asking for you."

"Me?"

"Uh-huh." He lit a cigarette. "He'd appreciate it if you could drop by."

"What for?"

"He didn't say. You're a detective, aren't you? Maybe he wants you to find something. What do you figure he might have lost?"

"I don't want to get in the middle of that."

"Don't tell me."

"Some Irish war, just what I need to cut myself in on."

He shrugged. "You don't have to go. He said to ask you to drop by any time after eight in the evening."

"I guess they sleep until then."

"If they sleep at all."

He drank some beer, wiped his upper lip with the back of his hand. I said, "You were there last night? What was it like?"

"What it's always like. I told you they patched the ceiling, did a good job of it as far as I could tell. Tim Pat and his brothers were their usual charming selves. I just said I'd pass the word to you next time I ran into you. You can go or not go."

"I don't think I will," I said.

But the next night around ten, ten-thirty, I figured what the hell and went over there. On the ground floor, the theater troupe was rehearsing Brendan Behan's *The Quare Fellow*. It was scheduled to open Thursday night. I rang the upstairs bell and waited until one of the brothers came downstairs and cracked the door. He told me they were closed, that they didn't open until two. I told him my name was Matthew Scudder and Tim Pat had said he wanted to see me.

"Oh, sure, an' I didn't now ye in that light," he said. "Come inside and I'll tell himself you're here."

I waited in the big room on the second floor. I was studying the ceiling, looking for patched bullet holes, when Tim Pat came in and switched on some more lights. He was wearing his usual garb, but without the butcher's apron.

"You're good to come," he said. "Ye'll have a drink with me? And your drink is bourbon, is it not?"

He poured drinks and we sat down at a table. It may have been the one his brother fell into when he came stumbling through the door. Tim Pat held his glass to the light, tipped it back and drained it.

He said, "Ye were here the night of the incident."

"Yes."

"One of those fine young lads left a hat behind, but

misfortunately his mother never got around to sewing a name tape in it, so it's impossible to return it to him."

"I see."

"If I only knew who he was and where to find him, I could see that he got what was rightfully his."

I'll bet you could, I thought.

"Ye were a policeman."

"Not anymore."

"Ye might hear something. People talk, don't they, and a man who keeps his eyes and ears open might do himself a bit of good."

I didn't say anything.

He groomed his beard with his fingertips. "My brothers and I," he said, his eyes fixed on a point over my shoulder, "would be greatly pleased to pay ten thousand dollars for the names and whereabouts of the two lads who visited us the other night."

"Just to return a hat."

"Why, we've a sense of obligation," he said. "Wasn't it your George Washington who walked miles through the snow to return a penny to a customer?"

"I think it was Abraham Lincoln."

"Of course it was. George Washington was the other, the cherry tree. 'Father, I cannot tell a lie.' This nation's heroes are great ones for honesty."

"They used to be."

"And then himself, tellin' us all he's not a crook. Jaysus." He shook his big head. "Well, then," he said. "Do ye think ye'll be able to help us out?"

"I don't see what help I could be."

"Ye were here and saw them."

"They were wearing masks and they had caps on their heads. In fact I could swear they both had their caps on when they left. You don't suppose you found somebody else's hat, do you?"

"Perhaps the lad dropped it on the stairs. If you hear anything, Matt, ye'll let us know?"

"Why not?"

"Are ye of Irish stock yourself, Matt?"

"No."

"I'd have thought maybe one of your forebears was from Kerry. The Kerryman is famous for answering a question with a question."

"I don't know who they were, Tim Pat."

"If you learn anything . . ."

"If I learn anything."

"Ye've no quarrel with the price? It's a fair price?"

"No quarrel," I said. "It's a very fair price."

It was a good price, the fairness of it notwithstanding. I said as much to Skip the next time I saw him.

"He didn't want to hire me," I said. "He wanted to post a reward. Ten K to the man who tells him who they are and where he can lay his hands on them."

"Would you do it?"

"What, go hunting for them? I told you the other day I wouldn't take the job for a fee. I'm certainly not going to go nosing around on the come."

He shook his head. "Suppose you found out without trying. You walked around the corner on the way to buy a paper and there they were."

"How would I recognize them?"

"How often do you see two guys wearing red kerchiefs for masks? No, seriously, say you recognized them. Or you got hold of the information, the word got out and some contact of yours from the old days put a flea in your ear. You used to have stool pigeons, didn't you?"

"Snitches," I said. "Every cop had them, you couldn't get anywhere without them. Still, I—"

"Forget *how* you find out," he said. "Just suppose it happened. Would you?"

"Would I—"

"Sell 'em out. Collect the ten grand."

"I don't know anything about them."

"Fine, let's say you don't know whether they're assholes or altar boys. What's the difference? Either way it's blood money, right? The Morrisseys find those kids, they gotta be dead as Kelsey's nuts, right?"

"I don't suppose Tim Pat wants to send them an invitation to a christening."

"Or ask 'em to join the Holy Name Society. Could you do it?"

I shook my head. "I can't answer that," I said. "It would depend on who they were and how bad I needed the money."

"I don't think you'd do it."

"I don't think I would either."

"I sure as shit wouldn't," he said. He tapped the ashes from his cigarette. "There's enough people who would."

"There's people who would kill for less than that."

"I was thinking that myself."

"There were a few cops in the room that night," I said. "You want to bet they'll know about the reward?"

"No bet."

"Say a cop finds out who the holdup men were. He can't make a collar. There's no crime, right? Nothing ever got reported, no witnesses, nothing. But he can turn the two bums over to Tim Pat and walk with half a year's pay."

"Knowing he's aided and abetted murder."

"I'm not saying everybody would do it. But you tell yourself the guys are scum, they've probably killed people themselves, they're a cinch to kill someone sooner or later, and it's not like you know for certain the Morrisseys are going to kill them. Maybe they'll just break a few bones, just scare 'em a little. Try to get their money back, something like that. You can tell yourself that."

"And believe it?"

"Most people believe what they want to believe."

"Yeah," he said. "Can't argue with that."

You decide something in your mind and then your body goes and decides something else. I wasn't going to have anything to do with Tim Pat's problem, and then I kept finding myself sniffing around it like a dog at a lamppost. The same night I assured Skip I wasn't playing, I wound up on Seventy-second Street at a place called Poogan's Pub, sitting at a rear table and buying iced Stolichnaya for a tiny albino Negro named Danny Boy Bell. Danny Boy was always interesting company, but he was also a prime snitch, an information broker who knew everyone and heard everything.

Of course he'd heard about the robbery at Morrissey's. He'd heard a wide range of figures quoted for the take, and for his own part guessed that the right number was somewhere between fifty and a hundred thousand dollars.

"Whoever took it," he said, "they're not spending it in the bars. My sense of it is that it's an Irish thing, Matthew. Irish Irish, not the local Harps. You know, it went down right in the middle of Westy country, but I can't see the Westies taking off Tim Pat like that."

The Westies are a loosely organized mob of toughs and killers, most of them Irish, and they've been operating in Hell's Kitchen since the turn of the century. Maybe longer, maybe since the Potato Famine.

"I don't know," I said. "With that kind of money involved—"

"If those two were Westies, if they were anybody from the neighborhood, it wouldn't be a secret for more than eight hours. Everybody on Tenth Avenue'd know it."

"You're right."

"Some kind of Irish thing, that's my best guess. You were there, you'd know this. The masks were red?"

"Red handkerchiefs."

"A shame. If they were green or orange they'd be making some sort of political statement. I understand the brothers are offering a generous reward. Is that what brings you here, Matthew?"

"Oh, no," I said. "Definitely not."

"Not doing a bit of exploratory work on speculation?"

"Absolutely not," I said.

Friday afternoon I was drinking in Armstrong's and fell into conversation with a couple of nurses at the next table. They had tickets for an off-off-Broadway show that night. Dolores couldn't go, and Fran really wanted to but she wasn't sure she felt like going by herself, and besides they had the extra ticket.

And of course the show turned out to be *The Quare Fellow*. It didn't relate in any way to the incident at Morrissey's, it was just coincidentally being performed downstairs of the after-hours joint, and it hadn't been my idea in the first place, but what was I doing there? I sat on a flimsy wooden folding chair and watched Behan's play about imprisoned criminals in Dublin and wondered what the hell I was doing in the audience.

Afterward Fran and I wound up at Miss Kitty's with a group that included two of the members of the cast. One of them, a slim red-haired girl with enormous green eyes, was Fran's friend Mary Margaret, and the reason why Fran had been so anxious to go. That was Fran's reason, but what was mine?

There was talk at the table of the robbery. I didn't raise the subject or contribute much to the discussion, but I couldn't stay out of it altogether because Fran told the group

I was a former police detective and asked for my professional opinion of the affair. My reply was as noncommittal as I could make it, and I avoided mentioning that I'd been an eyewitness to the holdup.

Skip was there, so busy behind the bar with the Friday-night crowd that I didn't bother to do more than wave hello at him. The place was mobbed and noisy, as it always was on weekends, but that was where everyone else had wanted to go, and I'd gone along.

Fran lived on Sixty-eighth between Columbus and Amsterdam. I walked her home, and at her door she said, "Matt, you were a sweetheart to keep me company. The play was okay, wasn't it?"

"It was fine."

"I thought Mary Margaret was good, anyway. Matt, would you mind awfully if I don't ask you to come up? I'm beat and I've got an early day tomorrow."

"That's okay," I said. "Now that you mention it, so do I."

"Being a detective?"

I shook my head. "Being a father."

The next morning Anita put the kids on the Long Island Rail Road and I picked them up at the station in Corona and took them to Shea and watched the Mets lose to the Astros. The boys would be going to camp for four weeks in August and they were excited about that. We ate hot dogs and peanuts and popcorn. They had Cokes, I had a couple of beers. There was some sort of special promotion that day, and the boys got free caps or pennants, I forget which.

Afterward I took them back to the city on the subway and to a movie at Loew's 83rd. We had pizza on Broadway after the film let out and took a cab back to my hotel, where I'd rented a twin-bedded room for them a floor below mine. They went to bed and I went up to my own room. After an hour I checked their room. They were sleeping soundly. I locked their door again and went around the corner to Armstrong's. I didn't stay long, maybe an hour. Then I went back to my hotel, checked the boys again, and went upstairs and to bed.

In the morning we went out for a big breakfast, pancakes and bacon and sausages. I took them up to the Museum of the American Indian in Washington Heights. There are a couple dozen museums in the city of New York, and when you leave your wife you get to discover them all.

It felt strange being in Washington Heights. It was in that neighborhood a few years earlier that I'd been having a few off-duty drinks when a couple of punks held up the bar and shot the bartender dead on their way out.

I went out into the street after them. There are a lot of hills in Washington Heights. They ran down one of them and I had to shoot downhill. I brought them both down, but one shot went wide and ricocheted, and it killed a small child named Estrellita Rivera.

Those things happen. There was a departmental hearing, there always is when you kill someone, and I was found to have acted properly and with justification.

Shortly thereafter I put in my papers and left the police department.

I can't say that one event caused the other. I can only say that the one led to the other. I had been the unwitting instrument of a child's death, and after that something was different for me. The life I had been living without complaint no longer seemed to suit me. I suppose it had ceased to suit me before then. I suppose the child's death precipitated a life change that was long overdue. But I can't say that for certain, either. Just that one thing led to another.

We took a train to Penn Station. I told the boys how good it had been to spend some time with them, and they told me what a good time they'd had. I put them on a train, made a phone call and told their mother what train they'd be on. She assured me she'd meet it, then mentioned hesitantly that it would be good if I sent money soon. Soon, I assured her.

I hung up and thought of the ten thousand dollars Tim Pat was offering. And shook my head, amused at the thought.

But that night I got restless and wound up down in the Village, stopping in a string of bars for one drink each. I took the A train to West Fourth Street and started at McBell's and worked my way west. Jimmy Day's, the 55, the Lion's Head, George Hertz's, the Corner Bistro. I told myself I was just having a couple of drinks, unwinding after the pressure of a weekend with my sons, settling myself down after awakening old memories with a visit to Washington Heights.

But I knew better. I was starting some half-assed purposeless investigation, trying to turn up a lead to the pair who'd hit Morrissey's.

I wound up in a gay bar called Sinthia's. Kenny, who owned the place, was minding the store, serving drinks to men in Levi's and ribbed tank tops. Kenny was slender, willowy, with dyed blond hair and a face that had been tucked and lifted enough to look no more than twenty-eight, which was about half as many years as Kenny had been on the planet.

"Matthew!" he called out. "You can all relax now, girls. Law and order has come to Grove Street."

Of course he didn't know anything about the robbery at Morrissey's. He didn't know Morrissey's to begin with; no gay man had to leave the Village to find a place where he could get a drink after closing. But the holdup men could have been gay as easily as not, and if they weren't spending their take elsewhere they might be spending it in the joints around Christopher Street, and anyhow that was the way you worked it, you nosed around, you worked all your sources, you put the word out and waited to see if anything came back to you.

But why was I doing this? Why was I wasting my time?

I don't know what would have happened—whether I would have kept at it or let go of it, whether I would have gotten someplace or ultimately turned away from a cold trail. I didn't seem to be getting anywhere, but that's often the way it is, and you go through the motions with no indication of progress until you get lucky and something breaks. Maybe something like that would have happened. Maybe not.

Instead, some other things happened to take my mind off Tim Pat Morrissey and his quest for vengeance.

For openers, somebody killed Tommy Tillary's wife.

4

Tuesday night I took Fran to dinner at the Thai restaurant Skip Devoe liked so much. Afterward I walked her home, with a stop for after-dinner drinks at Joey Farrell's. In front of her building she pleaded an early day again, and I left her there and walked back to Armstrong's with a stop or two en route. I was in a sour mood, and a stomachful of unfamiliar food didn't help any. I probably hit the bourbon a little harder than usual, rolling out of there around one or two. I took the long way home, picked up the *Daily News*, and sat on the edge of my bed in my underwear taking a quick look at a couple of stories.

On one of the inside pages I read about a Brooklyn woman who'd been killed in the course of a burglary. I was tired and I'd had a lot to drink and the name didn't register.

But I woke up the next morning with something buzzing in my mind, half dream and half memory. I sat up and reached for the paper and found the story.

Margaret Tillary, forty-seven, had been stabbed to death in the upstairs bedroom of her home on Colonial Road, in the Bay Ridge section of Brooklyn, evidently having

41

awakened in the course of a burglary. Her husband, securities salesman Thomas J. Tillary, had become concerned when his wife failed to answer the telephone Tuesday afternoon. He called a relative living nearby who entered the house, finding the premises ransacked and the woman dead.

"This is a good neighborhood," a neighbor was quoted as saying. "Things like this don't happen here." But a police source cited a marked increase in area burglaries in recent months, and another neighbor referred obliquely to the presence of a "bad element" in the neighborhood.

It's not a common name. There's a Tillary Street in Brooklyn, not far from the entrance to the Brooklyn Bridge, but I've no idea what war hero or ward heeler they named it after, or if he's a relative of Tommy's. There are several Tillerys in the Manhattan phone directory, spelled with an *e*. Thomas Tillary, securities salesman, Brooklyn—it seemed as though it had to be Telephone Tommy.

I took a shower and shaved and went out for breakfast. I thought about what I'd read and tried to figure out how I felt about it. It didn't seem real to me. I didn't know him well and I hadn't known her at all, had never known her name, had known only that she existed somewhere in Brooklyn.

I looked at my left hand, the ring finger. No ring, no mark. I had worn a wedding ring for years, and I had taken it off when I moved from Syosset to Manhattan. For months there had been a mark where the ring had been, and then one day I noticed that the mark was gone.

Tommy wore a ring. A yellow gold band, maybe three-eighths of an inch wide. And he wore a pinkie ring on his right hand, a high-school class ring, I think it must have been. I remembered it, sitting there over coffee in the Red Flame. A class ring with a blue stone on his right pinkie, a yellow gold band on his left ring finger.

I couldn't tell how I felt.

• • •

That afternoon I went to St. Paul's and lit a candle for Margaret Tillary. I had discovered churches in my retirement, and while I did not pray or attend services, I dropped in now and then and sat in the darkened silence. Sometimes I lit candles for people who had recently died, or for those longer dead who were on my mind. I don't know why I thought this was something I ought to do, nor do I know why I felt compelled to tuck a tenth of any income I received into the poor box of whatever church I next visited.

I sat in a rear pew and thought a bit about sudden death. When I left the church a light rain was falling. I crossed Ninth Avenue and ducked into Armstrong's. Dennis was behind the bar. I ordered bourbon neat, drank it straight down, and motioned for another and said I'd have a cup of coffee with it.

While I poured the bourbon into the coffee, he asked if I'd heard about Tillary. I said I'd read the story in the *News*.

"There's a piece in this afternoon's *Post*, too. Pretty much the same story. It happened the night before last is how they figure it. He evidently didn't make it home and he went straight to the office in the morning, and then after he called a few times to apologize and couldn't get through, he got worried."

"It said that in the paper?"

"Just about. That would have been the night before last. He didn't come in while I was here. Did you see him?"

I tried to remember. "I think so. The night before last, yeah, I think he was here with Carolyn."

"The Dixie Belle."

"That's the one."

"Wonder how she feels about now." He used thumb and forefinger to smooth the points of his wispy moustache. "Probably guilty for having her wish come true."

"You think she wanted the wife dead?"

"I don't know. Isn't that a girl's fantasy when she's running around with a married guy? Look, I'm not married, what do I know about these things?"

The story faded out of the papers during the next couple of days. There was a death notice in Thursday's *News*. Margaret Wayland Tillary, beloved wife of Thomas, mother of the late James Alan Tillary, aunt of Mrs. Richard Paulsen. There would be a wake that evening, a funeral service the following afternoon at Walter B. Cooke's, Fourth and Bay Ridge Avenues, in Brooklyn.

That night Billie Keegan said, "I haven't seen Tillary since it happened. I'm not sure we're gonna see him again." He poured himself a glass of JJ&S, the twelve-year-old Jameson that nobody else ever ordered. "I bet we don't see him with her again."

"The girlfriend?"

He nodded. "What's got to be on both their minds is he was with her when his wife was getting knifed to death in Brooklyn. And if he'd only been home where he was supposed to be, di dah di dah di dah. You're fooling around and you want a quick bounce and a couple of laughs, the last thing you need is something to remind you how you got your wife killed by fooling around."

I thought about it, nodded. "The wake was tonight," I said.

"Yeah? You go?" I shook my head. "I don't know anybody that went."

I left before closing. I had a drink at Polly's and another at Miss Kitty's. Skip was tense and remote. I sat at the bar and tried to ignore the man standing next to me without being actively hostile. He wanted to tell me how all the city's problems were the fault of the former mayor. I didn't necessarily disagree but I didn't want to hear about it.

I finished my drink and headed for the door. Halfway there Skip called my name. I turned and he motioned to me.

I walked back to the bar. He said, "This is the wrong time for it, but I'd like to talk to you soon."

"Oh?"

"Ask your advice, maybe throw a little work your way. You be around Jimmy's tomorrow afternoon?"

"Probably," I said. "If I don't go to the funeral."

"Who died?"

"Tillary's wife."

"Oh, the funeral's tomorrow? Are you thinking about going? I didn't know you were that close to the guy."

"I'm not."

"Then why would you want to go? Forget it, not my business. I'll look for you at Armstrong's around two, two-thirty. If you're not there I'll catch you some other time."

I was there when he came in the next day around two-thirty. I had just finished lunch and was sitting over a cup of coffee when Skip came in and scanned the room from the doorway. He saw me and came on over and sat down.

"You didn't go," he said. "Well, it's no day for a funeral. I was just over at the gym, I felt silly sitting in the sauna after. The whole city's a sauna. What have you got there, some of that famous Kentucky coffee of yours?"

"Just plain coffee."

"That'll never do." He turned, beckoned the waitress. "Let me have a Prior Dark," he told her, "and bring my father here something to put in his coffee."

She brought a shot for me and a beer for him. He poured it slowly against the side of the glass, examined the half-inch head, took a sip, put the glass down.

He said, "I might have a problem."

I didn't say anything.

"This is confidential, okay?"

"Sure."

"You know much about the bar business?"

"Just from the consumer's point of view."

"I like that. You know it's all cash."

"Of course."

"A lot of places take plastic. We don't. Strictly cash. Oh, if we know you we'll take your check, or if you run a tab, whatever. But it's basically a cash business. I'd say ninety-five percent of our gross is cash. As a matter of fact it's probably higher than that."

"And?"

He took out a cigarette, tapped the end against his thumbnail. "I hate talking about all this," he said.

"Then don't."

He lit the cigarette. "Everybody skims," he said. "A certain percentage of the take comes right off the top before it gets recorded. It doesn't get listed in the books, it doesn't get deposited, it doesn't exist. The dollar you don't declare is worth two dollars that you do, because you don't pay tax on it. You follow me?"

"It's not all that hard to follow, Skip."

"Everybody does it, Matt. The candy store, the newsie, everybody who takes in cash. Christ's sake, it's the American way—the president'd cheat on his taxes if he could get by with it."

"The last one did."

"Don't remind me. That asshole'd give tax fraud a bad name." He sucked hard on the cigarette. "We opened up, couple years ago, John kept the books. I yell at people, do the hiring and firing, he does the buying and keeps the books. Works out about right."

"And?"

"Get to the point, right? Fuck it. From the beginning we keep two sets of books, one for us and one for Uncle." His face darkened and he shook his head. "Never made sense to me. I figured keep one phony set and that's that, but he says you need honest books so you'll know how you're doing. That make sense to you? You count your money and you know how you're doing, you don't need two sets of books to tell you, but he's the guy with the business head, he knows these things, so I say fine, do it."

He picked up his glass, drank some beer. "They're gone," he said.

"The books."

"John comes in Saturday mornings, does the week's bookkeeping. Everything was fine this past Saturday. Day before yesterday he has to check something, looks for the books, no books."

"Both sets gone?"

"Only the dark set, the honest set." He drank some beer, wiped his mouth with the back of his hand. "He spent a day taking Valium and going nuts by himself, then told me yesterday. And I been going nuts ever since."

"How bad is it, Skip?"

"Aw, shit," he said. "It's pretty bad. We could go away for it."

"Really?"

He nodded. "It's all our records since we opened, and we been making money from the first week. I don't know why, it's just another joint, but we been pulling 'em in. And we've been stealing with both hands. They come up with the books, we're fucking *nailed*, you know? You can't call it a mistake, it's all down there in black and white, one set of figures, and there's another completely different set on each year's tax return. You can't even make up a story, all you can do is ask 'em where they want you, Atlanta or Leavenworth."

We sat silent for a few moments. I drank some of my coffee. He lit another cigarette and blew smoke at the ceiling. Music played on the tape deck, something contrapuntal with woodwinds.

I said, "What would you want me to do?"

"Find out who took 'em. Get 'em back."

"Maybe John got rattled, misplaced them. He could have—"

He was shaking his head. "I turned the office upside down yesterday afternoon. They're fuckin' gone."

"They just disappeared? No signs of force entry? Where did you keep 'em, under lock and key?"

"They're supposed to be locked up. Sometimes he would forget, leave 'em out, stick 'em in a desk drawer. You get careless, you know what I mean? You never have an incident, you take the whole thing for granted, and if you're rushed, you don't take the trouble to put things away where they belong. He tells me he locked up Saturday but in the next breath he admits maybe he didn't, it's a routine thing, he does the same thing every Saturday, so how do you remember one Saturday from the next? What's the difference? The stuff is capital-G Gone."

"So somebody took it."

"Right."

"If they go the IRS with it—"

"Then we're dead. That's all. They can plant us next to whatsisname's wife, Tillary's. You miss the funeral, don't worry about it. I'll understand."

"Was anything else missing, Skip?"

"Didn't seem to be."

"So it was a very specific theft. Somebody walked in, took the books, and left."

"Bingo."

I worked it out in my mind. "If it was somebody with a grudge against you, somebody you fired, say—"

"Yeah, I thought of that."

"If they go to the Feds, you'll know about it when a

couple of guys in suits come around and show you their ID. They'll take all your records, slap a lien on your bank accounts, and whatever else they do."

"Keep talking, Matt. You're really making my day."

"If it's not somebody who's got a hardon for you, then it's somebody looking to turn a dollar."

"By selling the books."

"Uh-huh."

"To us."

"You're the ideal customers."

"I thought of that. So did Kasabian. Sit tight, he tells me. Sit tight, and whoever took 'em'll get in touch, and we worry about it then. Just sit tight in the meantime. Tight's no problem, it's the sitting that's getting to me. Can you get bail for cheating on taxes?"

"Of course."

"Then I suppose I can get it and run out on it. Leave the country. Live the rest of my life in Nepal selling hash to hippies."

"All that's still a long ways off."

"I suppose." He looked thoughtfully at his cigarette, drowned it in the dregs of his beer. "I hate it when they do that," he said thoughtfully. "Send back glasses with butts floating in them. Disgusting." He looked at me, his eyes probing mine. "Anything you can do for me on this? I mean for hire."

"I don't see what. Not at this point."

"So in the meantime I just wait. That's always the hard part for me, always has been. I ran track in high school, the quarter-mile. I was lighter then. I smoked heavy, I smoked since I was thirteen, but you can do anything at that age and it doesn't touch you. Nothing touches kids, that's why they all think they're gonna live forever." He drew another cigarette halfway out of the pack, put it back again. "I loved the races, but waiting for the event to start, I hated that. Some guys would puke. I never puked but I used to feel like it. I would pee and then I'd think I had to pee again five minutes later." He shook his head at the memory. "And the same thing overseas, waiting to go into combat. I never minded combat, and there was a lot about it to mind. Things that bother me now, remembering them, but while they were going on it was a different story."

"I can understand that."

"Waiting, though, that was murder." He pushed his chair back. "What do I owe you, Matt?"

"For what? I didn't do anything."

"For the advice."

I waved the thought away. "You can buy me that drink," I said, "and that'll be fine."

"Done," he said. He stood up. "I may need a hand from you somewhere down the line."

"Sure," I said.

He stopped to talk to Dennis on the way out. I nursed my coffee. By the time I was done with it a woman two tables away had paid her check and left her newspaper behind. I read it, and had another cup of coffee with it, and a shot of bourbon to sweeten the coffee.

The afternoon crowd was starting to fill the room when I called the waitress over. I palmed her a buck and told her to put the check on my tab.

"No check," she said. "The gentleman paid it."

She was new, she didn't know Skip by name. "He wasn't supposed to do that," I said. "Anyway, I had a drink after he left. Put it on my tab, all right?"

"Talk to Dennis," she said.

She went to take somebody's order before I could reply. I went to the bar and crooked a finger for Dennis. "She tells me there's no check for my table," I said.

"She speaks the truth." He smiled. He often smiled, as if

much of what he saw amused him. "Devoe paid the check."

"He wasn't supposed to do that. Anyway, I had a drink after he left and told her to put it on my tab, and she said to see you. Is this something new? Don't I have a tab?"

His smile broadened. "Anytime you want one, but as a matter of fact you don't have one now. Mr. Devoe covered it. Wiped the slate clean."

"What did it come to?"

"Eighty dollars and change. I could probably come up with the exact figure if it mattered. Does it?"

"No."

"He gave me a hundred dollars to cover your tab, the check today, a tip for Lyddie and something to ease my own weariness of the soul. I suppose one could maintain that your most recent drink was not covered, but my inscrutable sense of the rightness of things is that it was." Another wide smile. "So you owe us nothing," he said.

I didn't argue. If there was one thing I learned in the NYPD, it was to take what people gave me.

5

I went back to my hotel, checked for mail and messages. There were none of either. The desk clerk, a loose-limbed black man from Antigua, said that he didn't mind the heat but he missed the ocean breezes.

I went upstairs and took a shower. My room was hot. There was an air-conditioner, but something was wrong with its cooling element. It moved the warm air around and gave it a chemical flavor but didn't do much about the heat or the humidity. I could shut it off and open the window from the top, but the air outside was no better. I stretched out and must have dozed off for an hour or so, and when I woke up I needed another shower.

I took it and then called Fran. Her roommate answered. I gave my name and waited what seemed like a long time for Fran to come to the phone.

I suggested dinner, and maybe a movie afterward if we felt up to it. "Oh, I'm afraid I can't tonight, Matt," she said. "I have other plans. Maybe some other time?"

I hung up regretting that I'd called. I checked the mirror, decided I didn't really need a shave after all, got dressed and got out of there.

It was hot on the street, but it would cool down in a couple of hours. Meanwhile, there were bars all over the place, and their air-conditioners all worked better than mine.

Curiously, I didn't hit it all that hard. I was in a surly mood, gruff and ill-tempered, and that usually led me to take my drinks fast. But I was restless, and as a result I moved around a lot. There were even a few bars that I walked into and out of without ordering anything.

At one point I almost got into a fight. In a joint on Tenth Avenue a rawboned drunk with a couple of teeth missing bumped into me and spilled part of his drink on me, then took exception to the way I accepted his apology. It was all over nothing—he was looking for a fight and I was very nearly ready to oblige him. Then one of his friends grabbed his arms from behind and another stepped between us, and I came to my senses and got out of there.

I walked east on Fifty-seventh. A couple of black hookers were working the pavement in front of the Holiday Inn. I noticed them more than I usually did. One, with a face like an ebony mask, challenged me with her eyes. I felt a rush of anger, and I didn't know who or what I was angry at.

I walked over to Ninth, up half a block to Armstrong's. I wasn't surprised to see Fran there. It was almost as if I had expected her to be there, seated at a table along the north wall. She had her back to me and hadn't noticed me come in.

Hers was a table for two, and her partner was no one I recognized. He had blond hair and eyebrows and an open young face, and he was wearing a slate-blue short-sleeved shirt with epaulets. I think they call it a safari shirt. He was smoking a pipe and drinking a beer. Her drink was something red in an oversize stemmed glass.

Probably a tequila sunrise. That was a big year for tequila sunrises.

I turned to the bar, and there was Carolyn. The tables were crowded but the bar was half empty, lightly attended for that hour on a Friday night. At her right, toward the door, a couple of beer drinkers stood talking baseball. To her left, there were three vacant stools in a row.

I took the middle one and ordered bourbon, a double with water back. Billie served it, saying something about the weather. I took a sip of my drink and shot a quick glance at Carolyn.

She didn't appear to be waiting for Tommy or for anyone else, nor did she look as though she'd just breezed in a few minutes ago. She was wearing yellow pedal pushers and a sleeveless lime-green blouse. Her light brown hair was combed to frame her little fox face. She was drinking something dark from a lowball glass.

At least it wasn't a tequila sunrise.

I drank some bourbon, glanced in spite of myself at Fran and was irritated with my own irritation. I'd had two dates with her, there was no great mutual attraction, no chemical magic, just two nights of leaving her at her door. And tonight I'd called her, late, and she'd said she had other plans, and here she was, drinking a tequila sunrise with her other plan.

Where did I get off being mad about that?

I thought, I'll bet she doesn't tell him she's got an early day tomorrow. I bet the White Hunter there doesn't have to say goodnight downstairs.

To my right, a voice with a Piedmont softness to it said, "I forget your name."

I looked up.

"I believe we were introduced," she said, "but I don't recall your name."

"It's Matthew Scudder," I said, "and you're right, Tommy introduced us. You're Carolyn."

"Carolyn Cheatham. Have you seen him?"

"Tommy? Not since it happened."

"Neither have I. Were you-all at the funeral?"

"No. I thought about going but I didn't get there."

"Why would you go? You never met her, did you?"

"No."

"Neither did I." She laughed. There wasn't much mirth in it. "Big surprise, I never met his wife. I would have gone this afternoon. But I didn't." She took her lower lip between her teeth. "Matt. Whyn't you buy me a drink? Or I'll buy you one, but come sit next to me so's I don't have to shout. Please?"

She was drinking Amaretto, a sweet almond-flavored liqueur that she took on the rocks. It tastes like dessert but it's almost as strong as whiskey.

"He told me not to come," she said. "To the funeral. It was someplace in Brooklyn, that's a whole foreign nation to me, Brooklyn, but a lot of people went from the office. I wouldn't have had to *know* how to get there, I could have had a ride, I could have been part of the office crowd, come to pay my respects along with everybody else. But he said not to, he said it wouldn't look right."

Her bare arms were lightly dusted with golden hair. She was wearing perfume, a floral scent with an undertaste of musk.

"He said it wouldn't look right," she said. "He said it was a matter of respect for the dead." She picked up her glass and stared into it.

She said, "Respect. What's the man care about respect? What's he so much as know about respect, for the dead or for the living? I would just have been part of the office crowd. We both work there at Tannahill, far as anyone knows we're just friends. Lord's sake, all we ever were is friends."

"Whatever you say."

"Well, *shit,*" she said, drawling it, giving the word an

extra syllable or two. "Ah *don't* mean to say Ah wasn't fucking him. Ah surely don't mean that. But all it ever was was laughs and good times. He was married and went home to mama most every night"—she drank some Amaretto— "and that was jes fine, believe me, because who in her right mind'd want Tommy Tillary around by the dawn's early light? Christ in the foothills, Matthew, did I spill this or drink it?"

We agreed that she was drinking them a little too fast. Sweet drinks, we assured each other, had a way of sneaking up on a person. It was this fancy New York Amaretto shit, she maintained. It wasn't like the bourbon she'd grown up on. You knew where you stood with bourbon.

I reminded her that I was a bourbon drinker myself, and it pleased her to learn this. Alliances have been forged on more tenuous bonds than that, and she sealed ours with a sip from my glass. I offered it to her, and she put her little hand on mine to steady the glass, sipping daintily at the liquor.

"Bourbon is low-down," she said. "You know what I mean?"

"Here I thought it was a gentleman's drink."

"It's for a gentleman likes to get down in the dirt. Scotch is vests and ties and prep school. Bourbon is an old boy ready to let the animal out, ready to let the nasty show. Bourbon is sitting up on a hot night and not minding if you sweat."

Nobody was sweating. We were in her apartment, sitting on her couch in a sunken living room set about a foot below the level of the kitchen and foyer. Her building was an Art Deco apartment house on Fifty-seventh just a few doors west of Ninth. A bottle of Maker's Mark from the store around the corner stood on top of her glass-and-wrought-iron coffee table. Her air-conditioner was on, quieter than mine and more effective. We were drinking out of rocks glasses but we weren't bothering with ice.

"You were a cop," she said. "Didn't he tell me that?"

"He could have."

"And now you're a detective?"

"In a way."

"Just so you're not a robber. Be something if I got myself stabbed by a burglar tonight, wouldn't it? He's with me and she gets killed, and then he's with her and *I* get killed. Except I don't guess he's with her right about now, is he. She's in the ground by now."

Her apartment was small but comfortable. The furniture had clean lines, the op art prints on the brick wall were framed simply in aluminum frames. From her window you could see the green copper roof of the Parc Vendome on the far corner.

"If a burglar came in here," she said, "I'd stand a better chance than she did."

"Because you've got me to protect you?"

"Mmmm," she said. "Mah hero."

We kissed then. I tipped up her chin and kissed her, and we moved into an easy clinch. I breathed in her perfume, felt her softness. We clung together for a moment or two, then withdrew and reached as if in synchronization for our drinks.

"Even if I was alone," she said, picking up the conversation as readily as she'd picked up the drink. "I could protect myself."

"You're a karate black belt."

"I'm a beaded belt, honey, to match my purse. No, I could protect myself with this here, just give me a minute and I'll show you."

A pair of modern matte-black step tables flanked the sofa. She leaned across me to grope for something in the drawer of the one on my side. She was sprawled facedown across my lap. An inch of golden skin showed between the tops of the yellow pedal pushers and the bottom of her green blouse. I put my hand on her behind.

"Now quit that, Matthew! I'll forget what I'm looking for."

"That's all right."

"No it's not. Here. See?"

She sat up, a gun in her hand. It was the same matte-black finish as the table. It was a revolver, and looked to be a .32. A small gun, all black, with a one-inch barrel.

"Maybe you should put that away," I said.

"I know how to behave around guns," she said. "I grew up in a house full of guns. Rifles, shotguns, handguns. My pa and both my brothers hunted. Quail, pheasants. Some ducks. I know about guns."

"Is that one loaded?"

"Wouldn't be much good if it wasn't, would it? Can't point at a burglar and say *bang*. He loaded it 'fore he gave it to me."

"Tommy gave it to you?"

"Uh-huh." She held the gun at arm's length, sighted across the room at an imaginary burglar. "Bang," she said. "He didn't leave me any shells, just the loaded gun. So if I was to shoot a burglar I'd have to ask him for more bullets the next day."

"Why'd he give it to you?"

"Not to go duck hunting." She laughed. "For protection," she said. "I said how I got nervous sometimes, a girl living alone in this city, and one time he brought me this here. He said he bought it for her, to have it for protection, but she wouldn't have any part of it, wouldn't even take it in her hand." She broke off and giggled.

"What's so funny?"

"Oh, that's what they all say. 'My wife won't even take it in her hand.' I got a dirty mind, Matthew."

"Nothing wrong with that."

"I told you bourbon was low-down. Brings out the beast in a person. You could kiss me."

"You could put the gun away."

"You got something against kissing a woman with a gun in her hand?" She rolled to her left, put the gun in the drawer and closed it. "I keep it in the bedside table," she explained, "so it'll be handy if I need it in a hurry. This here makes up into a bed."

"I don't believe you."

"You don't huh? Want me to prove it to you?"

"Maybe you'd better."

And so we did what grownups do when they find themselves alone together. The sofa opened up into an adequate bed and we lay upon it with the lights out and the room lit by a couple of candles in straw-wrapped wine bottles. Music played on an FM station. She had a sweet body, an eager mouth, perfect skin. She made a lot of enthusiastic noises and more than a few skillful moves, and afterward she cried some.

Then we talked and had a little more of the bourbon, and before long she dropped off to sleep. I covered her with the top sheet and a cotton blanket. I could have slept myself, but instead I put on my clothes and sent myself home. Because who in her right mind'd want Matt Scudder around by the dawn's early light?

On my way home I stopped at the little Syrian deli and had the clerk loosen the caps on two bottles of Molson Ale. I went up to my room and sat with my feet up on the windowsill and drank from one of the bottles.

I thought about Tillary. Where was he now? In the house where she died? Staying with friends or relatives?

I thought of him in the bars or Carolyn's bed while a

burglar was killing his wife, and I wondered what he thought about that. Or if he thought about it.

And my own thoughts turned suddenly to Anita, out there in Syosset with the boys. I had a moment of fear for her, seeing her menaced, drawing back in terror from some unseen danger. I recognized the fear as irrational, and I was able after a moment to know it for what it was, something I'd brought home with me, something that clung to me now along with Carolyn Cheatham's scent. I was carrying around Tommy Tillary's guilt by proxy.

Well, the hell with that. I didn't need his guilt. I had plenty of my own.

6

The weekend was quiet. I talked to my sons, but they didn't come in. Saturday afternoon I earned a hundred dollars by accompanying one of the partners in the antique shop down the block from Armstrong's. We cabbed together to East Seventy-fourth Street, where we collected clothing and other possessions from his ex-lover's apartment. The lover was thirty or forty pounds overweight, bitter and bitchy.

"I don't believe this, Gerald," he said. "Did you actually bring a bodyguard or is this my summer replacement? Either way I don't know whether to be flattered or insulted."

"Oh, I'm sure you'll work it out," Gerald told him.

In the cab back to the West Side Gerald said, "I really loved that cunt, Matthew, and I will be goddamned if I can figure out why. Thank you for this, Matthew. I could have hired a schlepper for five dollars an hour, but your presence was all the difference in the world. Did you see how ready he was to remember that the Handel lamp was his? The fucking *hell* it was his. When I met him he didn't know from Handel, not the lamps or the composer, either. All he

61

knew was to *hondle*. You know that word, *hondle?* It means to haggle over a price, like if I were to try to pay you fifty dollars now instead of the hundred we agreed on. I'm just joking, dear. I have no problem with paying you the hundred, I think you were worth every penny of it."

Sunday night Bobby Ruslander found me in Armstrong's. Skip was looking for me, he said. He was at Miss Kitty's, and if I got a minute why didn't I drop over? I had time then, and Bobby walked over there with me.

It was a little cooler; the worst of the heat wave had broken Saturday, and there had been some rain to cool the streets down a little. A fire truck raced past us as we waited for the light to change. When the siren died down, Bobby said, "Crazy business."

"Oh?"

"He'll tell you about it."

As we crossed the street he said, "I never see him like this, you know what I mean? He's always supercool, Arthur is."

"Nobody else calls him Arthur."

"Nobody ever did. Back when we're kids, nobody calls him Arthur. It was like going against type, you know? Everybody calls him Skip, I'm his best friend, *I* call him by his formal name."

When we got there Skip tossed Bobby a bar towel and asked him to take over for him. "He's a lousy bartender," he announced, "but he doesn't steal much."

"That's what you think," Bobby said.

We went in back and Skip closed the door. There were a couple of old desks, two swivel chairs and a straight-backed chair, a coatrack, a file cabinet, and a big old Mosler safe that was taller than I was. "That's where the books shoulda been," he said, pointing at the safe. "Except we're too smart for that, me and John. There's an audit, that's the first place they're gonna look, right? So all that's in there is a thousand in cash and some papers and shit, the lease on this place, the partnership agreement, his divorce papers, shit like that. Terrific. We saved that crap and let somebody walk off with the store."

He lit a cigarette. "Safe was here when we took the place," he said. "Left over from when the joint was a hardware store, and it cost more to move than it was worth, so we inherited it. Massive fucker, isn't it? You could put a body in there if you had one around. That way nobody'd steal it. He called, the fucker who stole the books."

"Oh?"

He nodded. "It's a ransom pitch. 'I got something of yours and you can have it back.'"

"He name a price?"

"No. Said he'll be in touch."

"You recognize the voice?"

"Uh-uh. Sounded phony."

"How do you mean?"

"Like it wasn't his real voice I was hearing. Anyway, I didn't recognize it." He clasped his hands, extended his arms to crack his knuckles. "I'm supposed to sit around until I hear from him."

"When did you get the call?"

"Couple hours ago. I was working, he called me here. Good start to the evening, I'll tell you."

"At least he's coming to you instead of sending the stuff straight to the IRS."

"Yeah, I thought of that. This way we get the chance to do something. If he went and dropped a dime on us, all we could do is bend over and take it."

"Did you talk to your partner?"

"Not yet. I called his house, he wasn't in."

"So you sit tight."

"Yeah. That's a switch. What the hell have I been doing,

hanging loose?'' There was a water tumbler on his desk, a third full with a brownish liquid. He took a last drag on his cigarette and dropped it into the glass. "Disgusting," he said. "I never want to see you do that, Matt. You don't smoke, do you?"

"Once in a great while."

"Yeah? You have one now and then and don't get hooked? I know a guy takes heroin that way. You know him, too, for that matter. But these little fuckers"—he tapped the pack—"I think they're more addictive than smack. You want one now?"

"No thanks."

He stood up. "The only things I don't get addicted to," he said, "are the ones I didn't like that much in the first place. Hey, thanks for coming by. There's nothing to do but wait, but I figured I wanted to keep you in the picture, let you know what's going on."

"That's fine," I said, "but I want you to know you don't owe me anything for it."

"What do you mean?"

"I mean don't go paying my bar tab for this."

"Are you sore?"

"No."

"It was just something I felt like doing."

"I appreciate it, but it wasn't necessary."

"Yeah, I guess." He shrugged. "When you're skimming you get to be very free with cash. You spend it on things that don't show. The hell with it. I can stand you a drink, though, can't I? In my own joint?"

"That you can do."

"C'mon then," he said, "before fucking Ruslander gives the whole store away."

Every time I went into Armstrong's I wondered if I'd run into Carolyn, and each time I was more relieved than disappointed when I didn't. I could have called her, but I sensed that it was perfectly appropriate not to. Friday night had been just what each of us had evidently wanted, and it looked as though it had been complete in itself for both of us, and I was glad of that. As a fringe benefit, I was over whatever had had me bugged about Fran, and it was beginning to look as though it had been nothing much more complicated than old-fashioned horniness. I suppose a half-hour with one of the streetwalkers would have served me as well, if less pleasurably.

I didn't run into Tommy, either, and that, too, was a relief, and in no sense disappointing.

Then Monday morning I picked up the *News* and read that they'd pulled in a pair of young Hispanics from Sunset Park for the Tillary burglary and homicide. The paper ran the usual photo—two skinny youths, their hair unruly, one of them trying to hide his face from the camera, the other smirking defiantly, and each of them handcuffed to a broad-shouldered grimfaced Irishman in a suit. There was a caption to tell you which ones were the good guys, but you didn't really need it.

I was in Armstrong's that afternoon when the phone rang. Dennis put down the glass he was wiping and answered it. "He was here a minute ago," he said. "I'll see if he stepped out." He covered the mouthpiece with his hand and looked quizzically at me. "Are you still here?" he asked. "Or did you slip away while my attention was somehow diverted?"

"Who wants to know?"

"Tommy Tillary."

You never know what a woman will decide to tell a man, or how a man will react to it. I didn't much want to find out, but I was better off learning over the phone than face-to-face. I nodded and Dennis passed the phone across the bar.

I said, "Matt Scudder, Tommy. I was sorry to hear about your wife."

"Thanks, Matt. Jesus, it feels like it happened a year ago. It was what, a little over a week?"

"At least they got the bastards."

There was a pause. Then he said, "Jesus. You haven't seen a paper, huh?"

"Sure I did. Two Spanish kids, had their pictures."

"I guess you read this morning's *News*."

"I generally do. Why?"

"But not this afternoon's *Post*."

"No. Why, what happened? They turn out to be clean?"

"Clean," he said, and snorted. Then he said, "I figured you'd know. The cops came by early this morning, before I saw the story in the *News*, so I didn't even know about the arrest. Shit. Be easier if you already knew this."

"I'm not following you, Tommy."

"The two Latin lovers. Clean? Shit, the men's room in the Times Square subway station, that's how clean they are. The cops hit their place and found stuff from my house everywhere they looked. Jewelry they had descriptions of, a stereo that I gave them the serial number, everything. Monogrammed shit. I mean that's how clean they were, for Christ's sake."

"So?"

"So they admitted the burglary but not the murder."

"Crooks do that all the time, Tommy."

"Lemme finish, huh? They admitted the burglary, but according to them it wasn't really a burglary. I was giving them all that stuff."

"And they just came to pick it up in the middle of the night."

"Yeah, right. No, their story was they were supposed to make it look like a burglary so I could collect from my insurance. I could claim a loss on top of what they were actually taking, and that way everybody's to the good."

"What did the actual loss amount to?"

"Shit, *I* don't know. There were twice as many things turned up at their place as I ever listed when I made out a report. There's things I missed a few days after I filled out the report and other stuff I didn't know was gone until the cops found them. And they took things weren't covered. There was a fur of Peg's, we were gonna get a floater on it and we never did. And some of her jewelry, same story. I got a standard homeowner's policy, it didn't cover anywheres near everything they took. They got a set of sterling, it came down to us from her aunt, I swear I forgot we owned the stuff. And *it* wasn't covered, either."

"It hardly sounds like an insurance setup."

"No, of course not. How the hell could it be? Anyway, the important thing is according to them the house was empty when they hit it. Peg wasn't home."

"And?"

"And I set them up is their story. They hit the place, they carted everything away, and then I came home with Peg and stabbed her six, eight times, whatever it was, and left her there so it looked like it happened during a burglary."

"How could the burglars testify that you stabbed your wife?"

"They couldn't. All they said was they didn't and she wasn't home when they were there and I had it arranged with them to do the burglary. The cops pieced the rest of it together."

"What did they do, arrest you?"

"No. They came over to the hotel where I'm staying, it was early, I was just out of the shower. Now this was the first I knew that the spics were arrested, let alone that they were trying to do a job on me. They just wanted to talk, the cops, and at first I talked to them, and then I started to get the drift of what they were trying to put on me. So I said I wasn't saying anything more without my lawyer present, and I called him, and he left half his breakfast on the table and came over in a hurry, and he wouldn't let me say a word."

"And they didn't take you in or book you?"

"No."

"But they didn't entirely buy your story either?"

"No way. I didn't really tell 'em a story because Kaplan wouldn't let me say anything. They didn't drag me in because they don't have a case yet, but according to Kaplan they're going to be building one if they can. They told me not to leave town. You believe it? My wife's dead, the *Post* headline says 'Quiz Husband in Burglary Murder,' and what the hell do they think I'm gonna do? Am I going fishing for fucking trout in Montana? 'Don't leave town.' You see this shit on television, you think nobody in real life talks like that. Maybe television's where they get it from."

I waited for him to tell me what he wanted from me. I didn't have long to wait.

"Why I called," he said, "is Kaplan thinks we ought to hire a detective. He figures maybe these guys talked around the neighborhood, maybe they bragged to their friends, maybe there's a way to prove they did the killing. He says the cops won't concentrate on that end if they're too busy trying to nail the lid shut on me."

I explained that I didn't have any official standing, that I had no license and filed no reports.

"That's okay," he insisted. "I told Kaplan what I want is somebody I can trust, somebody'll do a job for me. I don't think they're gonna have any kind of a case at all, Matt, because I can account for my time and I couldn'ta been where I woulda hadda be to do what they said I did. But the longer this shit drags on the worse it is for me. I want it cleared up, I want it in the papers that these Spanish assholes did it all and I had nothing to do with anything. I want that for me and for the people I do business with and for my relatives and Peg's relatives and all the wonderful people who voted for me. You remember the old 'Amateur Hour'? 'I want to thank mom and dad and Aunt Edith and my piano teacher Mrs. Pelton and all the wonderful people who voted for me.' Listen, you'll meet me and Kaplan in his office, hear what the man has to say, do me a hell of a big favor, and pick up a couple of bucks for yourself. What do you say, Matt?''

He wanted somebody he could trust. Had Carolyn from the Caroline told him how trustworthy I was?

What did I say? I said yes.

7

I took a train one stop into Brooklyn and met Tommy Tillary in Drew Kaplan's office on Court Street a few blocks from Brooklyn's Borough Hall. There was a Lebanese restaurant next door. At the corner a grocery store specializing in Middle Eastern imports stood next to an antique shop overflowing with stripped oak furniture and brass lamps and bedsteads. In front of Kaplan's building, a legless black man reposed on a platform with wheels. An open cigar box on one side of him held a couple of singles and a lot of coins. He was wearing horn-rimmed sunglasses, and a hand-lettered sign on the pavement in front of him said, "Don't Be Fooled by the Sunglasses. Not Blind Just No Legs."

Kaplan's office ran to wood paneling and leather chairs and oak file cabinets that might have come from the place on the corner. His name and the names of two partners were painted on the frosted glass of the hall door in old-fashioned gold and black lettering. Framed diplomas on the wall of his personal office showed he'd earned his B.A. at Adelphi, his LL.B. at Brooklyn Law. A lucite cube on top of a Victorian oak desk held photographs of his wife and young children. A bronzed railway spike served as a desktop paperweight. On the wall alongside the desk, a pendulum clock ticked away the afternoon.

Kaplan himself looked conservatively up-to-date in a tropical-weight gray pinstripe suit and a yellow pin-dot tie. He looked to be in his early thirties, which would fit the dates on the diplomas. He was shorter than I and of course much shorter than Tommy, trimly built, clean-shaven, with dark hair and eyes and a slightly lopsided smile. His handshake was medium-firm, his gaze direct but measuring, calculating.

Tommy wore his burgundy blazer over gray flannel trousers and white loafers. Strain showed at the corners of his blue eyes and around his mouth. His complexion was off, too, as if anxiety had caused the blood to draw inward, leaving the skin sallow.

"All we want you to do," Drew Kaplan said, "is find a key in one of their pants pockets, Herrera's or Cruz's, and trace it to a locker in Penn Station, and in the locker there's a foot-long knife with both their prints and her blood on it."

"Is that what it's going to take?"

He smiled. "Let's just say it wouldn't hurt. No, actually we're not in such bad shape. What they've got is some shaky testimony from a pair of Latins who've been in and out of trouble since they got weaned onto Tropicana. And they've got what looks to them like a good motive on Tommy's part."

"Which is?"

I was looking at Tommy when I asked. His eyes slipped away from mine. Kaplan said, "A marital triangle, a case of the shorts, and a strong money motive. Margaret Tillary came into some money this past spring upon the death of an aunt. The estate's not through probate yet but the value's somewhere in excess of half a million dollars."

"Be less than that when they get done hackin' away at it," Tommy said. "A whole lot less."

"Plus there's insurance. Tommy and his wife had a pair of straight-life policies, each naming the other as beneficiary, both with double-indemnity clauses and a face amount of"—he consulted a slip on his desk—"a hundred and fifty thousand dollars, which doubled for accidental death is three hundred thousand. At this point we've got what begins to look like seven, eight hundred thousand motives for murder."

"My lawyer talkin'," Tommy said.

"Same time, Tommy here's hurting a little for cash. He's having a bad year gambling, he's into the bookies and maybe they're starting to press him a little."

"Not so it amounts to anything," Tommy put in.

"I'm telling it the way the cops would tell it, all right? He owes some money around town, he's a couple of payments behind with the Buick. Meanwhile he's putting away this girl at the office, bouncing around the bars with her, sometimes not making it home altogether—"

"Hardly ever, Drew. I'd almost always make it home, an' if I couldn't grab a few hours in the sack I'd at least shower and change and have breakfast with Peg."

"What was breakfast? Dexamyl?"

"Sometimes. I had an office to go to, a job to do."

Kaplan sat on a corner of his desk, crossed his legs at the ankle. "That'll do for motive," he said. "What they don't bother to notice is a couple of things. One, he loved his wife, and how many husbands cheat? What is it they say? Ninety percent admit they cheat and ten percent lie about it? Two, he's got debts but he's not in a crunch. He's a guy makes good money over the year but he runs hot and cold, and for years he's been fat one month and strapped the next."

"You get used to it," Tommy said.

"Plus the numbers sound like a fortune, but they're not unusual figures. A half-million is substantial, but as Tommy said it won't net out to that much after taxes, and part of it consists of title to the house he's been occupying for years. A hundred fifty thousand dollars' insurance on a breadwinner isn't high by any means, and having the same coverage on the wife isn't uncommon, a lot of insurance agents try to write policies that way. They make it sound logically balanced, so you overlook the fact that you don't really need that kind of coverage on someone you don't depend upon for income." He spread his hands. "Anyway, the policies were taken out over ten years ago. This isn't something he went and set up last week."

He stood up, walked over to the window. Tommy had picked up the railway spike from the desk and was playing with it, slapping it against the palm of his hand, consciously or unconsciously matching the rhythm of the clock's pendulum.

Kaplan said, "One of the killers, Angel Herrera, except I suppose he pronounces it Ahn-hell, did some odd jobs at the Tillary house last March or April. Spring cleaning, he hauled stuff out of the basement and attic, did a little donkey work for hourly wages. According to Herrera, that's how Tommy knew to contact him to fake the burglary. According to common sense, that's how Herrera and his buddy Cruz knew the house and what was in it and how to gain access."

"How'd they do that?"

"Broke a small pane in the side door, reached in and unlocked it. Their story is Tommy left it open for them and must have broken the glass after. It's also their story that they left the place relatively neat."

"Looked like a cyclone hit it," Tommy said. "I had to go there. Made me sick to look at it."

"Their story is Tommy did that the same time he was murdering his wife. Except none of this works out if you take a good look at it. The times are all wrong. They went in around midnight, and the medical examiner places the time of death at between ten P.M. and four A.M. Now Tommy here never made it home from the office that evening. He worked past five, he met his friend for dinner, and he was with her in a variety of public places over the course of the evening." He looked over at his client. "We're lucky he's not much on discretion. His alibi'd be a whole lot thinner if he'd spent every minute in her apartment with the blinds drawn."

"I was discreet as far as Peg was concerned," Tommy said. "In Brooklyn I was a family man. What I did in the city never hurt her."

"After midnight his time's harder to account for," Kaplan went on. "The only substantiation for some of those hours is the girlfriend, because for a while they *were* in her apartment with the blinds drawn."

You didn't have to draw the blinds, I thought. Nobody could see in.

"Plus there was some time she couldn't account for."

"She fell asleep and I couldn't," Tommy said, "so I got dressed and went out for a couple of pops. But I wasn't gone that long, and she woke up when I got back. I had a helicopter, maybe I coulda got to Bay Ridge'n' back in that amount of time. Never do it in a Buick."

"The thing is," Kaplan said, "even supposing there was time, or discounting the girlfriend's alibi altogether and only accepting the times substantiated by unbiased witnesses, how could he possibly have done it? Say he sneaks home sometime after the Spanish kids have paid their visit and before four A.M., which was the latest the murder could have taken place. Where was she all this time? According to Cruz and Herrera, there was nobody home. Well, where did he find her to kill her? What did he do, haul her around in the trunk all night?"

"Let's say he killed her before they got there," I suggested.

"And I'm lookin' to *hire* this guy," Tommy said. "I got an instinct, you know what I mean?"

"Doesn't work," Kaplan said. "In the first place the times simply won't fit. He's alibied solid from before eight until past midnight, out in public with the girl. The M.E. says she was definitely alive at ten, that's the absolute earliest she could have been killed. Plus even forgetting the times it doesn't work. How could they go in, rob the whole house, and not see a dead woman in the bedroom? They were in that room, they were in possession of stolen articles from that room, I think they even found prints in there. Well, the police found the corpse of Margaret Tillary in that room, too, and it's the sort of thing they probably would have noticed."

"Maybe the body was covered up." I thought of Skip's big Mosler safe. "Locked in a closet they didn't look in."

He shook his head. "The cause of death was stabbing. There was a lot of blood and it was all over the place. The bed was soaked, the bedroom carpet." We both avoided looking at Tommy. "So she wasn't killed elsewhere," he concluded. "She was killed right there, and if it wasn't Herrera did it it was Cruz, and either way it wasn't Tommy."

I looked for a hole in it and couldn't find one. "Then I don't see what you need me for," I said. "The case against Tommy sounds pretty thin."

"So thin there isn't any case."

"Then—"

"The thing is," he said, "you get near a courtroom with something like this and even if you win you still lose. Because for the rest of your life all everybody remembers about you is you once stood trial for murdering your wife. Never mind that you won an acquittal. Everybody just figures some Jew lawyer bought a judge or conned a jury."

"So I'll get a guinea lawyer," Tommy said, "and they'll think he threatened the judge and beat up the jury."

"Besides," Kaplan said, "you never know which way a jury's going to jump. Remember, Tommy's alibi is he was with another woman at the time of the burglary. The woman's a colleague, they could choose to regard it as completely aboveboard, but did you see the piece in the *Post?* What juries'll go and do, they decide they don't believe the alibi because it's your girlfriend lying for you, and at the same time they label you a scumbag for getting your carrot scraped while your wife's getting killed."

"You keep it up," Tommy said, "I'll find my own self guilty, the way you make it sound."

"Plus he's hard to get a sympathetic jury for. He's a big handsome guy, a sharp dresser, and you'd love him in a gin joint but how much do you love him in a courtroom? He's a telephone securities salesman, perfectly respectable thing to be, calls you up, advises you how to invest your money. Fine. That means every clown who ever lost a hundred dollars on a stock tip or bought magazine subscriptions over the phone is going to walk into the courtroom with a hardon for him. I'm telling you, I want to stay the hell *out* of court. I'll *win* in court, I know that, or worse comes to worst I'll win on appeal, but who needs it? This is a case that shouldn't be in the first place, and what I'd love is to clear it up before they even go so far as presenting a bill to the grand jury."

"So from me you want—"

"Whatever you can find out, Matt. Whatever discredits Cruz and Herrera. I don't know what's there to find. I'd love it if you could find blood, their clothes with stains on it, anything like that. The point is that I don't know what's there to be found, and you were a cop and now you're working private, and you can get down in the streets and the bars and nose around. You familiar with Brooklyn?"

"Parts of it. I worked over here, off and on."

"So you can find your way around."

"Well enough. But wouldn't you be better off with a Spanish-speaker? I know enough to buy a beer in a bodega, but I'm a long way from fluent."

"Tommy says he wants somebody he can trust, and he was very adamant about calling you in. I think he's right. A personal relationship's worth more than a dime's worth of *'Me llamo Matteo y como está usted?'* "

"That's the truth," Tommy Tillary said. "Matt, I know I can count on you, and that's worth a lot."

I wanted to tell him all he could count on were his fingers, but why was I trying to talk myself out of a fee? His money was as good as anybody else's. I wasn't sure I liked him, but I was just as happy not to like the men I worked for. It bothered me less that way if I felt I was giving them less than full value.

And I didn't see how I could give him much. The case against him sounded loose enough to fall apart without my help. I wondered if Kaplan just wanted to create some activity to justify a high fee of his own, in the event that the whole thing blew itself out in a week's time. That was possible, and that wasn't my problem, either.

I said I would be glad to help. I said I hoped I would be able to come up with something useful.

Tommy said he was sure I could.

Drew Kaplan said, "Now you'll want a retainer. I suppose that'll be an advance against a per diem fee plus expenses, or do you bill at hourly rates? Why are you shaking your head?"

"I'm unlicensed," I said. "I have no official standing."

"That's no problem. We can carry you on the books as a consultant."

"I don't want to be on the books at all," I said. "I don't keep track of my time or expenses. I pay my own expenses out of my own pocket. I get paid in cash."

"How do you set your fees?"

"I think up a number. If I think I should have more coming when I'm finished, I say so. If you disagree, you don't have to pay me. I'm not going to take anybody to court."

"It seems a haphazard way to do business," Kaplan said.

"It's not a business. I do favors for friends."

"And take money for them."

"Is there anything wrong with taking money for a favor?"

"I don't suppose there is." He looked thoughtful. "How much would you expect for this favor?"

"I don't know what's involved," I said. "Suppose you let me have fifteen hundred dollars today. If things drag on and I feel entitled to more, I'll let you know."

"Fifteen hundred. And of course Tommy doesn't know exactly what he's getting for that."

"No," I said. "Neither do I."

Kaplan narrowed his eyes. "That seems high for a retainer," he said. "I'd have thought a third of that would be ample for starters."

I thought of my antique dealer friend. Did I know what it was to *hondle?* Kaplan evidently did.

"It's not that much," I said. "It's one percent of the insurance money, and that's part of the reason for hiring an investigator, isn't it? The company won't pay off until Tommy's in the clear."

Kaplan looked slightly startled. "That's true," he admitted, "but I don't know that it's the reason for hiring you. The company will pay up sooner or later. I don't think your fee is necessarily high, it just seemed a disproportionately large sum to lay out in advance, and—"

"Don't argue price," Tommy cut in. "The fee sounds fine to me, Matt. The only thing is, being a little short right now, and coming up with fifteen C in cash—"

"Maybe your lawyer will front it to you," I suggested.

Kaplan thought that was irregular. I went into the outer office while they talked it over. The receptionist was reading a copy of *Fate* magazine. A pair of hand-tinted etchings in antiqued frames showed scenes of nineteenth-century downtown Brooklyn. I was looking at them when Kaplan's door opened and he beckoned me back inside.

"Tommy's going to be able to borrow on the basis of his expectations from the insurance monies and his wife's estate," he said. "Meanwhile I can let you have the fifteen hundred. I hope you have no objection to signing a receipt?"

"None at all," I said. I counted the bills, twelve hundreds and six fifties, all circulated bills out of sequence. Everybody seems to have some cash around, even lawyers.

He wrote out a receipt and I signed it. He apologized for what he called a little awkwardness around the subject of my fee. "Lawyers are schooled to be very conventional human beings," he said. "I sometimes have a slow reaction time when it comes to adjusting to irregular procedure. I hope I wasn't offensive."

"Not at all."

"I'm glad of that. Now I won't be expecting written reports or a precise account of your movements, but you'll report to me as you go along and let me know what turns up? And please tell me too much rather than too little. It's hard to know what will prove useful."

"I know that myself."

"I'm sure you do." He walked me to the door. "And incidentally," he said, "your fee is only one-half of one percent of the insurance money. I think I mentioned that the policy had a double-indemnity clause, and murder is considered accidental."

"I know," I said. "I've always wondered why."

8

The Sixty-eighth Precinct is stationed on Sixty-fifth Street between Third and Fourth Avenues, straddling the approximate boundary of Bay Ridge and Sunset Park. On the south side of the street a housing project loomed; across from it, the station house looked like something from Picasso's cubist period, all blocky with cantilevered cubes and recessed areas. The structure reminded me of the building that houses the Two-three in East Harlem, and I learned later that the same architect designed them both.

The building was six years old then, according to the plaque in the entranceway that mentioned the architect, the police commissioner, the mayor, and a couple of other worthies making a bid for municipal immortality. I stood there and read the whole plaque as if it had a special message for me. Then I went up to the desk and said I was there to see Detective Calvin Neumann. The officer on duty made a phone call, then pointed me to the squad room.

The building's interior was clean and spacious and well lit. It had been open enough years, though, to begin to feel like what it was.

The squad room contained a bank of gray metal file cabinets, a row of green metal lockers, and twin rows of five-foot steel desks set back to back. A television set was on in one corner with nobody watching it. Half of the eight or ten desks were occupied. At the water cooler, a man in a suit talked with a man in his shirt sleeves. In the holding pen, a drunk sang something tuneless in Spanish.

I recognized one of the seated detectives but couldn't recall his name. He didn't look up. Across the room, another man looked familiar. I went up to a man I didn't know and he pointed out Neumann, two desks down on the opposite side.

He was filling in a form, and I stood while he finished what he was typing. He looked up then and said, "Scudder?" and pointed to a chair. He swiveled around to face me and waved a hand at the typewriter.

"They don't tell you," he said, "the hours you're gonna spend typing crud. Nobody out there realizes how much of this job is clerical."

"That's the part it's hard to get nostalgic about."

"I don't think I'd miss it myself." He yawned elaborately. "Eddie Koehler gave you high marks," he said. "I gave him a call like you suggested. He said you're okay."

"You know Eddie?"

He shook his head. "But I know what a lieutenant is," he said. "I haven't got a whole lot to give you, but you're welcome to it. You may not get the same cooperation from Brooklyn Homicide."

"Why's that?"

"They drew the case to start with. It got called in originally to the One-oh-four, which was actually wrong, it should have been ours, but that happens a lot. Then Brooklyn Homicide responded along with the One-oh-four, and they took the case away from the precinct guys."

"When did you come into it?"

"When a favorite snitch of mine came up with a lot of talk coming out of the bars and bakeries on Third under the expressway. A nice mink coat at a real good price, but you got to keep this quiet because there's a lot of heat. Well, July's a funny time to sell fur coats in Sunset Park. A guy buys a coat for his señora, he wants her to be able to wear it that night. So my guy comes to me with the impression that Miguelito Cruz has 'a houseful of stuff he's looking to sell and it just might be he hasn't got sales slips for many of the items. With the mink and a couple other items he mentioned, I remembered the Tillary job on Colonial Road, and it was enough to get a judge to issue a search warrant."

He ran a hand through his hair. It was medium brown, lighter where the sun had bleached it, and it was on the shaggy side. Cops were starting to wear their hair a little longer around about then, and the younger ones were beginning to show up in beards and moustaches. Neumann, though, was clean-shaven, his features regular except for a nose that had been broken and imperfectly reset.

"The stuff was in Cruz's house," he said. "He lives over on Fifty-first, the other side of the Gowanus Expressway. I have the address somewhere if you want it. Those are some pretty blighted blocks over by the Bush Terminal Warehouse, if you know where that is. A lot of empty lots and boarded-up buildings and others nobody bothered boarding up, or somebody opened them up again and there's junkies camped out there. Where Cruz lived wasn't so bad. You'll see it if you go over there."

"He live alone?"

He shook his head. "With his *abuela*. His grandmother. Little old lady, doesn't speak English, she probably ought to be in a home. Maybe they'll take her in at the Marien-Heim, it's right in the neighborhood. Old lady comes here from Puerto Rico, before she can learn English she winds up in a home with a German name. That's New York, right?'

"You found Tillary's possessions in the Cruz apartment?"

"Oh, yeah. No question. I mean the serial numbers matched on the record player. He tried to deny it. What else is new, right? 'Oh, I buy dis stuff on de street, it was some guy I met in a bar. I doan know hees name.' We told him, sure, Miguelito, but meanwhile a woman got cut bad in the house this stuff came out of, so it sure looks like you're gonna go away for murder one. The next minute he's copping to the burglary but insisting there was no dead woman when he was there."

"He must have known a woman got killed there."

"Of course, no matter who killed her. It was in the papers, right? One minute he says he didn't see the story, the next minute he didn't happen to recognize the address, you know how their stories keep changing."

"Where does Herrera come in?"

"They're cousins or something. Herrera lives in a furnished room on Forty-eighth between Fifth and Sixth just a couple of blocks from the park. Lived there, anyway. Right now they're both living at the Brooklyn House of Detention and they'll be living there until they move upstate."

"They both have sheets?"

"Be a surprise if they didn't, wouldn't it?" He grinned. "They're your typical fuckups. A few juvenile arrests for gang stuff. They both beat a burglary charge a year and a half ago, a judge ruled there wasn't probable cause to justify a frisk." He shook his head. "The fucking rules you have to play by. Anyway, they beat that one, and another time they got collared for burglary and plea-bargained it to criminal trespass and got suspended sentences for it. And another time, another burglary case, the evidence disappeared."

"It disappeared?"

"It got lost or misfiled or something, I don't know. It's a

miracle anybody ever goes to jail in this city. You really need a death wish to wind up in prison."

"So they did a fair amount of burglary."

"It looks like. In-and-out stuff, nickel-and-dime crap. Kick the door in, grab a radio, run into the street and sell it on the street for five or ten dollars. Cruz was worse than Herrera. Herrera worked from time to time, pushing a hand truck in the garment center or delivering lunches, minimum-wage stuff. I don't think Miguelito ever held a job."

"But neither of them ever killed anybody before."

"Cruz did."

"Oh?"

He nodded. "In a tavern fight, him and another asshole fighting over some woman."

"The papers didn't have that."

"It never got to court. There were no charges pressed. There were a dozen witnesses reporting that the dead guy went after Cruz first with a broken bottle."

"What weapon did Cruz use?"

"A knife. He said it wasn't his, and there were witnesses prepared to swear they'd seen somebody toss him the knife. And of course they hadn't happened to notice who it was did the tossing. We didn't have enough to make a case of weapon possession, let alone homicide."

"But Cruz normally carried a knife?"

"You'd be more likely to catch him leaving the house without underwear."

That was early afternoon, the day after I'd taken fifteen hundred dollars from Drew Kaplan. That morning I'd bought a money order and mailed it to Syosset. I paid my August rent in advance, settled a bar tab or two, and rode the BMT to Sunset Park.

It's in Brooklyn, of course, on the borough's western

edge, above Bay Ridge and south and west of Green-Wood Cemetery. These days there's a fair amount of brownstoning going on in Sunset Park, with young urban professionals fleeing the Manhattan rents and renovating the old row houses, gentrifying the neighborhood. Back then the upwardly mobile young had not yet discovered the place, and the population was a mixture of Latins and Scandinavians. Most of the former were Puerto Ricans, most of the latter Norwegians, and the balance was gradually shifting from Europe to the islands, from light to dark, but this was a process that had been going on for ages and there was nothing hurried about it.

I'd walked around some before my visit to the Six-eight, keeping mostly within a block or so of Fourth Avenue, the main commercial thoroughfare, and orienting myself intermittently by looking around for Saint Michael's Church. Few of the buildings stood more than three stories, and the egg-shaped church dome, set atop a two-hundred-foot tower, was visible a long ways off.

I walked north on Third Avenue now, on the right-hand side of the street, in the shade of the expressway overhead. As I neared Cruz's street I stopped in a couple of bars, more to immerse myself in the neighborhood than to ask any questions. I had a short shot of bourbon in one place, stuck to beer otherwise.

The block where Miguelito Cruz had lived with his grandmother was as Neumann described it. There were several vast vacant lots, one of them staked out in cyclone fencing, the others open and rubble-strewn. In one, small children played in the burned-out shell of a Volkswagen beetle. Four three-story buildings with scalloped brick fronts stood in a row on the north side of the block, closer to Second Avenue than to Third. The buildings abutting the group on either side had been torn down, and the newly exposed brick side walls looked raw except for the graffiti spray-painted on their lower portions.

Cruz had lived in the building closest to Second Avenue, closest too to the river. The vestibule was a lot of cracked and missing tiles and peeling paint. Six mailboxes were set into one wall, their locks broken and repaired and broken again. There were no bells to ring, nor was there a lock on the front door. I opened it and walked up two flights of stairs. The stairwell held cooking smells, rodent smells, a faint ammoniac reek of urine. All old buildings housing poor people smell like that. Rats die in the walls, kids and drunks piss. Cruz's building was no worse than thousands.

The grandmother lived on the top floor, in a perfectly neat railroad flat filled with holy pictures and little candle-illuminated shrines. If she spoke any English, she didn't let me know it.

No one answered my knock at the apartment across the hall.

I worked my way through the building. On the second floor, the apartment directly below the Cruz apartment was occupied by a very dark-skinned Hispanic woman with what looked like five children under six years old. A television set and a radio were playing in the front room, another radio in the kitchen. The children were in constant motion and at least two of them were crying or yelling at all times. The woman was cooperative enough, but she didn't have much English and it was impossible to concentrate on anything in there.

Across the hall, no one responded to my knock. I could hear a television set playing and went on knocking. Finally the door opened. An enormously fat man in his underwear opened the door and walked back inside without a word, evidently assuming I would follow. He led me through several rooms littered with old newspapers and empty Pabst Blue Ribbon cans to the front room, where he sat in a sprung armchair watching a game show. The color on his set was curiously distorted, giving the panelists faces that were red one moment and green the next.

He was white, with lank hair that had been blond once but was mostly gray now. It was hard to estimate his age because of the weight he was carrying, but he was probably somewhere between forty and sixty. He hadn't shaved in several days and may not have bathed or changed his bed linen in months. He stank, and his apartment stank, and I stayed there anyway and asked him questions. He had three beers left from a six-pack when I went in there, and he drank them one after another and padded barefoot through the apartment to return with a fresh six-pack from the refrigerator.

His name was Illing, he said, Paul Illing, and he had heard about Cruz, it was on television, and he thought it was terrible but he wasn't surprised, hell no. He'd lived here all his life, he told me, and this had been a nice neighborhood once, decent people, respected theirselves and respected their neighbors. But now you had the wrong element, and what could you expect?

"They live like animals," he told me. "You wouldn't believe it."

Angel Herrera's rooming house was a four-story red brick building, its ground floor given over to a coin laundry. Two men in their late twenties lounged on the stoop, drinking their beer from cans held in brown paper bags. I asked for Herrera's room. They decided I was a cop; the assumption showed in their faces, and the set of their shoulders. One of them told me to try the fourth floor.

There was a reek of marijuana smoke floating on top of the other smells in the hallway. A tiny woman, dark and bright-eyed, stood at the third-floor landing. She was wearing an apron and holding a folded copy of *El Diario*, one of the Spanish-language newspapers. I asked for Herrera's room.

"Twenny-two," she said, and pointed upstairs. "But he's not in." Her eyes fixed on mine. "You know where he is?"

"Yes."

"Then you know he is not here. His door is lock."

"Do you have the key?"

She looked at me sharply. "You a cop?"

"I used to be."

Her laugh was loud, unexpected. "Wha'd you get, laid off? They got no work for cops, all the crooks in jail? You want to go in Angel's room, come on, I let you in."

A cheap padlock secured the door of Room 22. She tried three keys before finding the right one, then opened the door and entered the room ahead of me. A cord hung from the bare-bulb ceiling fixture over the narrow iron bedstead. She pulled it, then raised a window shade to illuminate the room a little more.

I looked out the window, walked around the room, examined the contents of the closet and the small bureau. There were several photographs in drugstore frames on top of the bureau, and half a dozen unframed snapshots. Two different women, several children. In one snapshot, a man and woman in bathing suits squinted into the sun, the surf behind them. I showed the photograph to the woman and she identified the man as Herrera. I had seen his photo in the paper, along with Cruz and the two arresting officers, but he looked completely different in the snapshot.

The woman, I learned, was Herrera's girlfriend. The woman who appeared in some of the other photos with the children was Herrera's wife in Puerto Rico. He was a good boy, Herrera was, the woman assured me. He was polite, he kept his room neat, he didn't drink too much or play his radio loud late at night. And he loved his babies, he sent money home to Puerto Rico when he had it to send.

• • •

Fourth Avenue had churches on the average of one to a block—Norse Methodist, German Lutheran, Spanish Seventh-Day Adventists, and one called the Salem Tabernacle. They were all closed, and by the time I got to it, so was Saint Michael's. I was ecumenical enough in my tithing, but the Catholics got most of my money simply because they kept longer hours, but by the time I left Herrera's rooming house and stopped for a quick one at the bar on the corner, Saint Michael's was locked up as tight as its Protestant fellows.

Two blocks away, between a bodega and an OTB parlor, a gaunt Christ writhed on the cross in the window of a storefront *iglesia*. There were a couple of backless benches inside in front of a small altar, and on one of them two shapeless women in black huddled silent and motionless.

I slipped inside and sat on one of the benches myself for a few moments. I had my hundred-fifty-dollar tithe ready and I'd have been as happy giving it to this hole in the wall as to some more imposing and long-established firm, but I couldn't think of an inconspicuous way to manage it. There was no poor box in evidence, no receptacle designed to accommodate donations. I didn't want to call attention to myself by finding someone in charge and handing him the money, nor did I feel comfortable just leaving it on the bench, say, where anybody could pick it up and walk off with it.

I walked out of there no poorer than I'd walked in.

I spent the evening in Sunset Park.

I don't know if it was work, or if I even thought I was doing Tommy Tillary any good. I walked the streets and worked the bars, but I wasn't looking for anyone and I didn't ask a lot of questions.

On Sixtieth Street east of Fourth Avenue I found a dark

beery tavern called the Fjord. There were nautical decorations on the walls but they looked to have accumulated haphazardly over the years—a length of fishnet, a life preserver, and, curiously, a Minnesota Vikings football pennant. A black-and-white TV sat at one end of the bar, its volume turned down low. Old men sat with their shots and beers, not talking much, letting the night pass.

When I left there I flagged a gypsy cab and got the driver to take me to Colonial Road in Bay Ridge. I wanted to see the house where Tommy Tillary had lived, the house where his wife had died. But I wasn't sure of the address. That stretch of Colonial Road was mostly brick apartment houses and I was pretty sure that Tommy's place was a private house. There were a few such houses tucked in between the apartment buildings but I didn't have the number written down and wasn't sure of the cross streets. I told the cabdriver I was looking for the house where the woman was stabbed to death and he didn't know what the hell I was talking about, and seemed generally wary of me, as though I might do something unpredictable at any moment.

I suppose I was a little drunk. I sobered up on the way back to Manhattan. He wasn't that enthusiastic about taking me, but he set a price of ten dollars and I agreed to it and leaned back in my seat. He took the expressway, and en route I saw the tower of Saint Michael's and told the driver that it wasn't right, that churches should be open twenty-four hours a day. He didn't say anything, and I closed my eyes and when I opened them the cab was pulling up in front of my hotel.

There were a couple of messages for me at the desk. Tommy Tillary had called twice and wanted me to call him. Skip Devoe had called once.

It was too late to call Tommy, probably too late for Skip. Late enough, anyway, to call it a night.

9

I rode out to Brooklyn again the next day. I stayed on the train past the Sunset Park stations and got off at Bay Ridge Avenue. The subway entrance was right across the street from the funeral parlor Margaret Tillary had been buried from. Burial had been in Green-Wood Cemetery, two miles to the north. I turned and looked up Fourth Avenue, as if following the route of the funeral cortege with my eyes. Then I walked west on Bay Ridge Avenue toward the water.

At Third Avenue I looked to my left and saw the Verrazano Bridge off in the distance, spanning the Narrows between Brooklyn and Staten Island. I walked on, through a better neighborhood than the one I'd spent the previous day in, and at Colonial Road I turned right and walked until I found the Tillary house. I'd looked up the address before leaving my hotel and now found it easily. It may have been one of the houses I'd stared at the night before. The cab ride had since faded some from memory. It was indistinct, as if seen through a veil.

The house was a huge brick-and-frame affair three stories tall, just across the street from the southeast corner of Owl's

91

Head Park. Four-story apartment buildings of red brick flanked the house. It had a broad porch, an aluminum awning, a steeply pitched roof. I mounted the steps to the porch and rang the doorbell. A four-note chime sounded within.

No one answered. I tried the door and it was locked. The lock didn't look terribly challenging, but I had no reason to force it.

A driveway ran past the house on its left-hand side. It led past a side door, also locked, to a padlocked garage. The burglars had broken a pane of glass in the side door, and it had been since replaced with a rectangle of cardboard cut from a corrugated carton and secured with metallic tape.

I crossed the street and sat in the park for a while. Then I moved to where I could observe the Tillary house from the other side of the street. I was trying to visualize the burglary. Cruz and Herrera had had a car, and I wondered where they'd parked it. In the driveway, out of sight and close to the door they'd entered through? Or on the street, making a getaway a simpler matter? The garage could have been open then; maybe they stowed the car in it, so no one would see it in the driveway and wonder about it.

I had a lunch of beans and rice and hot sausage. I got to Saint Michael's by midafternoon. It was open this time, and I sat for a while in a pew off to the side, then lit a couple of candles. My $150 finally made it to the poor box.

I did what you do. Mostly, I walked around and knocked on doors and asked questions. I went back to both their residences, Herrera's and Cruz's. I talked to neighbors of Cruz's who hadn't been around the previous day, and I talked to some of the other tenants in Herrera's rooming house. I walked over to the Six-eight looking for Cal Neumann. He wasn't there, but I talked to a couple of cops in the station house and went out for coffee with one of them.

I made a couple of phone calls, but most of my activity was walking around and talking to people face-to-face, writing down bits and pieces in my notebook, going through the motions and trying not to question the point of my actions. I was amassing a certain amount of data but I had no idea whether or not it added up to anything. I didn't know what exactly I was looking for, or if there was anything there *to* look for. I suppose I was trying to perform enough action and produce enough information to justify, to myself and to Tommy and his lawyer, the fee I had already collected and largely dispersed.

By early evening I'd had enough. I took the train home. There was a message at the desk for me from Tommy Tillary, with his office number. I put it in my pocket and walked around the corner, and Billie Keegan told me Skip was looking for me.

"Everybody's looking for me," I said.

"It's nice to be wanted," Billie said. "I had an uncle was wanted in four states. You had a phone message, too. Where'd I put it?" He handed me a slip. Tommy Tillary again, but a different phone number this time. "Something to drink, Matt? Or did you just drop by to check your mail and messages?"

I'd been taking it easy in Brooklyn, mostly sticking with cups of coffee in bakeries and bodegas, drinking a little beer in the bars. I let Billie pour me a double bourbon and it went down easy.

"Looked for you today," Billie said. "Couple of us went out to the track. Thought you might want to come along."

"I had work to do," I said. "Anyway, I'm not much for horses."

"It's fun," he said, "if you don't take it serious."

• • •

The number Tommy Tillary left turned out to be a hotel switchboard in Murray Hill. He came on the line and asked if I could drop by the Hotel. "You know where it is? Thirty-seventh and Lex?"

"I ought to be able to find it."

"They got a bar downstairs, nice quiet little place. It's full of these Jap businessmen in Brooks Brothers suits. Every once in a while they put down their scotches long enough to take snapshots of each other. Then they smile and order more drinks. You'll love it."

I caught a cab and went over there, and he hadn't been exaggerating much. The cocktail lounge, plush and dimly lit, had a largely Japanese clientele that evening. Tommy was by himself at the bar, and when I walked in he pumped my hand and introduced me to the bartender.

We took our drinks to a table. "Crazy place," he said. "Look at that, will you? You thought I was kidding about the cameras, didn't you? I wonder what they do with all the pictures. You'd need a whole room in your house just to keep them, the way they click 'em off."

"There's no film in the cameras."

"Be a kick, wouldn't it?" He laughed. "No film in the cameras. Shit, they're probably not real Japs, either. Where I mostly been going, there's the Blueprint a block away on Park, and there's another place, a pub-type place, Dirty Dick's or something like that. But I'm staying here and I wanted you to be able to reach me. Is this okay for now or should we go somewhere else?"

"This is fine."

"You sure? I never had a detective work for me before, I want to make sure I keep him happy." He grinned, then let his face turn serious. "I was just wondering," he said, "if you were, you know, making any progress. Getting any-place."

I told him some of what I'd run into. He got very excited when he heard about the barroom stabbing.

"That's great," he said. "That ought to wrap it up for our little brown brothers, shouldn't it?"

"How do you figure that?"

"He's a knife artist," he said, "and he already killed somebody once and got away with it. Jesus, this is great stuff, Matt. I knew it was the right move to get you in on this. Have you talked to Kaplan yet?"

"No."

"That's what you want to do. This is the kind of stuff he can use."

I wondered at that. For openers, it struck me that Drew Kaplan should have been able to inform himself of Miguelito Cruz's no-bill for homicide without hiring a detective. Nor did it seem to me that the information would weigh heavily in a courtroom, or that you could even introduce it in court, for that matter. Anyway, Kaplan had said he was looking for something that would keep him and his client out of court in the first place, and I couldn't see how I'd uncovered anything that qualified.

"You want to fill Drew in on everything you come up with," Tommy assured me. "Some little bit you hand him, might not look like anything to you, and it might fit with something he already has and it's just what he needs, you know what I mean? Even if it looks like nothing all by itself."

"I can see how that would work."

"Sure. Call him once a day, give him whatever you got. I know you don't file reports, but you don't mind checking in regular by phone, do you?"

"No, of course not."

"Great," he said. "That's great, Matt. Let me get us a couple more of these." He went to the bar, came back with fresh drinks. "So you been out in my part of the world, huh? Like it out there?"

"I like your neighborhood better than Cruz and Herrera's."

"Shit, I hope so. What, were you out by the house? My house?"

I nodded. "To get a sense of it. You have a key, Tommy?"

"A key? You mean a house key? Sure, I'd have to have a key to my own house, wouldn't I? Why? You want a key to the place, Matt?"

"If you don't mind."

"Jesus, everybody's been through there, cops, insurance, not to mention the spics." He took a ring of keys from his pocket, removed one and held it out to me. "This is for the front door," he said. "You want the side door key too? That's how they went in, there's cardboard taped up where they broke a pane to let themselves in."

"I noticed it this afternoon."

"So what do you need with the key? Just pull off the cardboard and let yourself in. While you're at it, see if there's anything left worth stealing and carry it outta there in a pillowcase."

"Is that how they did it?"

"Who knows how they did it? That's how they do it on television, isn't it? Jesus, look at that, will ya? They take each other's pictures, they trade cameras and take 'em all over again. There's a lot of 'em stay at this hotel, that's why they come in here." He looked down at his hands, clasped loosely on the table in front of him. His pinkie ring had turned to one side and he reached to straighten it. "The hotel's not bad," he said, "but I can't stay here forever. You pay day rates, it adds up."

"Will you be moving back to Bay Ridge?"

He shook his head. "What do I need with a place like

that? It was too big for the two of us and I'd rattle around there by myself. Forgetting about the feelings connected with it."

"How did you come to have such a large house for two people, Tommy?"

"Well, it wasn't for two." He looked off, remembering. "It was Peg's aunt's house. What happened, she put up the money to buy the place. She had some insurance money left after she buried her husband some years ago, and we needed a place to live because we had the baby coming. You knew we had a kid that died?"

"I think there was something in the paper."

"In the death notice, yeah, I put it in. We had a boy, Jimmy. He wasn't right, he had congenital heart damage and some mental retardation. He died, it was just before his sixth birthday."

"That's hard, Tommy."

"It was harder for her. I think it woulda been worse than it was except he didn't live at home after the first few months. The medical problems, you couldn't really cope in a private home, you know what I mean? Plus the doctor took me aside and said, look, Mr. Tillary, the more your wife gets attached to the kid, the rougher it's gonna be on her when the inevitable happens. Because they knew he wasn't gonna live more than a couple of years."

Without saying anything he got up and brought back fresh drinks. "So it was the three of us," he went on, "me and Peg and the aunt, and she had her room and her own bath an' all on the third floor, an' it was still a big house for three people, but the two women, you know, they kept each other company. And then when the old woman died, well, we talked about moving, but Peg was used to the house and used to the neighborhood." He took a breath and let his shoulders drop. "What do I need, big house, drive back and forth or fight the subway, whole thing's a pain in the ass.

Soon as all this clears up I'll sell the place, find myself a little apartment in the city."

"What part of town?"

"You know, I don't even know. Around Gramercy Park is kind of nice. Or maybe the Upper East Side. Maybe buy a co-op in a decent building. I don't need a whole lot of space." He snorted. "I could move in with whatsername. You know. Carolyn."

"Oh?"

"You know we work at the same place. I see her there every day. 'I gave at the office.'" He sighed. "I been sort of stayin' away from the neighborhood until all of this is cleared up."

"Sure."

And then we got on the subject of churches, and I don't remember how. Something to the effect that bars kept better hours than churches, that churches closed early. "Well, they got to," he said, "on account of the crime problem. Matt, when we were kids, who ever heard of somebody stealing from a church?"

"I suppose it happened."

"I suppose it did but when did you ever hear of it? Nowadays you got a different class of people, they don't respect anything. Of course there's that church in Bensonhurst, I guess they keep whatever hours they want to."

"What do you mean?"

"I think it's Bensonhurst. Big church, I forget the name of it. Saint Something or other."

"That narrows it down."

"Don't you remember? Couple of years ago two black kids stole something off the altar. Gold candlesticks, whatever the hell it was. And it turns out Dominic Tutto's mother goes to mass there every morning. The capo, runs half of Brooklyn?"

"Oh, right."

"And the word went out, and a week later the candlesticks are back on the altar. Or whatever the hell they were. I think it was candlesticks."

"Whatever."

"And the punks who took 'em," he said, "disappeared. And the story I heard, well, you don't know if it was anything more than a story. I wasn't there, and I forget who I heard it from, but *he* wasn't there either, you know?"

"What did you hear?"

"I heard they hauled the two niggers to Tutto's basement," he said, "and hung 'em on meat hooks." A flashbulb winked two tables away from us. "And skinned 'em alive," he said. "But who knows? You hear all these stories, you don't know what to believe."

"You should've been with us this afternoon," Skip told me. "Me and Keegan and Ruslander, we took my car and drove out to the Big A." He drawled in imitation of W. C. Fields: "Participated in the sport of kings, made our contribution to the improvement of the breed, yes indeed."

"I was doing some work."

"I'd have been better off working. Fucking Keegan, he's got a pocket full of miniatures, he's knocking 'em off one a race, he's got his pockets full of these little bottles. And he's betting horses on the basis of their names. There's this plater, Jill the Queen, hasn't won anything since Victoria was the queen, and Keegan remembers this girl named Jill he had this mad passion for in the sixth grade. So of course he bets the horse."

"And the horse wins."

"Of *course* the horse wins. The horse wins at something like twelve-to-one, and Keegan's got a ten-dollar win ticket on her, and he's saying he made a mistake. What mistake? 'Her name was Rita,' he says. 'It was her sister's name was Jill. I remembered it wrong.'"

"That's Billie."

"Well, the whole afternoon was like that," Skip said. "He bets his old girlfriends and their sisters and he drinks half a quart of whiskey out of these little bottles, and Ruslander and I both lose I don't know, a hundred, hundred and fifty, and fucking Billie Keegan wins six hundred dollars by betting on girls' names."

"How did you and Ruslander pick horses?"

"Well, you know the actor. He hunches his shoulders and talks out of the side of his mouth like a tout, and he talks to a couple of horsey-looking guys and comes back with a tip. The guys he talks to are probably other actors."

"And you both followed his tips?"

"Are you crazy? I bet scientific."

"You read the form?"

"I can't make sense out of it. I watch which ones have the odds drop when the smart money comes in, and also I go down and watch 'em walk around, and I notice which one takes a good crap."

"Scientific."

"Absolutely. Who wants to invest serious money in some fucking constipated horse? Some steed wracked with irregularity? My horses"—he lowered his eyes, mock-shy—"are M/O-kay."

"And Keegan's crazy."

"You got it. The man trivializes a scientific pursuit." He leaned forward, ground out his cigarette. "Ah, Jesus, I love this life," he said. "I swear to God I was born for it. I spend half my life running my own saloon and the other half in other people's saloons, with a sunny afternoon away from it now and then to get close to nature and commune with God's handiwork." His eyes locked on mine. "I love it," he said levelly. "That's why I'm gonna pay those cock-suckers."

"You heard from them?"

"Before we left for the track. They presented their nonnegotiable demands."

"How much?"

"Enough to make my bets seem somehow beside the point. Who cares if you win or lose a hundred dollars? And I don't bet heavy, it's not fun once it gets into serious money. *They* want serious money."

"And you're going to pay it?"

He picked up his drink. "We're meeting with some people tomorrow. The lawyer, the accountants. That's if Kasabian stops throwing up."

"And then?"

"And then I suppose we try to negotiate the nonnegotiable, and then we fucking pay. What else are the lawyers and accountants going to tell us? Raise an army? Fight a guerrilla war? That's not the kind of answer you get from lawyers and accountants." He took another cigarette from the pack, tapped it, held it up, looked at it, tapped it again, then lit it. "I'm a machine that smokes and drinks," he said through a cloud of smoke, "and I'll tell you, I don't know why I fucking bother with any of it."

"A minute ago you loved this life."

"Was I the one who said that? You know the story about the guy bought a Volkswagen and his friend asks him how does he like it? 'Well, it's like eating pussy,' the guy says. 'I'm crazy about it, but I don't take a whole lot of pride in it.'"

10

I called Drew Kaplan the next morning before I went out to Brooklyn. His secretary said he was in a meeting, and could he call me back? I said I'd call him back, and I did forty minutes later when I got off the subway in Sunset Park. By then he'd gone for lunch. I told her I'd call back later.

That afternoon I managed to meet a woman who was friendly with Angel Herrera's girlfriend. She had strong Indio features and a face badly pitted by acne. She said it was a pity for Herrera that he had to go to jail, but it was probably good for her friend, because Herrera would never marry her or even live with her because he considered himself still married in Puerto Rico. "An' his wife divorce him, but he doan accept it," she said. "So my fren, she wanna get pregnant, but he doan get her pregnant and he woan marry her. What's she want with him, you know? Better for her if he goes away for a while. Better for everybody."

I called Kaplan again from a street corner phone booth and reached him this time. I got out my notebook and gave him what I had. None of it added up to anything as far as I could see, except for Cruz's prior arrest for manslaughter, which was something he should have known about, as he was quick enough to point out himself. "That's not something an investigator should have to come up with," he said. "They should have put that on the table. True, you can't introduce it in court, but there's ways to use it. You may have earned your fee with that little bit of information. Not that I want to discourage you from digging for more."

But when I'd hung up the phone I didn't really feel like digging for more. I went over to the Fjord and had a couple of drinks, but then a lanky kid with a lot of yellow hair and a blond Zapata moustache came in and tried to hustle me into a game on the shuffle-bowling machine. I wasn't interested and neither was anyone else, so he went and played the thing by himself, feigning noisy drunkenness, I suppose in an attempt to look like easy pickings. The noise drove me out of there, and I wound up walking all the way to Tommy's house on Colonial Road.

His key unlocked the front door. I walked in, half expecting the scene that had greeted the discoverer of Margaret Tillary's body, but of course things had been cleaned up and put right long ago, after the lab crew and the photographer had done their work and gone.

I walked through the rooms on the ground floor, found the side entrance that led to a vestibule off the kitchen, walked back through the kitchen and the dining room, trying to imagine myself into Cruz and Herrera's shoes as they moved through the rooms of the empty house.

Except it wouldn't have been empty. Margaret Tillary had been upstairs in her bedroom. Doing what? Sleeping? Watching television?

I climbed the stairs. A couple of the boards creaked underfoot. Had they done so the night of the burglary? Had Peg Tillary heard, and had she reacted? Maybe she thought it was Tommy's step, got out of bed to greet him. Maybe she knew it was someone else. Footsteps are recognizable to some people, and a stranger's footfall is unfamiliar, enough so sometimes to intrude on sleep.

She'd been killed in the bedroom. Up the stairs, open the door, find a woman cowering in there and stab her? Or maybe she'd come out of the bedroom door, expecting Tommy, or not expecting him but not thinking straight, confronting the burglar, people did that all the time, not thinking, outraged at the invasion of their home, acting as if their righteous indignation would serve them as armor.

Then she'd have seen the knife in his hand, and she'd have gone back inside the room, tried to shut the door, maybe, and he'd come in after her, and maybe she was screaming and he had to get to her to shut her up, and—

I kept seeing Anita backing away from a knife, kept turning the scene into our bedroom in Syosset.

Silly.

I walked over to one of the dressers, opened drawers, closed them. Her dresser, long and low. His was a highboy in the same French Provincial styling, part of a suite with the bed and a nightstand and a mirrored dressing table. I opened and closed drawers in his dresser. He'd left a lot of clothes behind, but he probably owned a lot of clothes.

I opened the closet door. She could have hidden in the closet, though not comfortably. It was full, the shelf loaded with a couple dozen shoe boxes, the rack packed with clothes on hangers. He must have taken a couple of suits and jackets with him, but the clothes he'd left behind were more than I owned.

There were bottles of perfume on the dressing table. I lifted the stopper of one and held it to my nose. The scent was lily-of-the-valley.

I was in the room for a long time. There are people who are psychically sensitive, they pick up things at a murder scene. Maybe everyone does, maybe the sensitive ones are simply better at figuring out what it is that they're attuned to. I had no illusions about my ability to glean vibrations from the room or the clothing or the furniture. Smell is the sense most directly hooked into the memory, but all her perfume did was remind me that an aunt of mine had smelled of that same floral scent.

I don't know what I thought I was doing there.

There was a television set in the bedroom. I turned it on, turned it off. She might have been watching it, she might not even have heard the burglar until he opened the door. But wouldn't he have heard the set? Why would he come into a room if he knew someone was there, when he could just slip away undetected?

Of course he could have had rape in mind. There hadn't been any rape, none detected in the autopsy, although that hardly proved the absence of intent. He might have achieved sexual release from the murder, might have been turned off by the violence, might have . . .

Tommy had slept in this room, had lived with the woman who smelled of lilies-of-the-valley. I knew him from the bars, I knew him with a girl on his arm and a drink in his hand and his laugh echoing off paneled walls. I didn't know him in a room like this, in a house like this.

I went in and out of other rooms on the second floor. In what I suppose was the upstairs sitting room, photos in silver frames were grouped on top of a mahogany radio-phonograph console. There was a formal wedding picture, Tommy in a tuxedo, the bride in white with her bouquet all pink and white. Tommy was lean in the photo, and impossibly young. He was sporting a crew cut, which looked outlandish in 1975, especially in counterpoint to the formal clothes.

Margaret Tillary—she might still have been Margaret Wayland when the photo was taken—had been a tall woman, with strong features even then. I looked at her and tried to imagine her with years added. She'd probably put on a few pounds over the years. Most people did.

Most of the other photos showed people I didn't recognize. Relatives, I suppose. I didn't notice any of the son Tommy'd told me about.

One door led to a linen closet, another to a bathroom. A third opened on a flight of stairs leading to the third floor. There was a bedroom up there, its window affording a good view of the park. I drew up an armchair, its seat and back worked in needlepoint, and watched the traffic on Colonial Road and a baseball game in the park.

I imagined the aunt sitting as I was sitting, watching the world through her window. If I'd heard her name I didn't remember it, and when I thought of her the image that came to mind was some sort of generic aunt, some combination of the various unidentifiable female faces in the photographs downstairs mixed, I suppose, with elements of some aunts of my own. She was gone now, this unnamed composite aunt, and her niece was gone, and before long the house would be sold and other people living in it.

And it would be a piece of work, too, removing the traces of the Tillary occupancy. The aunt's bedroom and bathroom took up the front third of the top floor; the rest was a large open space given over to storage, with trunks and cardboard cartons fitted in under the pitched roof along with pieces of furniture that had been removed from service. Some were covered with cloths. Others were not. Everything was lightly coated with dust, and you could smell the dust in the air.

I went back to the aunt's bedroom. Her clothes were still in the dresser and closet, her toilet articles in the bathroom medicine chest. Easy enough to leave everything, if they didn't need the room.

I wondered what Herrera had hauled away. That was how

he'd first come to the house, carting off jetsam after the aunt's death.

I sat in the chair again. I smelled the dust of the storage room, and the scent of the old woman's clothes, but I still held the lily-of-the-valley perfume in my nostrils and it overscored all of the other aromas. It cloyed now, and I wished I could stop smelling it. It seemed to me that I was smelling the memory of the scent more than the scent itself.

In the park across the street, two boys were playing a game of keep-away, with a third boy running vainly back and forth between them, trying to get the striped ball they tossed back and forth. I leaned forward, propping my elbows on the radiator to watch them. I tired of the game before they did. I left the chair facing the window and walked through the open area and down both flights of stairs.

I was in the living room, wondering what Tommy had around the house to drink and where he kept it, when someone cleared his throat a couple of yards behind me.

I froze.

11

"Yeah," a voice said. "I sort of figured it was you. Whyntcha sit down, Matt. You look white as a ghost. You look like you seen one."

I knew but couldn't place the voice. I turned, my breath still stuck in my chest, and I knew the man. He was sitting in an overstuffed armchair, deep in the room's long shadows. He was wearing a short-sleeved shirt open at the throat. His suit jacket was draped over the chair's arm, and the end of his tie peeped out of a pocket.

"Jack Diebold," I said.

"The same," he said. "How you doin', Matt? I got to tell you you'd make the world's worst cat burglar. You were clompin' around up there like the horse cavalry."

"You scared the shit out of me, Jack."

He laughed softly. "Well, what was I gonna do, Matt? A neighbor called in, lights on in the house, blah blah blah, and since I was handy and it was my case I took the squeal myself and came on over. I figured it was probably you. Guy from the Six-eight called me the other day, mentioned you were doin' something for this Tillary asshole."

108

"Neumann called you? You're at Brooklyn Homicide now?"

"Oh, a while now. I made Detective First, shit, it's been almost two years."

"Congratulations."

"Thanks. Anyway, I came over, but I don't know it's you and I don't want to charge the stairs and I thought, shit, we'll let Mohammad come to the mountain for a change. I didn't mean to scare you."

"The hell you didn't."

"Well, you walked right past me, for God's sake, and you looked so funny goin' about it. What were you lookin' for just now?"

"Just now? I was trying to guess where he keeps his liquor."

"Well, don't let me stop you. Find a couple of glasses too, while you're at it."

A pair of cut-glass decanters stood on a sideboard in the dining room. Little silver nameplates around their necks identified them as Scotch and Rye. You needed a key to remove them from their silver caddy. The sideboard itself held linen in its center drawers, glassware on the right-hand side, bottles of whiskey and cordials on the left. I found a fifth of Wild Turkey and a couple of glasses, showed the bottle to Diebold. He nodded and I poured drinks for both of us.

He was a big man a couple of years my senior. He'd lost some hair since I'd seen him last, and he was heavy, but then he'd always been heavy. He looked at his glass for a moment, raised it to me, took a sip.

"Good stuff," he said.

"Not bad."

"What were you doin' up there, Matt? Lookin' for clues?" He stretched the last word.

I shook my head. "Just getting the feel of it."

"You're working for Tillary."

I nodded. "He gave me the key."

"Shit, I don't care if you came down the chimney like Santy Claus. What's he want you to do for him?"

"Clear him."

"Clear him? The cocksucker's already clear enough to see through. No way we're gonna tag him for it."

"But you think he did it."

He gave me a sour look. "I don't think he did it," he said, "if doin' it means stickin' a knife in her. I'd love thinkin' he did but he's alibied better than a fuckin' Mafia don. He was out in public with this broad, a million people saw him, he's got charge-card receipts from a restaurant, for Christ's sake." He drank the rest of his whiskey. "I think he set her up."

"Hired them to kill her?"

"Something like that."

"They're not hired killers by trade, are they?"

"Shit, of course they're not. Cruz and Herrera, button men for the Sunset Park syndicate. Rubouts a specialty."

"But you think he hired them."

He came over and took the bottle from me, poured his glass half full. "He set them up," he said.

"How?"

He shook his head, impatient with the question. "I wish I was the first person to question them," he said. "The guys from the Six-eight went over with a burglary warrant, they didn't know when they went in where the stuff was from. So they already talked to the PRs before I got a crack at 'em."

"And?"

"First time out, they denied everything. 'I bought the stuff on the street.' You know how it goes."

"Of course."

"Then they didn't know anything about a woman who got killed. Now that was horseshit. They ran that story and then they changed it, or it died a natural death, because of course they knew, it was in the papers and on the television. Then the story was that there was no woman around when they did the job, and on top of that they were never upstairs of the first floor. Well, that's nice, but their fucking fingerprints were on the bedroom mirror and the dresser top and a couple of other places."

"You had prints putting them in the bedroom? I didn't know that."

"Maybe I shouldn't tell you. Except I can't see how it makes a difference. Yeah, we found prints."

"Whose? Herrera's or Cruz's?"

"Why?"

"Because I was figuring Cruz for the one who knifed her."

"Why him?"

"His record. And he carried a knife."

"A flick knife. He didn't use it on the woman."

"Oh?"

"She was killed with something had a blade six inches long and two or two-and-a-half inches wide. Whatever. A kitchen knife, it sounds like."

"You didn't recover it, though."

"No. She had a whole mess of knives in the kitchen, a couple of different sets. You keep house for twenty years, you accumulate knives. Tillary couldn't tell if one was missing. The lab took the ones we found, couldn't find blood on any of them."

"So you think—"

"That one of 'em picked up a knife in the kitchen and went upstairs with it and killed her and then threw it down a sewer somewhere, or in the river, or who knows where."

"Picked up a knife in the kitchen."

"Or brought it along. Cruz carried a flick knife as a

regular thing, but maybe he didn't want to use his own knife to kill the woman."

"Figuring he came here planning to do it."

"How else can you figure it?"

"I figure it was a burglary and they didn't know she was here."

"Yeah, well, you want to figure it that way because you're trying to clear the prick. He goes upstairs and takes a knife along with him. Why the knife?"

"In case someone's up there."

"Then why go upstairs?"

"He's looking for money. A lot of people keep cash in the bedroom. He opens the door, she's there, she panics, he panics—"

"And he kills her."

"Why not?"

"Shit, it sounds as good as anything else, Matt." He put his glass on the coffee table. "One more session with 'em," he said, "and they woulda spilled."

"They talked a lot as it was."

"I know. You know what's the most important thing to teach a new recruit? How to read 'em Miranda-Escobedo in such a way that they don't attach any significance to it. 'You have the right to remain silent. Now I want you to tell me what really went down.' One more time and they woulda seen that the way to cop out on Tillary was to say he hired them to kill her."

"That means admitting they did it."

"I know, but they were admitting a little more each time. I don't know. I think I could've got more out of them. But once they got legal counsel on the spot, shit, that's the end of our cozy little conversations."

"Why do you like Tillary for it? Just because he was playing around?"

"Everybody plays around."

"That's what I mean."

"The ones who kill their wives are the ones who aren't playing around and want to be. Or the ones who're in love with something sweet and young and want to marry it and keep it around forever. He's not in love with anybody but himself. Or doctors. Doctors are always killing their wives."

"Then—"

"We got tons of motive, Matt. He owed money that he didn't have. And she was gettin' ready to dump him."

"The girlfriend?"

"The wife."

"I never heard that."

"Who would you hear it from, him? She talked to a neighbor woman, she talked to a lawyer. The aunt dyin' made the difference. She came into the property, for one thing, and she didn't have the old woman around for company. Oh, we got lots of motive, my friend. If motive was enough to hang a man we could go shoppin' for a rope."

Jack Diebold said, "He's a friend of yours, huh? That's why you're involved?"

We had left the Tillary house somewhere in the early evening. I remember the sky was still light, but it was July and it stayed light well into the evening hours. I turned off the lights and put the bottle of Wild Turkey away. There wasn't much left in it. Diebold joked that I should wipe my prints off the bottle, and off the glasses we had used.

He was driving his own car, a Ford Fairlane that was showing a lot of rust. He chose the place, a plush steak-and-seafood restaurant near the approach to the Verrazano Bridge. They knew him there, and I sensed that there wouldn't be a check. Most cops have a certain number of restaurants where they can eat a certain number of free meals. This bothers some people, and I have never really understood why.

We ate well—shrimp cocktails, strip sirloins, hot pumpernickel rolls, stuffed baked potatoes. "When we were growin' up," Diebold said, "a man who ate like this was treating himself right. You never heard a goddamned word about cholesterol. Now it's all you hear."

"I know."

"I had a partner, I don't know if you ever knew him. Gerry O'Bannon. You know him?"

"I don't think so."

"Well, he got on this health kick. What started it was he quit smoking. I never smoked so I never had to quit, but he quit and then it was one thing after another. He lost a lot of weight, he changed his diet, he started jogging. He looked terrible, he looked all drawn, you know how guys get? But he was happy, he was really pleased with himself. Wouldn't go drinking, just order one beer and make it last, or he'd have one and then switch to club soda. The French stuff. Perrier?"

"Uh-huh."

"Very popular all of a sudden, it's plain soda water and it costs more than beer. Figure it out and explain it to me sometime. He shot himself."

"O'Bannon?"

"Yeah. I don't mean it's connected, losing the weight and drinking club soda and killing himself. The life you lead and the things you see, I'll tell you, a cop goes and eats his gun, I never figure it requires an explanation. You know what I mean?"

"I know what you mean."

He looked at me. "Yeah," he said. "Course you do." And then the conversation took a turn in another direction, and a little while later, with a slab of hot apple pie topped with cheddar in front of Diebold and coffee poured for both of us, he returned to the subject of Tommy Tillary, identifying him as my friend.

"Sort of a friend," I said. "I know him around the bars."

"Right, she lives up in your neighborhood, doesn't she? The girlfriend, I forget her name."

"Carolyn Cheatham."

"I wish she was all the alibi he had. But even if he got away from her for a few hours, what was the wife doing during the burglary? Waiting for Tommy to come home and kill her? I mean, take it to extremes, say she hides under the bed while they rifle the bedroom and get their prints on everything. They leave, she calls the cops, right?"

"He couldn't have killed her."

"I know, and it drives me crazy. How come you like him?"

"He's not a bad guy. And I'm getting paid for this, Jack. I'm doing him a favor, but it's one I'm getting paid for. And it's a waste of my time and his money anyway, because you haven't got a case against him."

"No."

"You don't, do you?"

"Not even close." He ate some pie, drank some coffee. "I'm glad you're getting paid. Not just because I like to see a guy turn a buck. I'd hate to see you bust your balls for him for free."

"I'm not busting anything."

"You know what I mean."

"Am I missing something, Jack?"

"Huh?"

"What did he do, steal baseballs from the Police Athletic League? How come you've got the red ass for him?"

He thought it over. His jaws worked. He frowned.

"Well, I'll tell you," he said at length. "He's a phony."

"He sells stock and shit over the phone. Of course he's a phony."

"More than that. I don't know how to explain it so it makes sense, but shit, you were a cop. You know how you get feelings."

"Of course."

"Well, I get a feeling with that guy. There's something about him that's wrong, something about her death."

"I'll tell you what it is," I said. "He's glad she's dead and he's pretending he isn't. It gets him out of a jam and he's glad, but he's acting like a sanctimonious son of a bitch and that's what you're responding to."

"Maybe that's part of it."

"I think it's the whole thing. You're sensing that he's acting guilty. Well, he is. He feels guilty. He's glad she's dead, but at the same time he lived with the woman for I forget how many years, he had a life with her, part of him was busy being a husband while the other part was running around on her—"

"Yeah, yeah, I follow you."

"So?"

"It's more than that."

"Why does it have to be more? Look, maybe he did set up Cruz and whatsisname—".

"Hernandez."

"No, not Hernandez. What the hell's his name?"

"Angel. Angel eyes."

"Herrera. Maybe he set them up to go in, rob the place. Maybe he even had it in the back of his mind she might get in the way."

"Keep going."

"Except it's too iffy, isn't it? I think he just feels guilty for wishing she'd get killed, or being glad of it after the fact, and you're picking up on the guilt and that's why you like him for the murder."

"No."

"You sure?"

"I'm not sure that I'm sure of anything. You know, I'm glad you're gettin' paid. I hope you're costin' him a ton."

"Not all that much."

"Well, soak him all you can. Because at least it's costin' him money, even if that's all it's costin' him, and it's money he doesn't have to pay. Because we can't touch him. Even if those two changed their story, admitted the killing and said he put 'em up to it, that's not enough to put him away. And they're *not* gonna change their story, and who would ever hire them to commit murder anyway, and they wouldn't take a contract like that. I *know* they wouldn't. Cruz is a mean little bastard but Herrera's just a stupid guy, and—aw, shit."

"What?"

"It just kills me to see him get away with it."

"But he didn't do it, Jack."

"He's gettin' away with *something*," he said, "and I hate to see it happen. You know what I hope? I hope he runs a red light sometime, in that fucking boat of his. What's it, a Buick he's got?"

"I think so."

"I hope he runs a light and I tag him for it, that's what I hope."

"Is that what Brooklyn Homicide does these days? A lot of traffic detail?"

"I just hope it happens," he said. "That's all."

12

Diebold insisted on driving me home. When I offered to take the subway he told me not to be ridiculous, that it was midnight already and I was in no condition for public transportation.

"You'll pass out," he said, "and some bum'll steal the shoes off your feet."

He was probably right. As it was I nodded off during the ride back to Manhattan, coming awake when he pulled up at the corner of Fifty-seventh and Ninth. I thanked him for the ride, asked him if he had time for a drink before he went back.

"Hey, enough's enough," he said. "I can't go all night like I used to."

"You know, I think I'll call it a night myself," I said.

But I didn't. I watched him pull away, started walking to my hotel, then turned and went around the corner to Armstrong's. The place was mostly empty. I went in, and Billie gave me a wave.

I went up to the bar. And she was there at the end of the bar, all alone, staring down into the glass on the bar in front of her. Carolyn Cheatham. I hadn't seen her since the night I'd gone home with her.

While I was trying to decide whether or not to say anything, she looked up and her eyes met mine. Her face was frozen with stubborn old pain. It took her a blink or two to recognize me, and when she did a muscle worked in her cheek and tears started to form in the corners of her eyes. She used the back of her hand to wipe them away. She'd been crying earlier; there was a tissue crumpled on the bar, black with mascara.

"My bourbon-drinking friend," she said. "Billie," she said, "this man is a gentleman. Will you please bring my gentleman friend a drink of good bourbon?"

Billie looked at me. I nodded. He brought a couple of ounces of bourbon and a mug of black coffee.

"I called you my gentleman friend," Carolyn Cheatham said, "but that has an unintentional connotation." She pronounced her words with a drunk's deliberate care. "You are a gentleman *and* a friend, but not a gentleman friend. My gentleman friend, on the other hand, is neither."

I drank some of the bourbon, poured some of it into the coffee.

"Billie," she said, "do you know how you can tell that Mr. Scudder is a gentleman?"

"He always removes his lady in the presence of a hat."

"He is a bourbon drinker," she said.

"That makes him a gentleman, huh, Carolyn?"

"It makes him a far cry removed from a hypocritical scotch-drinking son of a bitch."

She didn't speak in a loud voice, but there was enough edge to her words to shut down conversations across the room. There were only three or four tables occupied, and the people sitting at them all picked the same instant to stop talking. For a moment the taped music was startlingly audible. It was one of the few pieces I could identify, one of the Brandenburg concertos. They played it so often there that even I was now able to tell what it was.

Then Billie said, "Suppose a man drinks Irish whiskey, Carolyn. What does that make him?"

"An Irishman," she said.

"Makes sense."

"I'm drinking bourbon," she said, and shoved her glass forward a significant inch. "God damn it, I'm a *lady*."

He looked at her, then looked at me. I nodded, and he shrugged and poured for her.

"On me," I said.

"Thank you," she said. "Thank you, Matthew." And her eyes started to water, and she dug a fresh tissue from her bag.

She wanted to talk about Tommy. He was being nice to her, she said. Calling up, sending flowers. But it just wouldn't do if she made a scene around the office, and he just might have to testify how he spent the night his wife was killed, and he had to keep on the good side of her for the time being.

But he wouldn't see her because it wouldn't look right. Not for a new widower, not for a man who'd been virtually accused of complicity in his wife's death.

"He sends flowers with no card enclosed," she said. "He calls me from pay phones. The son of a bitch."

"Maybe the florist forgot to enclose a card."

"Oh, Matt. Don't make excuses for him."

"And he's in a hotel, of course he would use a pay phone."

"He could call from his room. He as much as said he didn't want the call to go through the hotel switchboard, in case the operator's listening in. There was no card with the flowers because he doesn't want anything in writing. He came to my apartment the other night, but he won't be seen with me, he won't go out with me, and—oh, the hypocrite. The scotch-drinking son of a bitch."

Billie called me aside. "I didn't want to put her out," he said, "a nice woman like that, shitfaced as she is. But I thought I was gonna have to. You'll see she gets home?"

"Sure."

First I had to let her buy us another round. She insisted. Then I got her out of there and walked her around the corner to her building. There was rain coming, you could smell it in the air, and when we went from Armstrong's air conditioning into the sultry humidity that heralds a summer storm it took some of the spirit out of her. She held my arm as we walked, gripped it with something on the edge of desperation. In the elevator she sagged against the back panel and braced her feet.

"Oh, God," she said.

I took the keys from her and unlocked her door. I got her inside. She half sat, half sprawled on the couch. Her eyes were open but I don't know if she saw much through them. I had to use the bathroom, and when I came back her eyes were closed and she was snoring lightly.

I got her shoes off, moved her to a chair, struggled with the couch until I managed to open it into a bed. I put her on it. I figured I ought to loosen her clothing, and while I was at it I undressed her completely. She remained unconscious throughout the operation, and I remembered what a mortician's assistant had told me once about the difficulty of dressing and undressing the dead. My gorge rose at the image and I thought I was going to be sick, but I sat down and my stomach settled itself.

I covered her with the top sheet, sat back down again. There was something else I'd wanted to do but I couldn't think what it was. I tried to think, and I guess I must have dozed off myself. I don't suppose I was out for more than a few minutes, just time enough to lose myself in a dream that fled from me the minute I opened my eyes and blinked it away.

I let myself out. Her door had a spring lock. There was a dead bolt you could engage with the key for extra security, but all I had to do was draw the door shut and it was locked, and reasonably secure. I took the elevator down and went outside.

The rain was holding off. At the corner of Ninth Avenue a jogger passed, running doggedly uptown against what little traffic there was. His T-shirt was gray with sweat and he looked ready to drop. I thought of O'Bannon, Jack Diebold's old partner, getting physically fit before blowing his brains out.

And then I remembered what I'd wanted to do at Carolyn's apartment. I'd been planning on taking away the little gun Tommy had given her. If she was going to drink like that and get depressed like that, she didn't need to have a weapon in the bedside table.

But the door was locked. And she was out cold, she wasn't going to wake up and kill herself.

I crossed the street. The steel gate was drawn most of the way across the front of Armstrong's, and the white globe lights over the front were out, but light showed from within. I walked over to the door, saw that the chairs were on top of the tables, ready for the Dominican kid who came in first thing in the morning to sweep the place out. I didn't see Billie at first, and then I saw him at a stool at the far end of the bar. The door was locked, but he spotted me and came over and let me in.

He locked the door again after I was through it, walked me over to the bar and slipped behind it. Without my saying anything he poured me a glass of bourbon. I curled my hand around it but didn't pick it up from the top of the bar.

"The coffee's all gone," he said.

"That's all right. I didn't want any more."

"She all right? Carolyn?"

"Well, she might have a hangover tomorrow."

"Just about everybody I know might have a hangover tomorrow," he said. "*I* might have a hangover tomorrow. It's gonna pour, I might as well sit in the house and eat aspirin all day."

Someone banged on the door. Billie shook his head at him, waved him away. The man knocked again. Billie ignored him.

"Can't they see the place is closed?" he complained. "Put your money away, Matt. We're closed, the register's locked up, it's private-party time." He held his glass to the light and looked at it. "Beautiful color," he said. "She's a pisser, old Carolyn. A bourbon drinker's a gentleman and a scotch drinker's—what did she say a scotch drinker was?"

"I think a hypocrite."

"So I gave her the straight line, didn't I? What's it make a man if he drinks Irish whiskey? An Irishman."

"Well, you asked."

"What else it makes him is drunk, but in a nice way. I only get drunk in the nicest possible way. Ah, Jesus, Matt, these are the best hours of the day. You can keep your Morrissey's. This is like having your own private after-hours, you know? The joint empty and dark, the music off, the chairs up, one or two people around for company, the rest of the world locked the hell out. Great, huh?"

"It's not bad."

"No, it's not."

He was freshening my drink. I didn't remember drinking it. I said, "You know, my trouble is I can't go home."

"That's what Thomas Wolfe said, 'You Can't Go Home Again.' That's everybody's trouble."

"No, I mean it. My feet keep taking me to a bar instead. I was out in Brooklyn, I got home late, I was tired, I was already half in the bag, I started to walk to my hotel and I turned around and came here instead. And just now I put her to sleep, Carolyn, and I had to drag myself out of there before I fell asleep in her chair, and instead of going home like a sane human being I came back here again like some dim homing pigeon."

"You're a swallow and this is Capistrano."

"Is that what I am? I don't know what the hell I am anymore."

"Oh, bullshit. You're a guy, a human being. Just another poor son of a bitch who doesn't want to be alone when the sacred ginmill closes."

"The what?" I started to laugh. "Is that what this place is? The sacred ginmill?"

"Don't you know the song?"

"What song?"

"The Van Ronk song. 'And so we've had another night—'" He broke off. "Hell, I can't sing, I can't even get the tune right. 'Last Call,' Dave Von Ronk. You don't know it?"

"I don't know what you're talking about."

"Well, *Christ*," he said. "You have got to hear it. You have by Christ got to hear this song. It's what we've been talking about, and on top of that it's the fucking national anthem. Come on."

"Come on and what?"

"Just come on," he said. He put a Piedmont Airlines flight bag on top of the bar, rooted around under the back bar and came up with two unopened bottles, one of the twelve-year-old Jameson Irish he favored and one of Jack Daniel's. "This okay?" he asked me.

"Okay for what?"

"For pouring over your head to kill the cooties. Is it okay to drink is my question. You've been drinking Forester, but I can't find an unopened bottle, and there's a law against carrying an opened bottle on the street."

"There is?"

"There ought to be. I never steal opened bottles. Will

you please answer a simple question? Is Jack Black all right?"

"Of course it's all right, but where the hell are we going?"

"My place," he said. "You've got to hear this record."

"Bartenders drink free," he said. "Even at home. It's a fringe benefit. Other people get pension plans and dental care. We get all the booze we can steal. You're gonna love this song, Matt."

We were in his apartment, an L-shaped studio with a parquet floor and a fireplace. He was on the twenty-second floor and his window looked south. He had a good view of the Empire State Building and, farther down on the right, the World Trade Center.

The place was sparsely furnished. There was a white mica platform bed and dresser in the sleeping alcove, a couch and a sling chair in the middle of the room. Books and records overflowed a bookcase and stood around in stacks on the floor. Stereo components were placed here and there—a turntable on an upended milk crate, speakers resting on the floor.

"Where did I put the thing?" Billie wondered.

I walked over to the window, looked out at the city. I was wearing a watch but I purposely didn't look at it because I didn't want to know what time it was. I suppose it must have been somewhere around four o'clock. It still wasn't raining.

"Here," he said, holding up an album. "Dave Van Ronk. You know him?"

"Never heard of him."

"Got a Dutch name, looks like a mick and I swear on the blues numbers he sounds just like a nigger. He's also one bitchin' guitar player but he doesn't play anything on this cut. 'Last Call.' He sings it al fresco."

"Okay."

"*Not* al fresco. I forget the expression. How do you say it when you sing without accompaniment?"

"What difference does it make?"

"How can I forget something like that? I got a mind like a fucking sieve. You're gonna love this song."

"That's if I ever get to hear it."

"A cappella. That's what it is, a cappella. As soon as I stopped actively trying to think of it, it popped right into my head. The Zen of Remembering. Where did I put the Irish?"

"Right behind you."

"Thanks. You all right with the Daniel's? Oh, you got the bottle right there. Okay, listen to this. Ooops, wrong groove. It's the last one on the album. Naturally, you couldn't have anything come after this one. *Listen.*"

> *And so we've had another night*
> *Of poetry and poses*
> *And each man knows he'll be alone*
> *When the sacred ginmill closes.*

The melody sounded like an Irish folk air. The singer did indeed sing without accompaniment, his voice rough but curiously gentle.

"Now listen to this," Billie said.

> *And so we'll drink the final glass*
> *Each to his joy and sorrow*
> *And hope the numbing drunk will last*
> *Till opening tomorrow*

"Jesus," Billie said.

> *And when we stumble back again*
> *Like paralytic dancers*

Each knows the question he must ask
And each man knows the answer

I had a bottle in one hand, a glass in the other. I poured from the bottle into the glass. "Catch this next part," Billie was saying.

And so we'll drink the final drink
That cuts the brain in sections
Where answers do not signify
And there aren't any questions

Billie was saying something but the words weren't registering. There was only the song.

I broke my heart the other day.
It will mend again tomorrow.
If I'd been drunk when I was born
I'd be ignorant of sorrow

"Play that again," I said.
"Wait. There's more."

And so we'll drink the final toast
That never can be spoken:
Here's to the heart that is wise enough
To know when it's better off broken

He said, "Well?"
"I'd like to hear it again."
" 'Play it again, Sam. You played it for her, you can play it for me. I can take it if she can.' Isn't it great?"
"Play it again, will you?"
We listened to it a couple of times through. Finally he took it off and returned it to its jacket and asked me if I

understood why he had to drag me up there and play it for me. I just nodded.

"Listen," he said, "you're welcome to crash here if you want. That couch is more comfortable than it looks."

"I can make it home."

"I don't know. Is it raining yet?" He looked out the window. "No, but it could start any minute."

"I'll chance it. I want to be at my place when I wake up."

"I got to respect a man who can plan that far in the future. You okay to go out on the street? Sure, you're okay. Here, I'll get you a paper bag, you can take the JD home with you. Or here, take the flight bag, they'll think you're a pilot."

"No, keep it, Billie."

"What do I want with it? I don't drink bourbon."

"Well, I've had enough."

"You might want a nightcap. You might want something in the morning. It's a doggie bag, for Christ's sake. When'd you get so fancy you can't take a doggie bag home with you?"

"Somebody told me it's illegal to carry an opened bottle on the street."

"Don't worry. It's a first offense, you're odds-on to get probation. Hey, Matt? Thanks for coming by."

I walked home with the song's phrases echoing in my mind, coming back at me in fragments. "If I'd been drunk when I was born I'd be ignorant of sorrow." Jesus.

I got back to my hotel, went straight upstairs without checking the desk for messages. I got out of my clothes, threw them on the chair, took one short pull straight from the bottle and got into bed.

Just as I was drifting off the rain started.

13

The rain kept up all weekend. It was lashing my window when I opened my eyes around noon Friday, but it must have been the phone that woke me. I sat on the edge of the bed and decided not to answer it, and after a few more rings it quit.

My head ached fiercely and my gut felt like it had taken somebody's best shot. I lay down again, got up quickly when the room started to spin. In the bathroom I washed down a couple of aspirin with a half-glass of water, but they came right back up again.

I remembered the bottle Billie had pressed on me. I looked around for it and finally found it in the flight bag. I couldn't remember putting it back after the last drink of the night, but then there were other things I couldn't recall either, like most of the walk home from his apartment. That sort of miniblackout didn't bother me much. When you drove cross-country you didn't remember every billboard, every mile of highway. Why bother recalling every minute of your life?

The bottle was a third gone, and that surprised me. I

129

could recall having had one drink with Billie while we listened to the record, then a short one before I turned the lights out. I didn't want one now, but there are the ones you want and the ones you need, and this came under the latter heading. I poured a short shot into the water glass and shuddered when I swallowed it. It didn't stay down either, but it fixed things so the next one did. And then I could swallow another couple of aspirins with another half-glass of water, and this time they stayed swallowed.

If I'd been drunk when I was born . . .

I stayed right there in my room. The weather gave me every reason to remain where I was, but I didn't really need an excuse. I had the sort of hangover I knew enough to treat with respect. If I'd ever felt that bad without having drunk the night before, I'd have gone straight to a hospital. As it was, I stayed put and treated myself like a man with an illness, which in retrospect would seem to have been more than metaphor.

The phone rang again later in the afternoon. I could have had the desk stop my calls, but I didn't feel equal to the conversation that would have required. It seemed easier to let it ring itself out.

It rang a third time in the early evening, and this time I picked it up. It was Skip Devoe.

"I was looking for you," he said. "You going to bounce around later?"

"I don't want to go out in this."

"Yeah, it's coming down again. It was slacking off for a while there and now it's teeming. The weather guy says we're gonna get a lot of it. We saw those guys yesterday."

"Already?"

"Not the guys in the black hats, not the bad guys. The lawyers and the accountants. Our accountant's armed with what he calls a Jewish revolver. You know what that is?"

"A fountain pen."

"You heard it, huh? Anyway, they all told us what we already knew, which is terrific, considering they'll bill us for the advice. We got to pay."

"Well, that's what you figured."

"Yeah, but it doesn't mean I like it. I spoke to the guy again, Mr. Voice on the Phone. I told old Telephone Tommy we needed the weekend to find the money."

"You told Tillary?"

"Tillary? What are you talking about?"

"You said—"

"Oh, right, I didn't even make the connection. No, not Tillary, I just said Telephone Tommy, I could have said Teddy or any name with a T. Which suddenly I can't think of. Name me some names start with T."

"Do I have to?"

There was a pause. "You don't feel so hot," he said.

"Keegan had me up till dawn listening to records," I said. "I'm not a hundred percent yet."

"Fucking Keegan," he said. "We all hit it pretty good, but he's gonna kill himself with it."

"He does keep at it."

"Yeah. Listen, I won't keep you. What I want to know, can you keep Monday open? The day and the night. Because I think that's when we're gonna move on this, and if we have to do it I'd just as soon get it over with."

"What do you want me to do?"

"We'll talk about that, iron it out. Okay?"

What did I have to do on Monday? I was still working for Tommy Tillary, but I didn't much care what hours I put in. My conversation with Jack Diebold had confirmed my own opinion that I was wasting my time and Tillary's money, that they didn't have a case against him and weren't likely to make one. Carolyn Cheatham's diatribe had left me not greatly inclined to do much for Tommy anyway, or to feel all that guilty about taking his money and giving him small value for it.

I had a couple of things to tell Drew Kaplan next time I talked to him. And I'd dig up a few more along the way. But I might not have to put in too many long hours in Sunset Park's bars and bodegas.

I told Skip Monday was wide open.

Later that evening I called the liquor store across the street. I ordered up two quarts of Early Times and asked them to have the kid stop at the deli and pick up a six-pack of ale and a couple of sandwiches. They knew me and knew I'd make it worth the delivery boy's while to give me special service, and I did. It was worth it to me.

I took it easy with the hard booze, drank a can of ale, and made myself eat half a sandwich. I took a hot shower, and that helped, and then I ate another half-sandwich and drank another can of ale.

I went to sleep, and when I woke up I put the TV on and watched Bogart and Ida Lupino, I guess it was, in *High Sierra*. I didn't pay a whole lot of attention to the movie but it was company. I went over to the window now and then and watched the rain. I ate part of the remaining sandwich, drank some more ale, and nipped a little from the bourbon bottle. When the movie ended I turned the set off and had a couple of aspirins and went back to bed.

Saturday I was a little more mobile. I needed a drink again on awakening but I made it a short one, and the first one stayed down this time. I had a shower, drank the last can of ale, and went downstairs and had breakfast at the Red Flame. I left half of the eggs but ate the potatoes and a double order of rye toast and drank a lot of coffee. I read the paper, or tried to. I couldn't make much sense out of what I read.

After breakfast I stopped in McGovern's for a quick one. Then I went around the corner to St. Paul's and sat there in the soft stillness for a half-hour or so.

Then back to the hotel.

I watched a baseball game in my room, and a fight on "Wide World of Sports," along with the arm-wrestling championship of the world and some women doing some kind of aquatic mono-ski exhibition. What they were doing was evidently very difficult, but not terribly interesting to look at. I turned them off and left. I dropped in at Armstrong's and talked to a couple of people, then went over to Joey Farrell's for a bowl of three-alarm chili and a couple of Carta Blancas.

I had a brandy with my coffee before returning to the hotel for the night. I had enough bourbon in the room to get me through Sunday but I stopped and picked up some beer because I was almost out and the stores can't sell it before noon on Sunday. Nobody knows why. Maybe the churches are behind it, maybe they want the faithful showing up with their hangovers sharp at the edges, maybe repentance is easier to sell to the severely afflicted.

I sipped and watched TV movies. I slept in front of the set, woke up in the middle of a war movie, had a shower and shaved and sat around in my underwear watching the end of that movie and the start of another, sipping bourbon and beer until I could go back to sleep again.

When I woke up again, it was Sunday afternoon and it was still raining.

Around three-thirty the phone rang. I picked it up on the third ring and said hello.

"Matthew?" It was a woman, and for an instant I thought it was Anita. Then she said, "I tried you day before yesterday, but there was no answer," and I heard the Tarheel in her voice.

"I want to thank you," she said.

"Nothing to thank me for, Carolyn."

"I want to thank you for being a gentleman," she said,

and her laughter came gently. "A bourbon-drinking gentleman. I seem to remember having a lot to say on that subject."

"As I recall, you were reasonably eloquent."

"And on other subjects as well. I apologized to Billie for being less than a lady and he assured me I was fine, but bartenders always tell you that, don't they? I want to thank you-all for seeing me home." A pause. "Uh, did we—"

"No."

A sigh. "Well, I'm glad of that, but only 'cause I'd hate to not remember it. I hope I wasn't too disgraceful, Matthew."

"You were perfectly fine."

"I was *not* perfectly fine. I remember that much. Matthew, I said some hard things about Tommy. I was bad-mouthing him something awful, and I hope you know that was just the drink talking."

"I never thought otherwise."

"He treats me fine, you know. He's a good man. He's got his faults. He's strong, but he has his weaknesses."

At a fellow police officer's wake, I once heard an Irish woman speak thus of the drink. "Sure, it's a strong man's weakness," she had said.

"He cares for me," Carolyn said. "Don't you pay any mind to what I said before."

I told her I'd never doubted he cared for her, and that I wasn't all that clear on what she had or hadn't said, that I'd been hitting it pretty hard that night myself.

Sunday night I walked over to Miss Kitty's. A light rain was falling but it didn't amount to much.

I'd stopped at Armstrong's first, briefly, and Miss Kitty's had the same Sunday-night feel to it. A handful of regulars and neighborhood people rode a mood that was the flip side of Thank God It's Friday. On the jukebox, a girl sang about having a brand-new pair of roller skates. Her voice seemed to slip in between the notes and find sounds that weren't on the scale.

I didn't know the bartender. When I asked for Skip he pointed toward the office in back.

Skip was there, and so was his partner. John Kasabian had a round face, and he wore wire-rimmed glasses with circular lenses that magnified his deep-set dark eyes. He was Skip's age or close to it, but he looked younger, an owlish schoolboy. He had tattoos on both forearms, and he didn't look at all to be the sort of person who got tattooed.

One tattoo was a conventional if garish representation of a snake entwined around a dagger. The snake was ready to strike, and the tip of the dagger dripped blood. The other tattoo was simpler, even tasteful: a chain-link bracelet encircling his right wrist. "If I'd at least had it on the other wrist," he had said, "at least the watch'd cover it."

I don't know how he really felt about the tattoos. He affected disdain for them, contempt for the young man who'd elected to get himself thus branded, and sometimes he did seem genuinely embarrassed by them. At other times I sensed that he was proud of them.

I didn't really know him all that well. His was a less expansive personality than Skip's. He didn't like to bounce around the bars, worked the early shift and did the marketing before that. And he wasn't the drinker his partner was. He liked his beer, but he didn't hit it the way Skip did.

"Matt," he said, and pointed to a chair. "Glad you're going to help us with this."

"Whatever I can."

"It's tomorrow night," Skip said. "We're supposed to be in this room, eight o'clock sharp, phone's gonna ring."

"And?"

"We get instructions. I should have a car ready. That's part of the instructions."

"Have you got a car?"

"I got my car, it's no hassle having it ready."

"Has John got a car?"

"I'll get it out of the garage," John said. "You think we might want to take two cars?"

"I don't know. He told you to have a car and I presume he told you to have the money ready—"

"Yeah, strangely enough he happened to mention it."

"—but he didn't give any indication of where he's going to want you to drive."

"None."

I thought about it. "What concerns me—"

"Is walking into something."

"That's right."

"I got the same concern. It's like walking point, you're out there and they can just bang away at you. It's bad enough paying ransom, but who knows if we're even gonna get what we pay for? It could wind up being a hijack, and they could waste us while they're at it."

"Why would they do that?"

"I don't know. 'Dead men tell no tales.' Isn't that what they say?"

"Maybe they do, but murder brings heat." I was trying to concentrate, and I wasn't thinking as clearly as I wanted to. I asked if I could have a beer.

"Oh, Jesus, where's my manners? What do you want, bourbon, cup of coffee?"

"I think just a beer."

Skip went to get it. While he was gone his partner said, "This is crazy. It's unreal, you know what I mean? Stolen books, extortion, voices over the phone. It has no reality."

"I guess."

"The money has no reality. I can't relate to it. The number—"

Skip brought me a bottle of Carlsberg and a bell-shaped glass. I sipped a little beer and frowned in what was supposed to be thought. Skip lit a cigarette, offered the pack to me, then said, "No, of course you don't want one, you don't smoke," and put the pack in his pocket.

I said, "It shouldn't be a hijack. But there's one way it could be."

"How's that?"

"If they haven't got the books."

"Of course they got the books. The books are gone and there's this voice on the phone."

"Suppose someone hasn't got the books, but knows that they're missing. If he doesn't have to prove possession of them, he's got a chance to take a few dollars off you."

"A few dollars," John Kasabian said.

Skip said, "Then who's got the books? The Feds? You mean they could have them all along and be preparing a case and in the meantime we're paying ransom to somebody who hasn't got shit." He stood up, walked around the desk. "I fuckin' love it," he said. "I love it so much I want to marry it, I want to have babies with it. Jesus."

"It's just a possibility, but I think we have to guard against it."

"How? Everything's set for tomorrow."

"When he calls, you have him read a page from the books."

He stared at me. "You just thought of that? Just now? Nobody move." Kasabian asked him where he was going. "To get two more of those Carlsbergs," he said. "The fucking beer stimulates thought. They should use it in their advertising."

He brought back two bottles. He sat on the edge of the desk with his feet swinging, sipping his beer straight from the brown bottle. Kasabian stayed in his chair and peeled the label from his bottle. He was in no hurry to drink it. We had our war council, making what plans we could. John and Skip were both coming along, and so of course was I.

"And I was thinking Bobby'd come," Skip said.

"Ruslander?"

"He's my best friend, he knows what's happening. I don't know if he could do much if the shit hit the fan, but who could? I'm gonna be armed, but if it's a trap I suppose they'll shoot first, so a lot of fucking good a gun's gonna do me. You got anybody you want to bring in on this?"

Kasabian shook his head. "I thought of my brother," he said. "First person I thought of, but what does Zeke need with this shit, you know?"

"What does anybody need with it? Matt, you got anybody you want to bring?"

"No."

"I was thinking maybe Billie Keegan," Skip said. "What do you think?"

"He's good company."

"Yeah, right. When you think about it, who the hell needs good company? What we need is heavy artillery and air support. Set up the meet and lay down a mortar barrage on their position. John, tell him about the spades with the mortar."

"Oh," Kasabian said.

"Tell him."

"It was just something I saw."

"Something he saw. Listen to this."

"It was whenever it was, a month or so ago. I was at my girl's house, she's on West End in the Eighties, I'm supposed to walk her dog, and I come out of the building and diagonally across the street there are these three black guys."

"So he turns around and goes back in the building," Skip offered.

"No, they didn't even look in my direction," Kasabian said. "They're wearing fatigue jackets, like, and one's got a cap. They look like soldiers."

"Tell him what they did."

"Well, it's hard to believe I really saw this," he said. He took off his glasses, massaged the bridge of his nose. "They took a look around, and if they saw me they decided I was nothing to worry about—"

"Shrewd judges of character," Skip put in.

"—and they set up this mortar, like they've done this drill a thousand times before, and one of them drops a shell in, and they lob a round into the Hudson, nice easy shot, they're on the corner and they can see clear to the river, and we all like check it out, and they still don't pay any attention to me, and they nod to each other and strip the mortar down and pack it up and walk off together."

"Jesus," I said.

"It happened so fast," he said, "and with so little fanfare, I wondered if I imagined it. But it happened."

"Did the round make a lot of noise?"

"No, not a whole lot. There was the sort of *whump!* sound a mortar makes on firing, and if there was an explosion when the round hit the water I didn't hear it."

"Probably a blank," Skip said. "They were probably, you know, testing the firing mechanism, checking out the trajectory."

"Yeah, but for what?"

"Well, shit," he said. "You never know when you're gonna need a mortar in this town." He tipped up his beer bottle, drank deeply, and drummed his heels against the side of the desk. "I don't know," he said, "I'm drinking this stuff but I'm not thinking any better than before. Matt, let's talk about money."

I thought he was referring to the ransom. But he meant money for me, and I was at a loss. I didn't know how to set a price, said something about being a friend.

He said, "So? This is what you do for a living, right? Do favors for friends?"

"Sure, but—"

"You're doing us a favor. Kasabian and I don't know what the hell we're doing. Am I right, John?"

"Absolutely."

"I'm not gonna give Bobby anything for coming, he wouldn't take it, and if Keegan comes along it won't be for the money. But you're a professional and a professional gets paid. Tillary's paying you, isn't he?"

"There's a difference."

"What's the difference?"

"You're a friend of mine."

"And he isn't?"

"Not in the same way. In fact I like him less and less. He's—"

"He's an asshole," Skip said. "No argument. Makes no difference." He opened a drawer in the desk, counted money, folded the bills, handed them to me. "Here," he said. "That's twenty-five there. Tell me if it's not enough."

"I don't know," I said slowly. "Twenty-five dollars doesn't seem like much, but—"

"It's twenty-five hundred, you dumb fuck." We all started laughing. " 'Twenty-five dollars doesn't seem like much.' Johnny, why did we have to hire a comedian? Seriously, Matt, is it okay?"

"Seriously, it seems a little high."

"You know what the ransom comes to?"

I shook my head. "Everybody's been careful not to mention it."

"Well, you don't mention rope in the house of the hanged, do you? We're paying those cocksuckers fifty grand."

"Jesus Christ," I said.

"His name came up already," Kasabian said. "He a friend of yours, by any chance? Bring him along tomorrow, he's got nothing else on for the evening."

14

I tried to make it an early night. I went home and went to bed, and somewhere around four I knew I wasn't going to be able to sleep. There was enough bourbon on hand to knock myself out, but I didn't want that, either. I didn't want to be hung over when we dealt with the blackmailers.

I got up and tried sitting around, but I couldn't sit still and there was nothing on television I was willing to watch. I got dressed and went out for a walk, and I was halfway there before I realized my feet were taking me to Morrissey's.

One of the brothers was on the downstairs door. He gave me a bright smile and let me in. Upstairs, another brother sat on a stool opposite the door. His right hand was concealed beneath his white butcher's apron, and I had been given to understand that there was a gun in it. I hadn't been to Morrissey's since Tim Pat had told me of the reward he and his brothers were offering, but I'd heard that the brothers took turns at guard duty, and that anyone who walked in the door was facing a loaded weapon. Opinions differed on the sort of weapon; I'd had various reports, ranging from revolver to automatic pistol to sawed-off shotgun. My thought was that you'd have to be crazy to plan on using a shotgun, sawed-off or otherwise, in a roomful of your own customers, but no one had ever established the Morrisseys' sanity.

I walked in and looked around the room, and Tim Pat saw me and motioned to me, and I took a step toward him when Skip Devoe called my name from a table in the front near the blacked-out window. He was sitting with Bobby Ruslander. I held up a hand, indicating I'd be with them in a minute, and Bobby put his hand to his mouth and a police whistle pierced the room, cutting off all conversation as cleanly as a gunshot. Skip and Bobby laughed, and the other drinkers realized the noise had been a joke, not an official raid, and, after a few people had assured Bobby he was an asshole, conversation resumed. I followed Tim Pat toward the rear of the room, where we stood on opposite sides of an empty table.

"We've not seen you here since we spoke," he said. "Do you bring me news?"

I told him I didn't have any news to bring him. "I just came in for a drink," I said.

"And you've heard nothing?"

"Not a thing. I went around, I talked to some people. If there were anything in the air I would have had word back by now. I think it must be some kind of Irish thing, Tim Pat."

"An Irish thing."

"Political," I said.

"Then we should have heard tell of it. Some braggart would have let a word slip." His fingertips caressed his beard. "They knew right where to go for the money," he mused. "And they even took the few dollars from the Norad jar."

"That's why I thought—"

"If it was Proddies we should have heard tell. Or if it was

a faction of our own." He smiled without humor. "We have our factional disagreements, don't you know. The Cause has more than one voice speakin' for it."

"So I've heard."

"If it were an 'Irish thing,'" he said, pronouncing the phrase deliberately, "there would be other incidents. But there's been only the one."

"That you know of," I said.

"Aye," he said. "That I know of."

I went over and joined Skip and Bobby. Bobby was wearing a gray sweat shirt with the sleeves cut off. Around his neck was a blue plastic whistle on one of those lanyards of plastic braid that boys make at summer camp.

"The actor is feeling his way into the role," Skip said, aiming a thumb at Bobby.

"Oh?"

"I got a call-back on a commercial," Bobby said. "I'm a basketball referee, I'm with these kids at a playground. They all tower over me, that's part of the point of it."

"Everybody towers over you," Skip said. "What are they supposed to be selling? Because if it's deodorant, you want to wear a different sweatshirt."

"It's brotherhood," Bobby said.

"Brotherhood?"

"Black kids, white kids, Spanish kids, all united in brotherhood as they drive for the fuckin' hoop. It's some public-service thing, show it during slow spots on the Joe Franklin show."

"You get paid for this?" Skip demanded.

"Oh, shit, yes. I think the agencies donate their time, and the TV stations run it free, but the talent gets paid."

"The talent," Skip said.

"*Le talent, c'est moi,*" Bobby said.

I ordered a drink. Skip and Bobby stayed with what they

had. Skip lit a cigarette and the smoke hung in the air. My drink came and I sipped it.

"I thought you were going to make it an early night," Skip said. I said I'd been unable to sleep. "Because of tomorrow?"

I shook my head. "Just not tired yet. Restless."

"I get that way. Hey, actor," he said. "What time's your audition?"

"Supposed to be two o'clock."

"Supposed to be?"

"You can get there and sit around a lot. I'm supposed to be there at two."

"You be done in time to give us a hand?"

"Oh, no problem," he said. "These agency cats, they got to catch the five forty-eight to Scarsdale. Couple of pops in the bar car, then find out how Jason and Tracy did in school today."

"Jason and Tracy are on summer break, dumbbell."

"So he's got to see the postcard they sent home from camp. They go to this fancy camp in Maine, the postcards are already written by the staff, all they gotta do is sign them."

My boys would be going to camp in a couple of weeks. One of them had woven me a lanyard like the one Bobby wore. I had it somewhere, packed away in a drawer or something. Or was it still in Syosset? If I were a proper father, I thought, I'd wear the damned thing, whistle and all.

Skip was telling Bobby that he needed his beauty sleep.

"I'm supposed to look like a jock," Bobby said.

"We don't get you outta here, you're gonna look more like a truss." He looked at his cigarette, dropped it in what was left of his drink. "I never want to see you do that," he told me. "I never want to see either of you do that. Disgusting habit."

• • •

The sky was lightening up outside. We walked slowly, not saying much. Bobby bobbed and weaved a ways ahead of us, dribbling an imaginary basketball, faking out an invisible opponent and driving for the hoop. Skip looked at me and shrugged. "What can I tell you?" he said. "The man is my friend. What else is there to say?"

"You're just jealous," Bobby said. "You got the height but you haven't got the moves. A good little man can fake you out of your socks."

"I wept because I had no shoes," Skip said solemnly, "and then I met a man who had no socks. What the hell was *that?*"

An explosion echoed half a mile or so to the north of us.

"Kasabian's mortar," Bobby said.

"Fucking draft-dodger," Skip said. "You wouldn't know a mortar from a pessary. I don't mean a pessary. What is it a pharmacist uses?"

"What the fuck are you talking about?"

"A pestle," Skip said. "You wouldn't know a mortar from a pestle. That's not what a mortar sounds like."

"Whatever you say."

"It sounded like blasting for a foundation," he said. "But it's too early, the neighbors would kill anybody started blasting at this hour. I'll tell you, I'm glad it's done raining."

"Yeah, we had enough of it, didn't we?"

"I suppose we needed it," he said. "That's always what they say, isn't it? Every time it rains its ass off, somebody says how we needed it. Because the reservoirs are drying up, or else the farmers need it or something."

"This is a wonderful conversation," Bobby said. "You'd never get a conversation like this in a less sophisticated city."

"Fuck you," Skip said. He lit a cigarette and started

coughing, got control of the cough and took another puff on the cigarette, this time without a cough. It was like a drink in the morning, I thought. Once you got one to stay down you were all right.

"The air's nice after a storm," Skip said. "I think it cleans it."

"Washes it," Bobby said.

"Maybe." He looked around. "I almost hate to say this," he said, "but it ought to be a beautiful day."

15

At six minutes past eight, the phone on Skip's desk rang. Billie Keegan had been talking about a girl he'd met the previous year on a three-week holiday in the west of Ireland. He stopped his story in midsentence. Skip put his hand on the phone and looked at me, and I reached for the phone that sat on top of the file cabinet. He nodded once, a quick bob of the head, and we lifted the two receivers in unison.

He said, "Yeah."

A male voice said, "Devoe?"

"Yeah."

"You have the money?"

"All set."

"Then get a pencil and write this down. You want to get in your car and drive to—"

"Hold on," Skip said. "First you got to prove you got what you say you got."

"What do you mean?"

"Read the entries for the first week of June. That's this June, June of '75."

There was a pause. Then the voice, taut now, said, "You don't give us orders, man. We're the ones say frog, you're the ones jump." Skip straightened up a little in his chair, leaned forward. I held up a hand to stop whatever he was about to say.

I said, "We want to confirm we're dealing with the right people. We want to buy it as long as we know you've got it to sell. Establish that much and we'll play out the hand."

"You're not Devoe speaking. Who the hell are you?"

"I'm a friend of Mr. Devoe's."

"You got a name, friend?"

"Scudder."

"Scudder. You want us to read something?"

Skip told him again what to read.

"Get back to you," the man said, and broke the connection.

Skip looked over at me, the receiver in his hand. I hung up the one I was holding. He passed his own from hand to hand like a hot potato. I had to tell him to hang up.

"Why'd they do that?" he wanted to know.

"Maybe they had to have a conference," I suggested. "Or get the books so they can read you what you want to hear."

"And maybe they never had them in the first place."

"I don't think so. They'd have tried to stall."

"Hanging up on somebody's a pretty good way to stall." He lit a cigarette, shoved the pack back into his shirt pocket. He was wearing a short-sleeved forest-green work shirt with *Alvin's Texaco Service* embroidered in yellow over the breast pocket. "Why hang up?" he said petulantly.

"Maybe he thought we could trace the call."

"Could we do that?"

"It's hard even when you've got the cops and the telephone company cooperating on it," I said. "It'd be out of the question for us. But they don't necessarily know that."

"Catch us tracing calls," John Kasabian put in. "We had our hands full installing the second phone this afternoon."

They had done that a few hours earlier, running wires from the terminal on the wall and hooking an extension phone borrowed from Kasabian's girl's apartment into the line so that Skip and I could be on the line at the same time. While Skip and John were doing that, Bobby had been auditioning for the role of referee in the brotherhood commercial and Billie Keegan had been finding someone to fill in for him behind the stick at Armstrong's. I'd used that time to stuff two hundred and fifty dollars into a parish fund box, light a couple of candles, and phone in another meaningless report to Drew Kaplan in Brooklyn. And now we were all five in Miss Kitty's back office, waiting for the phone to ring again.

"Sort of a southern accent," Skip said. "You happen to notice?"

"It sounded phony."

"Think so?"

"When he got angry," I said. "Or pretended to get angry, whatever it was. That bit about jump when he says frog."

"He wasn't the only one got angry just about then."

"I noticed. But when he first got angry the accent wasn't there, and when he started with the frog shit he was putting it on thicker than before, trying to sound country."

He frowned, summoning up the memory. "You're right," he said shortly.

"Was it the same guy you talked to before?"

"I don't know. His voice sounded phony before, but it wasn't the same as I was hearing tonight. Maybe he's a man of a thousand voices, all of them unconvincing."

"Guy could do voiceovers," Bobby suggested, "in fucking brotherhood commercials."

The phone rang again.

This time we made less of a thing out of synchronizing our answering, since I'd already made my presence known. When I had the receiver to my ear, Skip said, "Yeah?" and the voice I'd heard before asked what he was supposed to read. Skip told him and the voice began reading ledger entries. Skip had the fake set of books open on his desk and followed along on the page.

After half a minute the reader stopped and asked if we were satisfied. Skip looked as though he wanted to take exception to the word. Instead he shrugged and nodded, and I spoke up to say we were assured we were dealing with the right people.

"Then here's what you do," he said, and we both took up pencils and wrote down the directions.

"Two cars," Skip was saying. "All they know is me and Matt are coming, so the two of us'll go in my car. John, you take Billie and Bobby. What do you think, Matt, they'll follow us?"

I shook my head. "Somebody may be watching us leave here," I said. "John, why don't you three go ahead now. Your car's handy?"

"I'm parked two blocks from here."

"The three of you can drive out there now. Bobby, you and Bill walk on ahead and wait at the car. I'd just as soon you all didn't walk out together, just in case somebody's keeping an eye on the front door. You two wait ahead, and John, give them two, three minutes, and then meet them at the car."

"And then drive out to—where is it, Emmons Avenue?"

"In Sheepshead Bay. You know where that is?"

"Vaguely. I know it's the ass end of Brooklyn. I've gone out on fishing boats there, but somebody else drove and I didn't pay too much attention."

"You can take the Belt, the Shore Parkway."

"All right."

"Get off, let me think, probably the best place is Ocean Avenue. You'll probably see a sign."

"Hang on," Skip said. "I think I got a map someplace, I saw it the other day."

He found a Hagstrom street map of the borough and the three of us gave it some study. Bobby Ruslander leaned in over Kasabian's shoulder. Billie Keegan picked up a beer somebody had abandoned earlier and took a sip and made a face. We worked out a route, and Skip told John to take the map along with him.

"I can never fold these things right," Kasabian said.

Skip said, "Who cares how you fold the fucking thing?" He took the map away from his partner and began tearing it along some of its fold lines, handing a section some eight inches square to Kasabian and dropping the rest to the floor. "Here's Sheepshead Bay," he said. "You want to know where to get off the parkway, right? What do you need with all the rest of fucking Brooklyn?"

"Jesus," Kasabian said.

"I'm sorry, Johnny. I'm fuckin' twitchy. Johnny, you got a weapon?"

"I don't want anything."

Skip opened the desk drawer, put a blue-steel automatic pistol on top of the desk. "We keep it behind the bar," he told me, "case we want to blow our brains out when we count up the night's receipts. You don't want it, John?" Kasabian shook his head. "Matt?"

"I don't think I'll need it."

"You don't want to carry it?"

"I'd just as soon not."

He hefted the gun, looked for a place to put it. It was a .45 and it looked like the kind they issue to officers in the army. A big heavy gun, and what they called a forgiving one—its stopping power could compensate for poor aim, bringing a man down with a shoulder wound.

"Weighs a fucking ton," Skip said. He worked it underneath the waistband of his jeans and frowned at the way it looked. He tugged his shirt free of his belt, let it hang out over the gun. It wasn't the sort of shirt you wear out of your pants and it looked all wrong. "Jesus," he complained, "where am I gonna put the thing?"

"You'll work it out," Kasabian told him. "Meanwhile we ought to get going. Don't you think so, Matt?"

I agreed with him. We went over it one more time while Keegan and Ruslander walked on ahead. They would drive to Sheepshead Bay and park across the street from the restaurant, but not directly across the street. They would wait there, motor off, lights out, and keep an eye on the place and on us when we arrived.

"Don't try and do anything," I told him. "If you see anything suspicious, just observe it. Write down license numbers, anything like that."

"Should I try and follow them?"

"How would you know who you were following?" He shrugged. "Play it by ear," I said. "Mostly just be around, keep an eye open."

"Got it."

After he'd left Skip put an attaché case on top of the desk and popped the catches. Banded stacks of used currency filled the case. "That's what fifty grand looks like," he said. "Doesn't look like much, does it?"

"Just paper."

"It do anything for you, looking at it?"

"Not really."

"Me either." He put the .45 on top of the bills, closed the case. It didn't fit right. He rearranged the bills to make a little nest for the gun and closed it again.

"Just until we get in the car," he said. "I don't want to

walk down the street like Gary Cooper in *High Noon*." He tucked his shirt back into his pants. On the way to the car he said, "You'd think people'd be staring at me. I'm dressed like a grease monkey and carrying a case like a banker. Fucking New Yorkers, I could wear a gorilla suit and nobody'd look twice. Remind me, soon as we get in the car, I want to take the gun out of the case."

"All right."

"Bad enough if they pull something and shoot us. Be worse if they used my gun to do it."

His car was garaged on Fifty-fifth Street. He tipped the attendant a buck and drove around the corner, pulled up in front of a hydrant. He opened the attaché case and removed the pistol and checked the clip, then put the gun on the seat between us, thought better of it and wedged it down into the space between the cushion and the seat back.

The car was a Chevy Impala a couple of years old, long and low, loosely sprung. It was white, with a beige and white interior, and it looked as though it hadn't been through a car wash since it left Detroit. The ashtray overflowed with cigarette butts and the floor was deep in litter.

"Car's like my life," he said as we caught a light at Tenth Avenue.

"A comfortable mess. What do we do, take the same route we worked out for Kasabian?"

"No."

"You know a better way?"

"Not better, just different. Take the West Side Drive for now, but instead of the Belt we'll take local streets through Brooklyn."

"Be slower, won't it?"

"Probably. Let them get there ahead of us."

"Whatever you say. Any particular reason?"

"Might be easier this way to see if we're being followed."

"You think we are?"

"I don't see the point offhand, not when they know where we're going. But there's no way to know whether we're dealing with one man or an army."

"That's a point."

"Take a right the next corner, pick up the Drive at Fifty-sixth Street."

"Got it. Matt? You want something?"

"What do you mean?"

"You want a pop? Check the glove box, there ought to be something there."

There was a pint of Black & White in the glove compartment. Actually it wouldn't have been a pint, it would have been a tenth. I remember the bottle, green glass, curved slightly like a hip flask to fit comfortably in a pocket.

"I don't know about you," he said, "but I'm kind of wired. I don't want to get sloppy, but it might not hurt to have something to take the edge off."

"Just a short one," I agreed, and opened the bottle.

We took the West Side Drive to Canal Street, crossed into Brooklyn via the Manhattan Bridge, and took Flatbush Avenue until it crossed Ocean Avenue. We kept catching red lights, and several times I noticed his gaze fixing on the glove box. But he didn't say anything, and we left the bottle of Black & White untouched after the one short pull each of us had taken earlier.

He drove with his window rolled down all the way and his left elbow out the window, his fingertips resting on the roof, occasionally drumming the metal. Sometimes we made conversation and sometimes we rode along in silence.

At one point he said, "Matt, I want to know who set this

up. It's gotta be inside, don't you think? Somebody saw an opportunity and took it, somebody who took a look at the books and knew what he was looking at. Somebody who used to work for me, except how would they get back in? If I fired some asshole, some drunk bartender or spastic waitress, how do they wind up prancing into my office and waltzing out with my books? Can you figure that?"

"Your office isn't that hard to get into, Skip. Anybody familiar with the layout could head for the bathroom and slip into your office without anybody paying any attention."

"I suppose. I suppose I'm lucky they didn't piss in the top drawer while they were at it." He drew a cigarette from the pack in his breast pocket, tapped it against the steering wheel. "I owe Johnny five grand," he said.

"How's that?"

"The ransom. He came up with thirty and I put up twenty. His safe-deposit box was in better shape than mine. For all I know he's got another fifty tucked away, or maybe the thirty was enough to tap him." He braked, letting a gypsy cab change lanes in front of us. "Look at that asshole," he said, without rancor. "Do people drive like that everywhere or is it just Brooklyn? I swear everybody starts driving funny the minute you cross the river. What was I talking about?"

"The money Kasabian put up."

"Yeah. So he'll cut a few bills extra per week until he makes up the five-grand difference. Matt, I had twenty thousand dollars in a bank vault and now it's all packed up and ready for delivery, and in a few minutes I won't have it anymore, and it's got no reality. You know what I mean?"

"I think so."

"I don't mean it's just paper. It's more than paper, if it was just paper people wouldn't go so nuts over it. But it wasn't real when it was locked up tight in the bank and it won't be real when it's gone. I have to know who's doing this to me, Matt."

"Maybe we'll find out."

"I fucking have to know. I trust Kasabian, you know? This kind of business, you're dead if you can't trust your partner. Two guys in the bar business watching each other all the time, they're gonna go flat fucking nuts in six months. Never make it work, the place'll have the kind of vibe a Bowery bum wouldn't tolerate. On top of which you could watch your partner twenty-three hours a day and he could steal you blind in the hour he's got open. Kasabian does the buying, for Christ's sake. You know how deep you can stick it in when you're doing the buying for a joint?"

"What's your point, Skip?"

"My point is there's a voice in my head saying maybe this is a nice neat way for Johnny to take twenty grand off me, and it doesn't make any sense, Matt. He'd have to split it with a partner, he has to put up a lot of his own cash to do it, and why would he pick this way to steal from me? All aside from the fact that I trust him, I got no reason not to trust him, he's always been straight with me and if he wanted to rip me off there's a thousand easier ways that pay better and I'd never even know I was being taken. But I still get this voice, and I fuckin' bet he gets it, too, because I caught him looking at me a little different earlier, and I probably been looking at him the same way, and who *needs* this shit? I mean this is worse than what it's costing us. This is the kind of thing makes a joint close up overnight."

"I think that's Ocean Avenue coming up."

"Yeah? And to think we've only been driving for six days and six nights. I hang a left at Ocean?"

"You want to turn right."

"You sure?"

"Positive."

"I'm always lost in Brooklyn," he said. "I swear this

place was settled by the Ten Lost Tribes. They couldn't find their way back, they broke ground and built houses. Put in sewer lines, ran in electricity. All the comforts of home."

The restaurants on Emmons Avenue specialized in seafood. One of them, Lundy's, was a great barn of a place where serious eaters would tuck themselves in at big tables for enormous shore dinners. The place we were headed for was two blocks away at a corner. Carlo's Clam House was its name, and its red neon sign winked to show a clam opening and closing.

Kasabian was parked on the other side of the street a few doors up from the restaurant. We pulled up alongside him. Bobby was in the front passenger seat. Billie Keegan sat alone in the back. Kasabian, of course, was behind the wheel. Bobby said, "Took you long enough. If there's anything going on, you can't see it from here."

Skip nodded. We drove a half-block farther and he parked next to a hydrant. "They don't tow you out here," he said. "Do they?"

"I don't think so."

"All we need," he said. He killed the engine and we exchanged glances, and his eyes moved to the glove compartment.

He said, "You see Keegan? In the back seat there?"

"Uh-huh."

"You can bet he's had a couple since they left."

"Probably."

"We'll wait, right? Celebrate after."

"Sure."

He shoved the gun into the waistband of his pants, draped his shirt to conceal it. "Probably the style here," he said, opening the door, hefting the attaché case. "Sheepshead Bay, home of the flapping shirttail. You nervous, Matt?"

"A little."

"Good. I don't want to be the only one."

• • •

We walked across the wide street and approached the restaurant. The night was balmy and you could smell the salt water. I wondered for a moment if I should have been the one to take the gun. I wondered if he'd even fire the pistol, or if it was just there for comfort. I wondered if he'd be any good with it. He'd been in the service, but that didn't mean he was proficient with a handgun.

I'd been good with handguns. Barring ricochets, anyway.

"Catch the sign," he said. "Clam opening and closing, it's a goddamned obscenity. 'C'mere, honey, let's see you open your clam.' Place looks empty."

"It's Monday night and it's getting late."

"Midmorning's probably late out here. Gun weighs a ton, you ever notice? My pants feel like they're gonna get dragged down around my knees."

"You want to leave it in the car?"

"Are you kidding? 'This is your weapon, soldier. It could save your life.' I'm all right, Matt. I'm just running on nerves is all."

"Sure."

He reached the door first and held it for me. The place wasn't much more than a glorified diner, all formica and stainless steel, with a long lunch counter on our left and booths on the right and more tables in back. Four boys in their midteens sat at a booth near the front, eating french fries with their fingers from a communal platter. Farther back, a gray-haired woman with a lot of rings on both fingers was reading a hardcover book in a lending library's plastic cover.

The man behind the counter was tall and fat and completely bald. I suppose he shaved his head. Sweat was beaded on his forehead and had soaked through his shirt. The place was cool enough, with the air conditioning running full blast. There were two customers at the counter, one a round-shouldered man in a short-sleeved white shirt who looked like a failed accountant, the other a stolid girl with heavy legs and bad skin. At the rear of the counter the waitress was taking a cigarette break.

We took seats at the counter and ordered coffee. Someone had left that afternoon's *Post* on an adjoining stool. Skip picked it up, paged through it.

He lit a cigarette, smoked it, glancing every few seconds at the door. We both drank our coffee. He picked up a menu and ran his eyes over its listings. "They got a million different things," he said. "Name something, it's probably on here. Why am I looking? I couldn't eat."

He lit another cigarette, put his pack on the counter. I took one from it and put it between my lips. He raised his eyebrows but didn't say anything, just gave me a light. I took two, three puffs and put out the cigarette.

I must have heard the phone ring, but it didn't register until the waitress had already walked back to answer it and come forward to ask the round-shouldered man if he was Arthur Devoe. He looked astonished at the idea. Skip went to take the call and I tagged along.

He took the phone, listened for a moment, then began motioning for paper and pencil. I got my notebook and wrote down what he repeated to me.

A whoop of laughter came at us from the front of the restaurant. The kids were throwing french fries at each other. The counterman was leaning his bulk onto the formica, saying something to them. I turned my eyes from them and concentrated on writing down what Skip was saying.

16

Skip said, "Eighteenth and Ovington. You know where that is?"

"I think so. I know Ovington, it runs through Bay Ridge, but Eighteenth Avenue is west of there. I think that would put it in Bensonhurst, a little ways south of Washington Cemetery."

"How can anybody know all this shit? Did you say Eighteenth *Avenue?* They got avenues up to Eighteen?"

"I think they go up to Twenty-eight, but Twenty-eighth Avenue's only two blocks long. It runs from Cropsey to Stillwell."

"Where's that?"

"Coney Island. Not all that far from where we are now."

He waved a hand, dismissing the borough and all its unknowable streets. "You know where we're going," he said. "And we'll get the map from Kasabian. Oh, fuck. Is this going to be on the part of the map they're carrying?"

"Probably not."

"Fuck. What did I have to go and rip the map for? Jesus."

160

We were out of the restaurant by now. We stood in front, with the winking neon in back of us. Skip said, "Matt, I'm out of my element. Why'd they have us come here first, then call us up and send us to the church?"

"So they can get a look at us first, I guess. And interrupt our lines of communication."

"You think someone's looking at us right now? How'm I gonna tell Johnny to follow us? Is that what they oughta do, follow us?"

"They probably ought to go home."

"Why's that?"

"Because they'll be spotted following us, and they'll be spotted anyway when we tell them what's going on."

"You think we're being watched?"

"It's possible. It's one reason for them to set things up this way."

"Shit," he said. "I can't send Johnny home. If I suspect him, he probably suspects me at the same time, and I can't . . . Suppose we all go in one car?"

"Two cars would be better."

"You just said two cars won't work."

"We'll try it this way," I said, and took his arm to steer him. We walked not toward the car where Kasabian and the others were parked but to Skip's Impala. At my direction he started the car up, blinked the lights a couple of times, and drove to the corner, took a right, drove a block and pulled to the curb.

A few minutes later Kasabian's car pulled up beside us.

"You were right," Skip said to me. To the others he said, "You guys are smarter than I gave you credit. We got a phone call, they're sending us on a treasure hunt only we got the treasure. We're supposed to go to a church on Eighteenth Avenue and something."

"Ovington," I said.

No one knew where that was. "Follow us," I told them.

"Stay half a block to a block in back of us, and when we park go around the block and park behind us."

"Suppose we get lost?" Bobby wanted to know.

"Go home."

"How?"

"Just follow us," I said. "You won't get lost."

We took Coney Island Avenue and Kings Highway into Bay Parkway, and then we got disoriented and it took me a few blocks to get my bearings. We went across one of the numbered streets, caught Eighteenth Avenue, and found the church we were looking for on the corner of Ovington. In Bay Ridge, Ovington Avenue runs parallel to Bay Ridge Avenue a block to the south of it. Somewhere around Fort Hamilton Parkway it winds up still parallel to Bay Ridge Avenue but a block *north* of it, where Sixty-eighth Street used to be. Even when you know the area, this sort of thing can drive you crazy, and Brooklyn is full of it.

There was a No Parking zone directly across from the church, and Skip pulled the Chevy into it. He cut the lights, killed the engine. We sat in silence until Kasabian's car had moved up, passed us, and turned at the corner.

"Did he even see us?" Skip wondered. I said that they had, that was why they'd turned at the corner. "I guess," he said.

I turned and watched out the rear window. A couple of minutes later I saw their lights. They found a parking spot half a block back, and their lights went out.

The neighborhood was mostly prewar frame houses, large ones, set on lots with lawns and trees out in front. Skip said, "It doesn't look like New York out here. You know what I mean? It looks like some normal place in the rest of the country."

"A lot of Brooklyn is like this."

"Parts of Queens, too. Not where I grew up, but here and

there. You know what this reminds me of? Richmond Hill. You know Richmond Hill?"

"Not well."

"Track team had a meet out there once. We got the shit kicked out of us. The houses, though, they looked a lot like this." He dropped his cigarette out the window. "I guess we might as well do it," he said. "Right?"

"I don't like it," I said.

"*You* don't like it? I haven't liked it since the books disappeared."

"The other place was public," I said. I opened my notebook, read what I'd written down. "There's supposed to be a flight of steps on the left-hand side of the church leading down to the basement. The door's supposed to be open. I don't even see a light on, do you?"

"No."

"This looks like an awfully easy way to get sandbagged. I think you'd better stay here, Skip."

"You figure you're safer alone?"

I shook my head. "I figure we're both safer separated for the moment. The money stays with you. I want to go down there and see what kind of a reception they've got set up for us. If there looks to be a safe way to make the switch, I'll have them blink the lights three times."

"What lights?"

"Some light that you can see." I leaned across him, pointed. "Those are the basement windows down there. There must be lights, and you'll be able to see them."

"So you wink the lights three times and I bring the money. Suppose you don't like the setup?"

"Then I tell them I have to get you, and I come out and we drive back to Manhattan."

"Assuming we can find it." He frowned. "What if— never mind."

"What?"

"I was gonna say what if you don't come out."

"You'll find your way home sooner or later."

"Funny man. What are you doing?"

I'd popped the cover of the dome light and I was unscrewing the bulb. "In case they're watching," I said. "I don't want them to know when I open the door."

"The man thinks of everything. It's good you're not Polish, we'd need fifteen guys to turn the car while you held onto the bulb. You want the gun, Matt?"

"I don't think so."

"'Bare-handed, he went up alone against an army.' Take the fucking gun, will you?"

"Gimme."

"And how about a quick one?"

I reached for the glove box.

I got out and stayed low, keeping the car between me and the church basement windows. I walked half a block to the other car and ran down the situation for them. I had Kasabian stay with the car and told him to start the motor when he saw Skip enter the church. I sent the other two around the block on foot. If the other side made their getaway through a rear exit of the church and over a fence and through a yard, Bobby and Billie might be able to spot them. I didn't know that they could do much, but maybe one of them could come up with a license-plate number.

I returned to the Impala and told Skip what I'd done. I put the bulb back in the dome light, and when I opened the door again it went on, lighting up the car's interior. I swung the door shut and crossed the street.

The gun was tucked into the waistband of my slacks, the butt protruding, the whole thing positioned for a draw across the front of my body. I'd have preferred to have it riding in a holster on my hip but I didn't have the choice. It got in the way as I walked, and when I was in the shadows at the side of the church I drew the gun and walked along holding it, but I didn't like that either, and I put it back where I'd had it.

The flight of stairs was steep. Concrete steps with a rusted iron railing that was loosely mounted into the surrounding brick. A bolt or two had evidently worked loose. I walked down the steps and felt myself disappearing into the darkness. There was a door at the bottom. I groped until I found the knob and I hesitated with my hand on it, listening carefully, trying to hear something within.

Nothing.

I turned the knob, eased the door inward just far enough to be sure that it was unlocked. Then I drew it shut and knocked on it.

Nothing.

I knocked again. This time I heard movement inside, and a voice called out something unintelligible. I turned the knob again and stepped through the doorway.

The time I'd spent in the pitch-dark stairwell had worked to my advantage. A little light filtered into the basement through the windows at the front, and my pupils had dilated enough to make use of it. I was standing in a room that must have measured about thirty by fifty feet. There were chairs and tables scattered around the floor. I pulled the door closed after me and moved into the shadows against one wall.

A voice said, "Devoe?"

"Scudder," I said.

"Where's Devoe?"

"In the car."

"It doesn't matter," another voice said. I couldn't recognize either of them as the one I'd heard over the phone, but it had been disguised, and for all I knew these voices were disguised, too. They didn't sound like New York but they didn't sound like anyplace else in particular, either.

The first speaker said, "You bring the money, Scudder?"

"It's in the car."

"With Devoe."

"With Devoe," I agreed.

Still just the two speakers. One was at the far end of the room, the other to his right. I could place them by their voices but the darkness shrouded them, and one of them sounded as if he might be speaking from behind something, some upended table or something of the sort. If they came out where I could see them, I could draw the gun and throw down on them, shoot them if I had to. On the other hand, it was more than possible that they already had guns trained on me and could drop me where I stood before I got the gun out of my pants. And even if I shot first and got them both, there could be another couple of armed men standing in the shadows, and they could shoot me full of holes before I even knew they existed.

Besides, I didn't want to shoot anybody. I just wanted to trade the money for the books and get the hell out of there.

"Tell your friend to bring the money," one of them said. I decided he might have been the voice on the phone, if he were to let his speech soften into a southern accent. "Unless he wants the books sent to the IRS."

"He doesn't want that," I said. "But he's not going to walk into a blind alley, either."

"Keep talking."

"First of all, put a light on. We don't want to do business in the dark."

There was a whispered conference, then a fair amount of moving around. One of them flicked a wall switch and a fluorescent fixture in the center of the ceiling came on one tube at a time. There was a flickering quality to its light, the way fluorescents get when they're starting to go.

I blinked, as much at what I saw as at the flickering light.

For a moment I thought they were hippies or mountain men, some curious breed. Then I realized they were disguised.

There were two of them, shorter than I, slender in build. Both wore full beards and fright wigs that started low on their foreheads and concealed not only their hair but the whole shapes of their heads. Between the low hairline and the beginning of the beard, each wore an oval mask over the eyes and the top half of the nose. The taller of the two, the one who'd turned on the light, had a chrome-yellow wig and a black face mask. The other, half concealed by a table with chairs stacked on it, sported dark brown hair and a white mask. Both had black beards, and the short one had a gun in his hand.

With the light on, I think we all three felt vulnerable, almost naked. I know I did, and there was a tension in their stance that indicated the same feeling. The one with the gun was not exactly training it on me, but neither was he pointing it in another direction altogether. Darkness had protected all three of us, and now we'd flicked it aside.

"The trouble is we're afraid of each other," I told him. "You're afraid we'll try to get the books without paying for them. We're afraid you'll rip us off for the money and give us nothing in return, hold us up again with the books or peddle them to somebody else."

The tall one shook his head. "This is a one-time deal."

"For both of us. We pay once and that's all. If you made a copy of the books, get rid of it."

"No copies."

"Good," I said. "You have the books here?" The short one with the dark wig shoved a navy-blue laundry bag across the room with his foot. His partner hefted it, put it back on the floor. I said it could be anything, it could be laundry, and would they show me what was in the bag.

"When we see money," the tall one said, "you get to see the books."

"I don't want to examine them. Just take them out of the sack before I tell my friend to bring the money."

They looked at each other. The one with the gun shrugged. He moved the pistol to cover me while the other one worked the drawstring on the laundry bag and withdrew a hinged-post bound ledger similar to the set of fake books I'd seen on Skip's desk.

"All right," I said. "Flick the light on and off three times."

"Who are you signaling?"

"The Coast Guard."

They exchanged glances, and the one by the light switch worked it up and down three times. The fluorescent fixture winked on and off in ragged fashion. The three of us stood awkwardly and waited what seemed like a long time. I wondered if Skip had seen the signal, wondered if he'd had enough time alone in the car to lose his nerve.

Then I heard him on the stairs and at the door. I called out to him to come in. The door opened and he entered, the attaché case in his left hand.

He looked at me, then caught sight of the two of them in their beards and wigs and masks.

"Jesus," he said.

I said, "Each side will have one man to make the exchange and one to cover him. That way nobody will be able to take anybody off and the books and money will pass at the same time."

The taller one, the one at the light switch, said, "You sound like an old hand at this."

"I had time to think about it. Skip, I'll back you up. Bring the case over here, set it down by me. Good. Now you and one of our friends can set up a table in the middle of the room and clear some of the other furniture out from around it."

The two of them looked at each other, and predictably the

taller one kicked the laundry bag over to his partner and came forward. He asked what I wanted him to do and I put him and Skip to work rearranging the furniture.

"I don't know what the union's going to say about this," he said. The beard hid his mouth, and the mask covered him around the eyes, but I sensed he was smiling.

At my direction, he and Skip positioned a table in the center of the room, almost directly beneath the overhead light fixture. The table was eight feet long and four feet wide, placed to divide their side of the room from ours.

I got down on one knee, crouched behind a nest of chairs. At the far end of the room, the one with the gun was similarly concealing himself. I called Skip back for the case full of money, sent the tall yellow-haired fellow for the books. Moving deliberately, each carried his part of the bargain to one end of the long table. Skip set the case down first, worked the buttons to release the catches. The man in the blond wig slipped the set of books out of the bag and put them down gently, then stepped back, his hands hovering.

I had each of them retreat a few yards, then switch ends of the table. Skip opened the heavy ledger, made sure the books were the ones he'd negotiated for. His opposite number opened the attaché case and took out a banded stack of bills. He riffled through it, put it back, took up another stack.

"Books are okay," Skip announced. He closed the heavy volume, got it into the laundry bag, hoisted it and started back toward me.

The one with the gun said, "Hold it."

"What for?"

"Stay where you are until he counts it."

"I got to stand here while he counts fifty grand? Be serious."

"Take a fast count," the one with the gun told his partner.

"Make sure it's all money. We don't want to go home with a bag full of cut-up newspaper."

"I'd really do that," Skip said. "I'd really walk up into a gun with a case full of fucking Monopoly money. Point that thing somewhere else, will you? It's getting on my nerves."

There was no answer. Skip held his position, balanced on the balls of his feet. My back was cramping and my knee, the one I was kneeling on, was giving me a little trouble. Time came to a stop while the yellow-haired one flipped through the packets of money, assuring himself that none of it consisted of cut paper or one-dollar bills. He probably did this as quickly as he could but it seemed forever before he was satisfied, closing the case and engaging the clasps.

"All right," I said. "Now the two of you—"

Skip said, "Wait a minute. We get the laundry bag and they get the attaché case, right?"

"So?"

"So it seems uneven. That case was close to a hundred bucks and it's less than two years old, and how much could a laundry bag be worth? A couple of bucks, right?"

"What are you getting at, Devoe?"

"You could throw in something," he said, his voice tightening. "You could tell me who set this up."

They both looked hard at him.

"I don't know you," he said. "I don't know either of you. You ripped me off, fine, maybe your kid sister needs an operation or something. I mean everybody's gotta make a living, right?"

No answer.

"But somebody set this up, somebody I know, somebody who knows me. Tell me who. That's all."

There was a long silence. Then the one with the brown wig said, "Forget it," flat, final. Skip's shoulders dropped in resignation.

"We try," he said.

And he and the man in the yellow wig backed away from the table, one with the attaché case and one with the laundry bag. I called the shots, sending Skip to the door he'd come in, watching the other move not surprisingly through a curtained archway in the rear. Skip had the door open and was backing through it when the one in the dark wig said, "Hold it."

His long-barreled pistol had swung around to cover Skip, and for a moment I thought he was going to shoot. I got both hands on the .45 and took a bead on him. Then his gun swung to the side and he raised it and said, "We leave first. Stay where you are for ten minutes. You got that?"

"All right," I said.

He pointed the gun at the ceiling, fired twice. The fluorescent tubes exploded overhead, plunging the room into darkness. The gunshots were loud and the exploding tubes were louder, but for some reason neither the noise nor the darkness rattled me. I watched as he moved to the archway, a shadow among shadows, and the .45 stayed centered on him and my finger stayed on the trigger.

We didn't wait ten minutes as instructed. We got out of there in a hurry, Skip lugging the books in the laundry bag, me with the gun still clutched in one hand. Before we could cross the street to the Chevy, Kasabian had put his car in gear and roared down the block, pulling up next to us with a great screech of brakes. We piled into the back seat and told him to go around the block, but the car was already in motion before we got the words out.

We took a left and then another left. On Seventeenth Avenue, we found Bobby Ruslander hanging on to a tree with one hand, struggling to catch his breath. Across the street, Billie Keegan took a few slow steps toward us, then paused to cup his hands around a match and light a cigarette.

Bobby said, "Oh, Jesus, am I out of shape. They came tearin' out of that driveway, had to be them, they had the case with the money. I was four houses down, I saw 'em but I didn't want to run up on 'em right away, you know? I think one of 'em was carrying a gun."

"Didn't you hear the shots?"

He hadn't, nor had either of the others. I wasn't surprised. The dark-haired gunman had used a small-caliber pistol, and while the noise was loud enough in a closed room, it wouldn't have been likely to carry very far.

"They jumped into this car," Bobby said, pointing to where it had been parked, "and they got out in a hurry and left rubber. I started moving once they were in the car, figuring I could get a look at the plate number, and I chased 'em and the light was rotten and—" He shrugged. "Nothing," he said.

Skip said, "Least you tried."

"I'm so out of shape," Bobby said. He slapped himself across the belly. "No legs, no wind, and my eyes aren't so good, either. I couldn't referee a real basketball game, running up and down the court. I'd fuckin' die."

"You could have blown your whistle," Skip suggested.

"Jesus, if I'd had it with me I might have. You think they would have stopped and surrendered?"

"I think they'd probably have shot you," I said. "Forget the plate number."

"At least I tried," he said. He looked over at Billie. "Keegan there, he was closer to them and he didn't budge. Just sat under the tree like Ferdinand the bull, smelling the flowers."

"Smelling the dogshit," Keegan said. "We have to work with the materials at hand."

"Been working on those minibottles, Billie?"

"Just maintaining," Keegan said.

I asked Bobby if he got the make of the car. He pursed his

lips, blew out, shook his head. "Dark late-model sedan," he said. "They all look alike these days anyway."

"That's the truth," Kasabian said, and Skip agreed with him. I started to form another question when Billie Keegan announced that the car was a Mercury Marquis, three or four years old, black or navy blue.

We all stopped and looked at him. His face carefully expressionless, he took a scrap of paper from his breast pocket, unfolded it. "LJK-914," he read. "Does that mean anything to any of you?" And while we went on staring at him, he said, "That's the license number. New York plates. I wrote down all the makes and plate numbers earlier to keep from dying of boredom. It seemed easier than chasing cars like a fucking cocker spaniel."

"Fucking Billie Keegan," Skip said with wonder, and went over and hugged him.

"You gentlemen will rush to judgment of the man who drinks a bit," Keegan said. He took a miniature bottle from a pocket, twisted the cap until the seal broke, tipped back his head and drank the whiskey down.

"Maintenance," he said. "That's all."

17

Bobby couldn't get over it. He seemed almost hurt by Billie's ingenuity. "Why didn't you say something?" he demanded. "I could have been writing down numbers the same time, we could have covered more of them."

Keegan shrugged. "I figured I'd keep it to myself," he said. "So that when they ran past all these cars and caught a bus on Jerome Avenue I wouldn't look like an asshole."

"Jerome Avenue's in the Bronx," somebody said. Billie said he knew where Jerome Avenue was, that he had an uncle used to live on Jerome Avenue. I asked if the pair had been wearing their disguises when they emerged from the driveway.

"I don't know," Bobby said. "What were they supposed to look like? They had little masks on." He made twin circles of his thumbs and forefingers, held them to his face in imitation of the masks.

"Were they wearing beards?"

"Of course they were wearing beards. What do you think, they stopped to shave?"

"The beards were fake," Skip said.

174

"Oh."

"They have the wigs on, too? One dark and one light?"

"I guess. I didn't know they were wigs. I—there wasn't a hell of a lot of light, Arthur. Streetlamps there and there, but they came out that driveway and ran to their car, and they didn't exactly pause and hold a press conference, pose for the photographers."

I said, "We'd better get out of here."

"Why's that? I like standing around in the middle of Brooklyn, it reminds me of hanging out on the corner when I was a boy. You're thinking cops?"

"Well, there were gunshots. No point being conspicuous."

"Makes sense."

We walked over to Kasabian's car, got in, and circled the block again. We caught a red light, and I gave Kasabian directions back to Manhattan. We had the books in hand, we'd paid the ransom, and we were all alive to tell or not tell the tale. Besides that, we had Keegan's drunken resourcefulness to celebrate. All of this changed our mood for the better, and I was now able to provide clear directions back to the city and Kasabian for his part was able to absorb them.

As we neared the church, we saw a handful of people in front of it, men in undershirts, teenagers, all of them standing around as if waiting for someone. Somewhere in the distance, I heard the undulating siren of a blue-and-white.

I wanted to tell Kasabian to drive us all home, that we could come back tomorrow for Skip's car. But it was parked next to a hydrant, it would stand out. He pulled up—he may not have put the crowd and the siren together—and Skip and I got out. One of the men across the street, balding and beer-gutted, was looking us over.

I called out, asked him what was up. He wanted to know if I was from the precinct. I shook my head.

"Somebody busted into the church," he said. "Kids, probably. We got the exits covered, the cops coming."

"Kids," I said heavily, and he laughed.

"I think I was more nervous just now than I was in the church basement," Skip said, after we'd driven a few blocks. "I'm standing with a laundry bag over my shoulder like I just committed a burglary and you've got a forty-five in your belt. I figured we're in great shape if they see the gun."

"I forgot it was there."

"And we just got out of a car full of drunks. Another point in our favor."

"Keegan was the only one who was drunk."

"And he was the brilliant one. Figure that out, will you? Speaking of drinking—"

I got the scotch from the glove compartment and uncapped it for him. He took a long pull, handed it to me. We passed it back and forth until it was gone, and Skip said, "Fuck Brooklyn," and tossed it out the window. I'd have been just as happy if he hadn't—we had booze on our breath, an unlicensed gun in our possession, and no good way to account for our presence—but I kept it to myself.

"They were pretty professional," Skip said. "The disguises, everything. Why did he shoot the light out?"

"To slow us down."

"I thought he was going to shoot me for a minute there. Matt?"

"What?"

"How come you didn't shoot him?"

"When he was aiming at you? I might have, if I sensed he was about to shoot. I had him covered. As it stood, if I shot him he would shoot you."

"I mean after that. After he shot the light out. You still had him covered. You were aiming at him when he went out the door."

I took a moment to answer. I said, "You decided to pay the ransom to keep the books away from the IRS. What do you think happens if you're tagged to a shooting in a church in Bensonhurst?"

"Jesus, I wasn't thinking."

"And shooting him wouldn't have recovered the money, anyway. It was already out the back door with the other one."

"I know. I really wasn't thinking. The thing is, *I* mighta shot him. Not because it was the right thing to do, but in the heat of the moment."

"Well," I said. "You never know what you'll do in the heat of the moment."

The next light we caught, I got out my notebook and began sketching. Skip asked me what I was drawing.

"Ears," I said.

"How's that?"

"Something an instructor told us when I was at the Police Academy. The shapes of people's ears are very distinctive and it's something that's rarely disguised or changed by plastic surgery. There wasn't a hell of a lot to see of these two. I want to make sketches of their ears before I forget."

"You remember what their ears looked like?"

"Well, I made a point of remembering."

"Oh, that makes a difference." He drew on his cigarette. "I couldn't swear they *had* ears. Didn't the wigs cover them? I guess not, or you wouldn't be drawing pictures. You can't check their ears in some file, can you? Like fingerprints?"

"I just want to have a way to recognize them," I said. "I think I might know their voices, if they were using their real ones tonight, and I think they probably were. As far as their height, one was around five-nine or -ten and the other was either a little shorter or it looked that way because he was standing farther back." I shook my head at my notebook. "I don't know which set of ears went with which of them. I should have done this right away. That kind of memory fades on you fast."

"You think it matters, Matt?"

"What their ears look like?" I considered. "Probably not," I granted. "At least ninety percent of what you do in an investigation doesn't lead anywhere. Make that ninety-five percent—the people you talk to, the things you take time to check. But if you do enough things, the one thing that does work is in there."

"You miss it?"

"Being a cop? Not often."

"I can see where a person would miss it," he said. "Anyway, I didn't mean just ears. I mean is there a point to the whole thing? They did us a dirty and they got away with it. You think the license plate will lead anywhere?"

"No. I think they were smart enough to use a stolen car."

"That's what I think, too. I didn't want to say anything because I wanted to feel good back there, and I didn't want to piss on Billie's parade, but the trouble they took, disguises, sending us all around the barn before we got to the right place, I don't think they're gonna get tripped up by a license number."

"Sometimes it happens."

"I guess. Maybe we're better off if they stole a car."

"How do you figure that?"

"Maybe they'll get picked up in it, some sharp-eyed patrolman who looked at the hot-car list. Is that what they call it?"

"The hot-car sheet. It takes a while for a car to get on it, though."

"Maybe they planned in advance. Stole the car a week ago, took it in for a tune-up. What else could they get charged with? Desecrating a church?"

"Oh, Jesus," I said.

"What's the matter?"

"That church."

"What about it?"

"Stop the car, Skip."

"Huh?"

"Stop the car a minute, all right?"

"You serious?" He looked at me. "You're serious," he said, and pulled over to the curb.

I closed my eyes, tried to bring things into focus. "The church," I said. "What kind of church was it, did you happen to notice?"

"They all look the same to me. It was, I don't know, brick, stone. What the hell's the difference?"

"I mean was it Protestant or Catholic or what?"

"How would I know which it was?"

"There was one of those signs out in front. A glass case with white letters on a black background, tells you when the services are and what the sermon's going to be about."

"It's always about the same thing. Figure out all the things you like to do and don't do 'em."

I could close my eyes and see the damn thing but I couldn't bring the letters into focus. "You didn't notice?"

"I had things on my mind, Matt. What fucking difference does it make?"

"Was it Catholic?"

"*I* don't know. You got something for or against Catholic? The nuns hit you with a ruler when you were a kid? 'Impure thoughts, *wham*, take that, you little bastard.' You gonna be a while, Matt?" I had my eyes closed, wrestling with memory, and I didn't answer him. "Because there's a liquor store across the street, and much as I hate to spend money in Brooklyn, I think I'm gonna. All right?"

"Sure."

"You can pretend it's altar wine," he said.

He returned with a pint of Teacher's in a brown bag. He cracked the seal and uncapped the bottle without removing it from the bag, took a drink and gave it to me. I held on to it for a moment, then drank.

"We can go now," I said.

"Go where?"

"Home. Back to Manhattan."

"We don't have to go back, make a novena or something?"

"The church was some kind of Lutheran."

"And that means we can go to Manhattan."

"Right."

He started the engine, pulled out from the curb. He reached out a hand and I gave him the bottle and he drank and handed it back to me.

He said, "I don't mean to pry, Detective Scudder, but—"

"But what was all that about?"

"Yeah."

"I feel silly mentioning it," I said. "It's something Tillary told me a few days ago. I don't even know if it was true, but it was supposed to be a church in Bensonhurst."

"A Catholic one."

"It would have to be," I said, and I told him the story Tommy had told me, of the two kids who'd burglarized a Mafia capo's mother's church, and what had supposedly been done to them in return.

Skip said, "Really? It really happened?"

"I don't know. Neither does Tommy. Stories get around."

"Hung on meat hooks and fucking skinned alive—"

"It might appeal to Tutto. They call him Dom the

Butcher. I think he's got interests in the wholesale meat industry."

"Jesus. If that was his church—"

"His mother's church."

"Whatever. You gonna hang on to that bottle until the glass melts?"

"Sorry."

"If that was his church, or his mother's church, or whatever it was—"

"I wouldn't want him to know we were there tonight while it got shot up. Not that it's the same as burglarizing the premises, but he still might take it personally. Who knows how he'd react?"

"Jesus."

"But it was definitely a Protestant church and his mother would go to a Catholic one. Even if it was Catholic, there's probably four or five Catholic churches in Bensonhurst. Maybe more, I don't know."

"Someday we'll have to count 'em." He drew on his cigarette, coughed, tossed it out the window. "Why would anybody do something like that?"

"You mean—"

"I mean hang two kids up and fucking skin 'em, that's what I mean. Why would somebody do that, two kids that all they did was stole some shit from a church?"

"I don't know," I said. "I know why Tutto probably thought he was doing it."

"Why?"

"To teach them a lesson."

He thought about this. "Well, I bet it worked," he said. "I bet those little fuckers never rob another church."

18

By the time we were back home the pint of Teacher's was empty. I hadn't had much of it. Skip had kept chipping away at it, finally flipping it empty into the back seat. I guess he only threw them out the window on the other side of the river.

We hadn't talked much since our conversation about Dom the Butcher. The booze was working in him now, showing up a little in his driving. He ran a couple of lights and took a corner a little wildly, but we didn't hit anything or anybody. Nor did we get flagged down by a traffic cop. You just about had to run down a nun to get cited for a moving violation that year in the city of New York.

When we'd pulled up in front of Miss Kitty's he leaned forward and put his elbows on the steering wheel. "Well, the joint's still open," he said. "I got a guy working the bar tonight, he probably took as much off of us as the boys from Bensonhurst. Come on in, I want to put the books away."

In his office, I suggested he might want to put the ledger in the safe. He gave me a look and worked the combination dial. "Just overnight," he said. "Tomorrow all this shit

182

goes down a couple different incinerators. No more honest books. All you do is leave yourself wide open."

He put the books in the safe and started to close the big door. I put a hand on his arm to stop him. "Maybe this should go in there," I said, and handed him the .45.

"Forgot about that," he said. "It doesn't go in the safe. You gonna tell a holdup man, 'Please excuse me a minute, I wanna get the gun from the safe, blow your head off'? We keep it behind the bar." He took it from me, then looked around for an inconspicuous way to carry it. There was a white paper bag on the desk, stained from the takeout coffee and sandwiches it had once held, and Skip put the gun in it.

"There," he said. He closed the safe, spun the dial, tugged the handle to make sure the lock had engaged. "Perfect," he said. "Now let me buy you a drink."

We went out front and he slipped behind the bar, pouring out two drinks of the same scotch we'd had in the car. "Maybe you wanted bourbon," he said. "I didn't think, didn't think when I bought the bottle, either."

"This is fine."

"You sure?" He moved off, put the gun somewhere behind the bar. The bartender he had on that night came over and wanted a conference with him, and they walked off and spoke for a few minutes. Skip came back and finished his drink and said he wanted to put his car in the parking garage before somebody towed it, but he'd be back in a few minutes. Or I could come along for the ride.

"You go ahead," I told him. "I may go on home myself."

"Make it an early night?"

"Not the worst idea."

"No. Well, if you're gone when I get back I'll see you tomorrow."

• • •

I didn't go right home. I hit a few joints first. Not Armstrong's. I didn't want any conversation. I didn't want to get drunk, either. I'm not sure what I wanted.

I was leaving Polly's Cage when I saw a car that looked like Tommy's Buick cruising west on Fifty-seventh. I didn't get a good look at the person behind the wheel. I walked along after it, saw it pull into a parking space in the middle of the next block. By the time the driver got out and locked up, I was close enough to see it was Tommy. He was wearing a jacket and tie and carrying two packages. One, fan-shaped, looked to be flowers.

I watched him enter Carolyn's building.

For some reason I went and stood on the sidewalk across the street from her building. I picked out her window, or what I decided was her window. Her light was on. I stood there for quite a while, until the light went out.

I went to a pay phone, called 411. The Information operator reported to me that she did indeed have a listing for Carolyn Cheatham at the address I gave her, but that the number was unpublished. I called again, got a different operator, and went through the procedure a policeman uses to get an unlisted number. I got it and wrote it down in my notebook, on the same page with my witless little sketch of ears. They were, I thought, rather unremarkable ears. They would pass in a crowd.

I put a dime in the phone and dialed the number. It rang four or five times, and then she picked it up and said hello. I don't know what the hell else I expected. I didn't say anything, and she said hello a second time and broke the connection.

I felt tight across my upper back and in my shoulders. I wanted to go to some bucket of blood and get in a fight. I wanted to hit something.

Where had the anger come from? I wanted to go up there and pull him off of her and hit him in the face, but what the hell had he done? A few days ago I'd been angry with him for neglecting her. Now I was enraged because he wasn't.

Was I jealous? But why? I wasn't interested in her.

Crazy.

I went and looked at her window again. The light was still out. An ambulance from Roosevelt sped down Ninth Avenue, its siren wailing. Rock music blared on the radio of a car waiting for the light to change. Then the car sped away and the ambulance siren faded in the distance, and for a moment the city seemed utterly silent. Then the silence, too, was gone, as I became aware again of all the background noises that never completely disappear.

That song Keegan had played for me came into my mind. Not all of it. I couldn't get the tune right and I only remembered snatches of the lyrics. Something about a night of poetry and poses. Well, you could call it that. And knowing you're all alone when the sacred ginmill closes.

I picked up some beer on the way home.

19

The Sixth Precinct is housed on West Tenth Street between Bleecker and Hudson, in the Village. Years before, when I did a tour of duty there, it was in an ornate structure farther west on Charles Street. That building has since been converted into co-op apartments, and named the Gendarme.

The new station house is an ugly modern building that no one will ever carve into apartments. I was there a little before noon on Tuesday and I walked past the front desk and straight to Eddie Koehler's office. I didn't have to ask, I knew where it was.

He looked up from a report he'd been reading, blinked at me. "Thing about that door," he said, "anybody could walk through it."

"You're looking good, Eddie."

"Well, you know. Clean living. Sit down, Matt."

I sat, and we talked a little. We went back a long ways, Eddie and I. When the small talk faded, he said, "You just happened to be in the neighborhood, right?"

"I just thought of you and figured you needed a new hat."

"In this weather?"

"Maybe a panama. Nice straw, keep the sun off."

"Maybe a pith helmet. But in thith neighborhood," he said, "Thome of the girlth would make dirty crackth."

I had my notebook out. "A license number," I said. "I thought maybe you could check it for me."

"You mean call Motor Vehicles?"

"First check the hot-car sheet."

"What's it, a hit-and-run? Your client wants to know who hit him, maybe take quiet cash instead of press charges?"

"You've got a great imagination."

"You got a license number and I should check the hot cars before anything else? Shit. What's the number?"

I read it out to him. He jotted it down and pushed away from his desk. "Be a minute," he said.

While he was gone I looked at my ear drawings. Ears really do look different. The thing is you have to train yourself to notice them.

He wasn't gone long. He came back and dropped into his swivel chair. "Not on the sheet," he said.

"Could you check the registration with Motor Vehicles?"

"I could, but I don't have to. They don't always get on the sheet so quick. So I called in, and it's hot, all right, it'll be listed on the next sheet. It was phoned in last night, stolen late afternoon or early evening."

"It figured," I said.

" 'Seventy-three Mercury, right? Sedan, dark blue?"

"That's right."

"That what you wanted?"

"Where was it stolen from?"

"Somewhere in Brooklyn. Ocean Parkway, the high numbers, it must be pretty far out."

"Makes sense."

"It does?" he said. "Why?"

I shook my head. "It's nothing," I said. "I thought the

car might be important, but if it's stolen it doesn't lead anywhere." I took out my wallet, drew out a twenty and a five, the traditional price of a hat in police parlance. I put the bills on his desk. He covered them with his hand but did not pick them up.

"Now I got a question," he said.

"Oh?"

"Why?"

"That's private," I said. "I'm working for someone, I can't—"

He was shaking his head. "Why spend twenty-five dollars on something you coulda got for nothing over the telephone? Jesus Christ, Matt, how many years did you carry a shield that you don't remember how to get a listing out of the DMV? You call up, you identify yourself, you know the drill, don't you?"

"I thought it was hot."

"So you want to check hot cars first, you call somebody in the Department. You're a police officer on a stakeout, whatever you want to say, you just spotted a car you think might be hot, and could they check it for you? That saves you running down here and saves you the price of a hat on top of it."

"That's impersonating an officer," I said.

"Oh, really?" He patted the money. "This," he said, "is *bribing* an officer, you want to get technical. You pick a funny place to draw the line."

The conversation was making me uncomfortable. I had impersonated an officer less than twelve hours ago, getting Carolyn Cheatham's unlisted number from Information. I said, "Maybe I missed the sight of you, Eddie. How's that?"

"Maybe. Maybe your brain's getting rusty."

"That's possible."

"Maybe you should lay off the booze and rejoin the human race. Is that possible?"

I stood up. "Always a pleasure, Eddie." He had more to say, but I didn't have to stay there and listen to it.

There was a church nearby, Saint Veronica's, a red-brick pile on Christopher Street near the river. A derelict had arranged himself on the steps, an empty bottle of Night Train still clutched in his hand. The thought came to me that Eddie had phoned ahead and had the man placed there, a grim example of what could lie in store for me. I didn't know whether to laugh or to shudder.

I climbed the steps and went inside. The church was cavernous and empty. I found a seat and closed my eyes for a minute. I thought about my two clients, Tommy and Skip, and the ineffectual work I was performing for each of them. Tommy didn't need my help and wasn't getting it. As for Skip, perhaps I'd helped make the exchange go smoothly, but I'd made mistakes. For God's sake, I should have had Billie and Bobby taking down license numbers, I shouldn't have left it for Billie to think of on his own.

I was almost glad the car had turned out to be stolen. So that Keegan's clue wouldn't lead anywhere and my lack of foresight would be less significant.

Stupid. Anyway, I'd posted them there, hadn't I? They wouldn't have seen the car, let alone got the number, if they'd been with Kasabian on the other side of the block.

I went and put a dollar in the slot and lit a candle. A woman was kneeling a few yards to my left. When she rose to her full height I saw she was a transsexual. She stood two inches taller than I. Her features were a mix of Latin and Oriental, her shoulders and upper arms were muscular, and her breasts were the size of cantaloupes, straining the polka-dot sun halter.

"Well, hello," she said.

"Hello."

"Have you come to light a candle to Saint Veronica? Do you know anything about her?"

"No."

"Neither do I. But I prefer to think of her"—she arranged a strand of hair to fall across her forehead—"as Saint Veronica *Lake*."

The N train took me to within a few blocks of the church at Ovington and Eighteenth Avenue. A rather scattered woman in paint-spattered jeans and an army shirt pointed me to the pastor's office. There was no one at the desk, just a pudgy young man with an open freckled face. He had one foot on the arm of a chair and was tuning a guitar.

I asked where the pastor was.

"That's me," he said, straightening up. "How can I help you?"

I said I understood he'd had some minor vandalism in the basement the previous evening. He grinned at me. "Is that what it was? Someone seems to have shot up our light fixture. The damage won't amount to much. Would you like to see where it happened?"

We didn't have to use the stairs I'd gone down last night. We walked down an inside staircase and a hallway, entering the room through the curtained archway our wigged and bearded friends had used to make their departure. The room had been straightened since then, the chairs stacked, the tables folded. Daylight filtered in through the windows.

"That's the fixture, of course," he said, pointing. "There was glass on the floor but it's been swept up. I suppose you've seen the police report."

I didn't say anything, just looked around.

"You are with the police, aren't you?"

He wasn't probing. He simply wanted to be reassured. But something stopped me. Maybe the tail end of my conversation with Eddie Koehler.

"No," I said. "I'm not."

"Oh? Then your interest is—"

"I was here last night."

He looked at me, waiting for me to go on. He was, I thought, a very patient young man. You sensed that he wanted to hear what you had to say, and in your own good time. I suppose that quality would be a useful one for a minister.

I said, "I used to be a cop. I'm a private detective now." That was perhaps technically incorrect, but close enough to the truth. "I was here last night on behalf of a client, seeking to exchange money for some goods of the client's that were being held for ransom."

"I see."

"The other parties, the criminals who had stolen my client's goods in the first place, selected this location for the exchange. They were the ones who did the shooting."

"I see," he said again. "Was anyone . . . shot? The police looked for bloodstains. I don't know that all wounds bleed."

"No one was shot. There were only two shots fired and they both went into the ceiling."

He sighed. "That's a relief. Well, Mr. Uh—"

"Scudder. Matthew Scudder."

"And I'm Nelson Fuhrmann. I guess we missed introducing ourselves earlier." He ran a hand over a freckled forehead. "I gather the police don't know about any of this."

"No, they don't."

"And you'd rather they didn't."

"It would certainly be simpler if they didn't."

He considered, nodded. "I doubt I'd have occasion to communicate it to them anyway," he said. "I don't suppose they'll come around again, do you? It's no major crime."

"Somebody might follow up. But don't be surprised if you never hear further."

"They'll file a report," he said, "and that will be that." He sighed again. "Well, Mr. Scudder, you must have had a reason to take the chance that I *would* mention your visit to the police. What is it you're hoping to find out?"

"I'd like to know who they were."

"The villains?" He laughed. "I don't know what else to call them. If I were a policeman I suppose I'd call them perpetrators."

"You could call them sinners."

"Ah, but we're all that, aren't we?" He smiled at me. "You don't know their identity?"

"No. And they wore disguises, wigs and false beards, so I don't even know what they looked like."

"I don't see how I could help you. You don't suppose they're connected with the church, do you?"

"I'm almost certain they're not. But they picked this place, Reverend Fuhrmann, and—"

"Call me Nelson."

"—and it suggests a familiarity with the church, and with this room in particular. Did the cops find any evidence of forced entry?"

"I don't believe so, no."

"Mind if I look at the door?" I examined the lock of the door leading to the outside stairs. If it had been tampered with, I couldn't see it. I asked him what other doors led to the outside, and he took me around and we checked, and none of them bore the scars of illegal entry.

"The police said a door must have been left open," he said.

"That would be a logical guess if this were just a case of vandalism or malicious mischief. A couple of kids happen to find a door left unlocked, go inside, horse around a little. But this was planned and arranged. I don't think our sinners could count on the door being left open. Or is locking up a hit-or-miss business here?"

He shook his head. "No, we always lock up. We have to, even in a decent neighborhood like this one. Two doors were open when the police arrived last night, this one and the one in the rear. We certainly wouldn't have left both doors unlocked."

"If one was open, the other could be unlocked from inside without a key."

"Oh, of course. Still—"

"There must be a lot of keys in circulation, reverend. I'm sure a lot of community groups use the space."

"Oh, absolutely," he said. "We feel it's part of our function to make our space available when we don't require it for our own purposes. And the rent we collect for it is an important part of our income."

"So the basement is often in use at night."

"Oh, it certainly is. Let's see, AA meets in this room every Thursday night, and there's an Al-Anon group that uses the room on Tuesdays, they'll be here tonight, come to think of it. And Fridays, who's here Fridays? This space has been put to no end of uses in the few years I've been here. We had a little theater group doing their rehearsals, we have a monthly cub scout meeting when the whole pack assembles together, we have—well, you can see that there are a lot of different groups with access to the premises."

"But no one meets here on Monday nights."

"No. There was a women's consciousness-raising group that met here Mondays up until about three months ago, but I believe they decided to meet in one another's homes instead." He cocked his head. "You're suggesting that the, uh, sinners would have had to be in a position to know the space would be empty last night."

"I was thinking that."

"But they could have called and asked. Anyone could

have called and posed as someone interested in the space, and checking on its availability."

"Did you get any calls like that?"

"Oh, we get them all the time," he said. "It's not something anyone here would bother to remember."

"Why are you comin' around here all the time?" the woman wanted to know. "Askin' everybody about Mickey Mouse."

"Who?"

She let out a laugh. "Miguelito Cruz. Miguelito means Little Michael, you know? Like Mickey. People call him Mickey Mouse. *I* do, anyway."

We were in a Puerto Rican bar on Fourth Avenue, nestled between a shop that sold botanicals and one that rented formal wear. I'd gotten back on the N train after my visit to the Lutheran church in Bensonhurst, intending to ride it back into the city, but instead I found myself rising abruptly at Fifty-third Street in Sunset Park and leaving the train there. I had nothing else to do with the day, no logical direction to take in Skip's behalf, and I thought I might as well put in some time justifying my fee from Tommy Tillary.

Besides, it was lunchtime, and a plate of black beans and rice sounded good to me.

It tasted as good as it sounded. I washed it down with a bottle of cold beer, then ordered flan for dessert and had a couple of cups of espresso. The Italians give you a thimble of the stuff; the Puerto Ricans pour you a full cup of it.

Then I barhopped, staying with beers and making them last, and now I'd met this woman who wanted to know why I was interested in Mickey Mouse. She was around thirty-five, with dark hair and eyes and a hardness to her face that matched the hardness in her voice. Her voice, scarred by cigarettes and booze and hot food, was the sort that would cut glass.

Her eyes were large and soft, and what showed of her body suggested that it would have a softness to match the eyes. She was wearing a lot of bright colors. Her hair was wrapped up in a hot-pink scarf, her blouse was an electric blue, her hip-hugging slacks canary yellow, her high-heeled shoes Day-Glo orange. The blouse was unbuttoned far enough to reveal the swell of her full breasts. Her skin was like copper, but with a blush to it, as if lighted from within.

I said, "You know Mickey Mouse?"

"Sure I know him. I see him all the time in the cartoons. He is one funny mouse."

"I mean Miguelito Cruz. You know that Mickey Mouse?"

"You a cop?"

"No."

"You look like one, you move like one, you ask questions like one."

"I used to be a cop."

"They kick you out for stealin'?" She laughed, showing a couple of gold teeth. "Takin' bribes?"

I shook my head. "Shooting kids," I said.

She laughed louder. "No way," she said. "They don't kick you out for that. They give you a promotion, make you the chief."

There was no island accent in her speech. She was a Brooklyn girl from the jump. I asked her again if she knew Cruz.

"Why?"

"Forget it."

"Huh?"

"Forget it," I said, and turned a shoulder to her and went back to my beer. I didn't figure she'd leave it alone. I watched out of the corner of my eye. She was drinking something colorful through a straw, and as I watched she sucked up the last of it.

"Hey," she said. "Buy me a drink?"

I looked at her. The dark eyes didn't waver. I motioned to the bartender, a sullen fat man who gazed on the world with a look of universal disapproval. He made her whatever the hell she was drinking. He needed most of the bottles on the back bar to do it. He put it in front of her and looked at me, and I held my glass aloft to show I was all right.

"I know him pretty good," she said.

"Yeah? Does he ever smile?"

"I don't mean him, I mean Mickey Mouse."

"Uh-huh."

"Whattaya mean, 'uh-huh'? He's a baby. When he grows up, then he can come see me. *If* he grows up."

"Tell me about him."

"What's to tell?" She sipped her drink. "He gets in trouble showin' everybody how he's so tough and so smart. But he's not so tough, you know, and he's not so smart either." Her mouth softened. "He is nice-lookin', though. Always the nice clothes, always the hair combed neat, always a fresh shave." Her hand reached to stroke my cheek. "Smooth, you know? And he's little, and he's cute, and you want to reach out and give him a hug, just wrap him up and take him home."

"But you never did?"

She laughed again. "Hey, man, I got all the troubles I need."

"You figure him for trouble?"

"If I ever took him home," she said, "he'd be all the time thinkin', 'Now how am I gonna get this bitch to let me put her on the street?'"

"He's a pimp? I never heard that."

"If you're thinkin' about a pimp with the purple hat and the Eldorado, forget it." She laughed. "That's what Mickey

Rat wishes he was. One time he hits on this new girl, she's fresh up from Santurce, from a village near Santurce, you know? Very green, and she's not Señorita Einstein to start with, you know? And he gets her to turn tricks for him, you know, workin' outta her apartment, seein' one or two guys a day, guys he finds and brings up to her.''

"'Hey, Joe, you wanna fock my seestair?'"

"You do one lousy PR accent, man. But you got the idea. She works about two weeks, you know, and she gets sick of it, and she takes the plane back to the island. And that's the story of Mickey the pimp."

By then she needed another drink and I was ready for a beer myself. She had the bartender bring us a little bag of plantain chips and split the side seam so the chips spilled out on the bar between us. They tasted like a cross between potato chips and wood shavings.

Mickey Mouse's trouble, she told me, was how hard he worked trying to prove something. In high school he had proved his toughness by going into Manhattan with a couple of buddies, roaming the crooked streets of the West Village in search of homosexuals to beat up.

She said, "He was the bait, you know? Small and pretty. And then when they got the guy, he was the guy who went crazy, almost wanted to kill him. Guys who went with him, first time they said he had heart, but later they started to say he had no brains." She shook her head. "So I never took him home," she said. "He's cute, but cute disappears when you turn the lights out, you know? I don't think he woulda done me much good." She extended a painted nail, touched my chin. "You don't want a man that's too cute, you know?"

It was an overture, and one I somehow knew I didn't want to follow up on. The realization brought a wave of sadness rolling in on me out of nowhere. I had nothing for this woman and she had nothing for me. I didn't even know her name; if we'd introduced ourselves I couldn't remember it. And I didn't think we had. The only names mentioned had been Miguelito Cruz and Mickey Mouse.

I mentioned another, Angel Herrera's. She didn't want to talk about Herrera. He was nice, she said. He was not so cute and maybe not so smart, but maybe that was better. But she didn't want to talk about Herrera.

I told her I had to go. I put a bill on the bar and instructed the bartender to keep her glass full. She laughed, either mocking me or enjoying the humor of the situation, I don't know which. Her laughter sounded like someone pouring a sack of broken glass down a staircase. It followed me to the door and out.

20

When I got back to my hotel there was a message from Anita and another from Skip. I called Syosset first, talked with Anita and the boys. I talked with her about money, saying I'd collected a fee and would be sending some soon. I talked with my sons about baseball, and about the camp they'd be going to soon.

I called Skip at Miss Kitty's. Someone else answered the phone and I held while they summoned him.

"I want to get together with you," he said. "I'm working tonight. You want to come by afterward?"

"All right."

"What time is it now? Ten to nine? I've been on less than two hours? Feels like five. Matt, what I'll do, I'll close up around two. Come by then and we'll have a few."

I watched the Mets. They were out of town. Chicago, I think. I kept my eyes on the screen but I couldn't keep my mind on the game.

There was a beer left over from the night before. I sipped at it during the game, but I couldn't work up much enthusiasm for it, either. After the game ended I watched

199

about half of the newscast, then turned the set off and stretched out on the bed.

I had a paperback edition of *The Lives of the Saints*, and at one point I looked up Saint Veronica. I read that there was no great certainty that she had existed, but that she was supposed to have been a Jerusalem woman who wiped Christ's sweating face with a cloth while he was suffering on his way to Calvary, and that an image of his face remained on the cloth.

I pictured the act that had brought her twenty centuries of fame, and I had to laugh. The woman I was seeing, reaching out to soothe His brow, had the face and hairstyle of Veronica Lake.

Miss Kitty's was closed when I got there, and for a moment I thought that Skip had said the hell with it and gone home. Then I saw that the iron gates, though drawn, were not secured by a padlock, and that a low-wattage bulb glowed behind the bar. I slid the accordion gates open a foot or so and knocked, and he came and opened up for me, then rearranged the gates and turned the key in the door.

He looked tired. He clapped me on the shoulder, told me it was good to see me, led me to the end of the bar farthest from the door. Without asking he poured me a long drink of Wild Turkey, then topped up his own glass with scotch.

"First of the day," I said.

"Yeah? I'm impressed. Of course the day's only two hours and ten minutes old."

I shook my head. "First since I woke up. I had some beer, but not too much of that, either." I drank off some of my bourbon. It had a good bite to it.

"Yeah, well, I'm the same way," he said. "I have days when I don't drink. I even have days when I don't have so much as a beer. You know what it is? For you and me, drinking's something we choose to do. It's a choice."

"There's mornings when I don't think it was the most brilliant choice I could have made."

"Jesus, tell me about it. But even so it's a choice for us. That's the difference between you and me and a guy like Billie Keegan."

"You think so?"

"Don't you? Matt, the man is always drinking. I mean, take last night. All the rest of us, okay, we're pretty heavy drinkers, but we took it easy last night, right? Because it's sometimes appropriate and sometimes not. Am I right?"

"I guess."

"Afterward, another story. Afterward a man wants to unwind, loosen up. But Keegan was shitfaced before we got there, for God's sake."

"Then he turned out to be the hero."

"Yeah, go figure that one. Uh, the plate number, did you—"

"Stolen."

"Shit. Well, we figured that."

"Sure."

He drank some of his drink. "Keegan," he said, "*has* to drink. For myself, I could stop anytime. I don't, because I happen to like what the stuff does for me. But I could stop anytime, and I figure you're the same."

"Oh, I would think so."

"Of course you are. Now Keegan, I don't know. I don't like to call the man an alcoholic—"

"That's a hell of a thing to call a man."

"I agree with you. I'm not saying that's what he is, and God knows I like the man, but I think he's got a problem." He straightened up. "The hell with it. He could be a fucking Bowery bum, I still wish the car hadn't been stolen. C'mon back, we'll spread out and relax a little."

In the office, with the two whiskey bottles on the desk between us, he leaned back in his chair and put his feet up. "You checked the license number," he said. "So I guess you're already working on it."

I nodded. "I went out to Brooklyn, too."

"Where? Not where we were last night?"

"The church."

"What did you think you stood to learn there? You figure one of them left his wallet on the floor?"

"You never know what you'll find, Skip. You have to look around."

"I suppose. I wouldn't know where to start."

"You start anyplace. And do anything you think of."

"You learn anything?"

"A few things."

"Like what? Never mind, I don't want to be sitting on your shoulder while you do all this. You find out anything useful?"

"Maybe. You don't always know until later on what's useful and what isn't. You can look at it that everything you learn is useful. For instance, just knowing that the car was stolen tells me something, even if it doesn't tell me who was driving it."

"At least you can rule out the owner. Now you know one person out of eight million couldn't have done it. Who was the owner? Some old lady, only drives it to bingo?"

"I don't know, but it was lifted from Ocean Parkway, not far from the clam bar they sent us to first."

"Means they live out in Brooklyn?"

"Or they drove their own car out there, parked it and stole the one we saw. Or they went out on the subway or took a cab. Or—"

"So we don't know a whole lot."

"Not yet."

He leaned back with his hands behind his head. "Bobby got another call-back on that commercial," he said. "The basketball referee in the fight against prejudice? He's got to go in again tomorrow. It's now down to him and four other guys so they want to look at everybody again."

"That's good, I guess."

"How can you tell? You believe a profession like that, running your ass off and fighting the competition so you can be on the tube for twenty seconds. You know how many actors it takes to change a light bulb? Nine. One to climb up and replace it and eight others to stand around the ladder and say, 'That should be *me* up there!'"

"That's not bad."

"Well, credit where it's due, it was the actor told me the joke." He touched up his drink, sat back in his chair. "Matt, that was strange last night. That was fucking strange last night."

"In the church basement."

A nod. "Those disguises of theirs. What they needed was Groucho noses and moustaches and glasses, you know the kind the kids wear. Because it was like that, the wigs and beards, they didn't even come close to looking real, but they weren't funny. The gun kept it from being funny."

"Why'd they wear disguises?"

"So we wouldn't recognize them. Why does anybody wear a disguise?"

"Would you have recognized them?"

"I don't know, I didn't get to see them without the disguises. What are we here, Abbott and Costello?"

"I don't think they recognized us," I said. "When I went into the basement, one of them called out your name. It was dark, but they'd had time for their eyes to get used to it. You and I don't look alike."

"I'm the pretty one." He drew on his cigarette, blew out a great cloud of smoke. "What are you getting at?"

"I don't know. I'm just wondering why they would bother with disguises if we didn't know them in the first place."

"To make it harder to find them later, I suppose."

"I guess. But why should they think we'd bother to look for them? There's not a hell of a lot we can do to them. We made a deal, traded money for your books. What did you wind up doing with the books, incidentally?"

"Burned them, like I said. And what do you mean, there's nothing we could do to them? We could murder them in their beds."

"Sure."

"Find the right church, take a shit on the altar, and tell Dominic Tutto they did it. That has a certain charm, now that I think of it. Fix 'em up, get 'em a date with the Butcher. Maybe they wore disguises for the same reason they stole the car. Because they're pros."

"They look familiar to you, Skip?"

"You mean looking past the wigs and beards and shit? I don't know that I could *see* past it. I didn't recognize the voices."

"No."

"There *was* something familiar about them, but I don't know what it was. The way they moved, maybe. That's it."

"I think I know what you mean."

"An economy of motion. You could almost say they were light on their feet." He laughed. "Call 'em up, see if they want to go dancing."

My glass was empty. I poured a little bourbon into it, sat back, and sipped it slowly. Skip drowned his cigarette in a coffee cup and told me, inevitably, that he never wanted to see me do the same. I assured him he wasn't likely to. He lit another cigarette and we sat there in a comfortable silence.

After a while he said, "You want to explain something to me, forget about disguises. Tell me why they shot the lights out."

"To cover their exit. Give them a step or two on us."

"You think they thought we were gonna come stampeding after them? Chase armed men through backyards and driveways?"

"Maybe they wanted it dark, thought they stood a better chance that way." I frowned. "All he had to do was take a step and flick the switch. You know the worst thing about the gunshots?"

"Yeah, they scared the shit out of me."

"They drew heat. One thing a pro knows is you don't do anything that brings the cops. Not if you can help it."

"Maybe they figured it was worth it. It was a warning: 'Don't try to get even.'"

"Maybe."

"A little touch of the dramatic."

"Maybe."

"And God knows it was dramatic enough. When the gun was aimed at me I thought I was gonna get shot. I really did. Then when he shot up the ceiling instead I didn't know whether to shit or go blind. What's the matter?"

"Oh, for Christ's sake," I said.

"What?"

"He pointed the gun at you and then he fired two shots into the ceiling."

"Is that something we're supposed to have overlooked? What do you think we've been talking about?"

I held up a hand. "Think a minute," I said. "I'd been thinking of him shooting out the lights, that's why I missed it."

"Missed what? Matt, I don't—"

"Where have you been lately that somebody pointed a gun at someone but didn't shoot him? And fired two bullets into the ceiling?"

"Jesus Christ."

"Well?"

"Jesus Christ on stilts. Frank and Jesse."

"What do you think?"

"I don't know what I think. It's such a crazy thought. They didn't sound Irish."

"How do we know they were Irish at Morrissey's?"

"We don't. I guess I assumed it. Those handkerchief masks, and taking the money for Northern Relief, and the whole sense that it was political. They had that same economy of movement, you know? The way they were so precise, they didn't take extra steps, they moved through that whole robbery like somebody choreographed it."

"Maybe they're dancers."

"Right," he said. "*Ballet Desperadoes of '75*. I'm still trying to wrap my mind around all of this. Two clowns in red hankies take off the Morrissey brothers for fifty grand, and then they jack off me and Kasabian for—hey, it's the same amount. A subtle pattern begins to emerge."

"We don't know what the Morrisseys lost."

"No, and they didn't know what was gonna be in the safe, but a pattern's a pattern. I'll take it. What about their ears? You got pictures of their ears from last night. Are those the ears of Frank and Jesse?" He started to laugh. "I can't believe the lines I'm speaking. 'Are those the ears of Frank and Jesse?' Sentence sounds like it was translated from another language. Are they?"

"Skip, I never noticed their ears."

"I thought you detectives are working all the time."

"I was trying to figure out how to get out of the line of fire. If I was thinking of anything. They were fair-skinned, Frank and Jesse. And they were fair last night."

"Fair and warmer. You see their eyes?"

"I didn't see the color."

"I was close enough to see the eyes of the one who made the trade with me. But if I saw them I wasn't paying attention. Not that it makes any difference. Did either of them speak a word at Morrissey's?"

"I don't think so."

He closed his eyes. "I'm trying to remember. I think the whole thing was pantomime. Two gunshots and then silence until they were out the door and down the stairs."

"That's how I remember it."

He stood up, paced around the room. "It's crazy," he said. "Hey, maybe we can stop looking for the viper in my bosom. We're not looking at an inside job. We're dealing with a daring gang of two who're specializing in taking off bars in Hell's Kitchen. You don't suppose that local Irish gang, what do they call them—"

"The Westies. No, we'd have heard. Or Morrissey would

have heard. That reward of his would have smoked it out in a day if any of them had anything to do with it." I picked up my glass and drank what was in it. God, it tasted good right now. We had them, I knew we did. I didn't know a single goddamned thing about them I hadn't known an hour ago but now I knew that I was going to bag them.

"That's why they wore disguises," I said. "Oh, they might have worn them anyway, but that's why they didn't want us to get a look at them. They made a mistake. We're going to get them."

"Jesus, look at you, Matt. Like an old firehouse dog when the alarm goes off. How the hell are you going to get them? You still don't know who they are."

"I know they're Frank and Jesse."

"So? Morrissey's been trying to find Frank and Jesse for a long time. Fact he tried to get you to go looking for them. What gives you the edge now?"

I poured myself just one more little slug of the Wild Turkey. I said, "When you plant a bug on a car and then you want to pick it up, you need two cars. One won't do it, but with two you can triangulate on the signal and home in on it."

"I'm missing something."

"It's not quite the same thing, but it's close. We've got them at Morrissey's, and we've got them in that church basement in Bensonhurst. That's two points of reference. Now we can home in on them, we can triangulate on their signal. Two bullets in the ceiling—it's their fucking trademark. You'd think they wanted to get caught, giving the job a signature like that."

"Yeah, I feel sorry for 'em," he said. "I bet they're really shitting in their pants. So far they only made a hundred grand this month. What they don't realize is Matt "Bulldog" Scudder is on their trail, and the poor bastards won't get to spend a dime of it."

21

The telephone woke me. I sat up, blinked at daylight. It went on ringing.

I picked it up. Tommy Tillary said, "Matt, that cop was here. He came here, can you believe it?"

"Where?"

"The office, I'm at my office. You know him. At least he said he knew you. A detective, a very unpleasant man."

"I don't know who you're talking about, Tommy."

"I forget his name. He said—"

"What did he say?"

"He said the two of you were in my house together."

"Jack Diebold."

"That's it. He was right then? You were in my house together?"

I rubbed my temples, reached over and looked at my watch. It was a few minutes past ten. I tried to figure out when I'd gone to sleep.

"We didn't go there together," I said. "I was there, checking the setting, and he turned up. I used to know him years ago."

It was no use. I couldn't remember anything after I'd assured Skip that Frank and Jesse were living on borrowed time. Maybe I went home right away, maybe I sat drinking with him until dawn. I had no way of knowing.

"Matt? He's been bothering Carolyn."

"Bothering her?"

My door was bolted. That was a good sign. I couldn't have been in too bad shape if I'd remembered to bolt the door. On the other hand, my pants were tossed over the chair. It would have been better if they'd been hung in the closet. Then again, they weren't in a tangled heap on the floor, nor was I still wearing them. The great detective, sifting clues, trying to find out how bad he'd been last night.

"Bothering her. Called her a couple of times and went over to her place once. Insinuating things, you know, like she's covering for me. Matt, all it's doing is upsetting Carolyn, plus it makes things awkward for me around the office."

"I can see how it would."

"Matt, I gather you knew him of old. Do you think you could get him to lay off me?"

"Jesus, Tommy, I don't see how. A cop doesn't ease up on a homicide investigation as a favor to an old friend."

"Oh, I wouldn't suggest anything out of line, Matt. Don't get me wrong. But a homicide investigation is one thing and harassment's another, don't you agree?" He didn't give me a chance to answer. "The thing is, the guy's got it in for me. He's got it in his head I'm a lowlife, and if you could just, you know, have a word with him. Tell him I'm good people."

I tried to remember what I'd told Jack about Tommy. I couldn't recall, but I didn't think it amounted to much in the way of a character reference.

"And touch base with Drew, just as a favor to me, okay? He was asking me just yesterday what I'd heard from you, if you'd come up with anything. I know you're working hard for me, Matt, and we might as well let him know, too. Keep him in the picture, you know what I mean?"

"Sure, Tommy."

After he hung up I chased two aspirins with a glass of water from the tap. I had a shower and was halfway through with my shave before I realized I'd virtually agreed to try to talk Jack Diebold into letting up on Tommy. For the first time I realized how good the son of a bitch must be at getting people to buy his real-estate syndications, or whatever the hell he was peddling. It was just as everybody said. He was very persuasive over the telephone.

Outside the day was clear, the sun brighter than it needed to be. I stopped at McGovern's for one quick one, just a bracer. I bought a paper from the bag lady on the corner, tossed her a buck and walked away wrapped in a fog of blessings. Well, I'd take her blessing. I could use all the help I could get.

I had coffee and an English muffin at the Red Flame and read the paper. It bothered me that I couldn't remember leaving Skip's office. I told myself I couldn't have been too bad because I didn't have all that bad of a hangover, but there wasn't necessarily any correlation there. Sometimes I awoke clearheaded and physically fit after a night of ugly drinking and a large memory gap. Other times a hangover that kept me in bed all day would follow a night when I hadn't even felt drunk and nothing untoward had taken place, no memory lost.

Never mind. Forget it.

I ordered a refill on the coffee and thought about my discourse on triangulating on the two men we had taken to calling Frank and Jesse. I remembered the confidence I had felt and wondered what had become of it. Maybe I'd had a plan, maybe I'd come up with a brilliant insight and had known just how to track them down. I looked in my notebook on the chance that I'd written down a passing thought that I'd since forgotten. No such luck. There were no entries after I'd left the bar in Sunset Park.

But I did have that entry, notes on Mickey Mouse and his adolescent career as a fag-basher in the Village. So many working-class teenagers take up that sport, sure that they're acting on genuine outrage and confirming their manliness in the process, never realizing they're trying to kill a part of themselves they don't dare acknowledge. Sometimes they overachieve, maiming or killing a gay man. I'd made a couple of arrests in cases like that, and on every occasion the boys had been astonished to find out that they were in genuine trouble, that we cops were not on their side, that they might actually go away for what they'd done.

I started to put my notebook away, then went over and put a dime in the phone instead. I looked up Drew Kaplan's number and dialed it. I thought of the woman who'd told me about Mickey Mouse, glad I didn't have to see her bright clothing on a morning like this one.

"Scudder," I said, when the girl rang me through to Kaplan. "I don't know if it helps, but I've got a little more proof that our friends aren't choirboys."

Afterward I went for a long walk. I walked down Ninth Avenue, stopping at Miss Kitty's to say a quick hello to John Kasabian, but I didn't stay long. I dropped into a church on Forty-second Street, then continued on downtown, past the rear entrance of the Port Authority bus terminal, down through Hell's Kitchen and Chelsea to the Village. I walked through the meatpacking district and stopped at a butchers' bar on the corner of Washington and Thirteenth and stood among men in bloody aprons drinking shots with short beer chasers. I went outside and watched carcasses of beef and lamb suspended on steel hooks, with flies buzzing around them in the heat of the midday sun.

I walked some more and got out of the sun to have a drink at the Corner Bistro on Jane and Fourth and another at the Cookie Bar on Hudson. I sat at a table at the White Horse and ate a hamburger and drank a beer.

Through all of this I kept running things through my mind.

I swear to God I don't know how anybody ever figures anything out, myself included. I'll watch a movie in which someone explains how he figured something out, fitting clues together until a solution appeared, and it will make perfect sense to me as I listen along.

But in my own work it is rarely like that. When I was on the force most of my cases moved toward solution (if they moved that way at all) in one of two ways. Either I didn't know the answer at all until a fresh piece of information made itself instantly evident, or I knew all along who had done whatever had been done, and all that was ever needed was sufficient evidence to prove it in court. In the tiny percentage of cases where I actually worked out a solution, I did so by a process I did not understand then and do not understand now. I took what I had and stared at it and stared at it and stared at it, and all of a sudden I saw the same thing in a new light, and the answer was in my hand.

Have you ever worked a jigsaw puzzle? And have you then been stuck for the moment, and kept taking up pieces and holding them this way and that, until finally you take up a piece you must have already held between thumb and forefinger a hundred times, one you've turned this way and that, fitted here and fitted there? And this time the piece drops neatly into place, it fits where you'd swear you tried it a minute ago, fits perfectly, fits in a way that should have been obvious all along.

I was at a table in the White Horse, a table in which

someone had carved his initials, a dark brown table with the varnish wearing thin here and there. I had finished my hamburger, I had finished my beer, I was drinking a cup of coffee with a discreet shot of bourbon in it. Shreds and images flitted through my mind. I heard Nelson Fuhrmann talking about all the people with access to the basement of his church. I saw Billie Keegan draw a record from its jacket and place it on a turntable. I watched Bobby Ruslander put the blue whistle between his lips. I saw the yellow-wigged sinner, Frank or Jesse, grudgingly agree to move furniture. I watched *The Quare Fellow* with Fran the nurse, walked with her and her friends to Miss Kitty's.

There was a moment when I didn't have the answer, and then there was a moment when I did.

I can't say I did anything to make this happen. I didn't work anything out. I kept picking up pieces of the puzzle, I kept turning them this way and that, and all of a sudden I had the whole puzzle, with one piece after another locking effortlessly and infallibly into place.

Had I thought of all this the night before, with all my thoughts unraveled in blackout like Penelope's tapestry? I don't really think so, although such is the nature of blackouts that I shall never be able to say with certainty one way or the other. Yet it almost felt that way. The answers as they came were so obvious—just as with a jigsaw puzzle, once the piece fits you can't believe you didn't see it right away. They were so obvious I felt as though I were discovering something I had known all along.

I called Nelson Fuhrmann. He didn't have the information I wanted, but his secretary gave me a phone number, and I managed to reach a woman who was able to answer some of my questions.

I started to phone Eddie Koehler, then realized I was only a couple of blocks from the Sixth Precinct. I walked over there, found him at his desk, and told him he had a chance to earn the rest of the hat I'd bought him the day before. He made a couple of telephone calls without leaving his desk, and when I left there I had a few more entries in my notebook.

I made phone calls of my own from a booth on the corner, then walked over to Hudson and caught a cab uptown. I got out at the corner of Eleventh Avenue and Fifty-first Street and walked toward the river. I stopped in front of Morrissey's, but I didn't bang on the door or ring the bell. Instead I took a moment to read the poster for the theater downstairs. *The Quare Fellow* had finished its brief run. A play by John B. Keane was scheduled to open the following night. *The Man from Clare*, it was called. There was a photograph of the actor who was to play the leading role. He had wiry red hair and a haunted, brooding face.

I tried the door to the theater. It was locked. I knocked on it, and when that brought no response I knocked on it some more. Eventually it opened.

A very short woman in her mid-twenties looked up at me. "I'm sorry," she said. "The box office will be open tomorrow during the afternoon. We're shorthanded right now and we're in final rehearsals and—"

I told her I hadn't come to buy tickets. "I just need a couple minutes of your time," I said.

"That's all anybody ever needs, and there's not enough of my time to go around." She said the line airily, as if a playwright had written it for her. "I'm sorry," she said more matter-of-factly. "It'll have to be some other time."

"No, it'll have to be now."

"My god, what is this? You're not the police, are you? What did we do, forget to pay somebody off?"

"I'm working for the fellow upstairs," I said, gesturing. "He'd want you to cooperate with me."

"Mr. Morrissey?"

"Call Tim Pat and ask him, if you want. My name is Scudder."

From the rear of the theater, someone with a rich brogue called out, "Mary Jean, what in Christ's fucking name is taking you so long?"

She rolled her eyes, sighed, and held the door open for me.

After I left the Irish theater I called Skip at his apartment and looked for him at his saloon. Kasabian suggested I try the gym.

I tried Armstrong's first. He wasn't there, and hadn't been in, but Dennis said someone else had. "A fellow was looking for you," he told me.

"Who?"

"He didn't leave his name."

"What did he look like?"

He considered the question. "If you were choosing up sides for a game of cops and robbers," he said thoughtfully, "you would not pick him to be one of the robbers."

"Did he leave a message?"

"No. Or a tip."

I went to Skip's gym, a large open second-floor loft on Broadway over a delicatessen. A bowling alley had gone broke there a year or two earlier, and the gym had the air of a place that wouldn't outlast the term of its lease. A couple of men were working out with free weights. A black man, glossy with sweat, struggled with bench presses while a white partner spotted him. On the right, a big man stood flat-footed, working the heavy bag with both hands.

I found Skip doing pulldowns on the lat machine. He was wearing gray sweat pants and no shirt and he was sweating fiercely. The muscles worked in his back and shoulders and upper arms. I stood a few yards off watching while he finished a set. I called his name, and he turned and saw me and smiled in surprise, then did another set of pulldowns before rising and coming over to take my hand.

He said, "What's up? How'd you find me here?"

"Your partner's suggestion."

"Well, your timing's good. I can use a break. Let me get my cigarettes."

There was an area where you could smoke, a couple of armchairs grouped around a water cooler. He lit up and said, "It helps, working out. I had a head and a half when I woke up. We kicked it around last night, didn't we? You get home all right?"

"Why, was I in bad shape?"

"No worse'n I was. You were feeling pretty good. The way you were talking, Frank and Jesse had their tits in the wringer and you were ready to start cranking."

"You think I was a little optimistic?"

"Hey, that's okay." He drew on his Camel. "Me, I'm starting to feel human again. You get the blood moving, sweat out some of the poison, it makes a difference. You ever work with weights, Matt?"

"Not in years and years."

"But you used to?"

"Oh, a hundred years ago I thought I might like to box a little."

"You serious? You used to duke it out?"

"This was in high school. I started hanging out at the Y gym, lifting a little, training. Then I had a couple of PAL fights and I found out I didn't like getting hit in the face. And I was clumsy in the ring, and I *felt* clumsy, and I didn't like that."

"So you got a job where they let you carry a gun instead."

"And a badge and a stick."

He laughed. "The runner and the boxer," he said. "Look at them now. You came up here for a reason."

"Uh-huh."

"And?"

"I know who they are."

"Frank and Jesse? You're kidding."

"No."

"Who are they? And how did you manage it? And—"

"I wondered if we could get the crew together tonight. After closing time, say."

"The crew? Who do you mean?"

"Everybody we had with us chasing around Brooklyn the other night. We need some manpower, and there's no point involving new people."

"We need manpower? What are we going to do?"

"Nothing tonight, but I'd like to hold a war council. If that's all right with you."

He jabbed his cigarette into an ashtray. "All right with me?" he said. "Of course it's all right with me. Who do you want, the Magnificent Seven? No, there were five of us. The Magnificent Seven Minus Two. You, me, Kasabian, Keegan and Ruslander. What's tonight, Wednesday? Billie'll close around one-thirty if I ask him nice. I'll call Bobby, I'll talk to John. You really know who they are?"

"I really do."

"I mean do you know specifically or—"

"The whole thing," I said. "Names, addresses, the works."

"The whole shmear. So who are they?"

"I'll come by your office around two."

"You fuck. Suppose you get hit by a bus between now and then?"

"Then the secret dies with me."

"You prick. I'm gonna do some bench presses. You want to try a set of bench presses, just sort of warm up your muscles?"

"No," I said. "I want to go have a drink."

• • •

I didn't have the drink. I looked into one bar but it was crowded, and when I got back to my hotel Jack Diebold was sitting in a chair in the lobby.

I said, "I figured it was you."

"What, the Chinese bartender describe me?"

"He's Filipino. He said a fat old man who didn't leave a tip."

"Who tips at bars?"

"Everybody."

"Are you serious? I tip at tables, I don't tip standing up at a bar. I didn't think anybody did."

"Oh, come on. Where have you been doing your drinking, the Blarney Stone? The White Rose?"

He looked at me. "You're in a funny mood," he said. "Bouncy, peppy."

"Well, I'm right in the middle of something."

"Oh?"

"You know how it is when it all falls into place and things break apart for you? I had an afternoon like that."

"We're not talking about the same case, are we?"

I looked at him. "You haven't been talking about anything," I said. "What case are you—oh, Tommy, Christ. No, I'm not talking about that. There's nothing there to crack."

"I know."

I remembered how my day had started. "He called me this morning," I said. "To complain about you."

"Did he now."

"You're harassing him, he said."

"Yeah, and a hot lot of good it's doing me."

"I'm supposed to give you a character reference, tell you he's really good people."

"Is that right. Well, is he really good people?"

"No, he's an asshole. But I could be prejudiced."

"Sure. After all, he's your client."

"Right." During all of this he had gotten up from his chair and the two of us had walked to the sidewalk in front of the hotel. At the curb, a cabdriver and the driver of a florist's delivery van were having an argument.

I said, "Jack, why'd you come looking for me today?"

"Happened to be in the neighborhood and I thought of you."

"Uh-huh."

"Oh, hell," he said. "I wondered if you had anything."

"On Tillary? There's not going to be anything on him, and if I found it—he *is* my client."

"I meant did you find anything on the Spanish kids." He sighed. "Because I'm starting to get worried that we're gonna lose that one in court."

"Seriously? You've got them admitting to the burglary."

"Yeah, and if they plead to burglary that's the end of it. But the DA's office wants to go for some kind of homicide charge, and if it goes to trial I could see losin' the whole thing."

"You've got stolen goods ID'd with serial numbers found in their residence, you've got fingerprints, you've—"

"Aw, shit," he said. "You know what can happen in a courtroom. All of a sudden the stolen goods isn't evidence anymore because there's some technicality about the search, they found a stolen typewriter when they were only empowered to search for a stolen adding machine, whatever the hell it was. And the fingerprints, well, the one was over there months ago hauling trash for Tillary, that would account for the prints, right? I can see a smart lawyer kicking holes in a solid case. And I just thought, well, if you ran into something good, I'd like to know about it. And it helps your client if it locks up Cruz and Herrera, right?"

"I suppose so. But I haven't got anything."

"Not a thing?"

"Not as far as I can see."

I wound up taking him to Armstrong's and buying us both a couple of drinks. I tipped Dennis a pound just for the pleasure of seeing Jack's reaction. Then I went back to my hotel and left a call at the desk for one in the morning, and set my alarm clock for insurance.

I took a shower and sat on the edge of my bed, looking out at the city. The sky was darkening, turning that cobalt blue it shows all too briefly.

I lay down, stretched out, not really expecting to sleep. The next thing I knew the phone was ringing, and I had no sooner answered it and hung it up again than my clock sounded. I put on my clothes, splashed a little cold water on my face, and went out to earn my money.

22

When I got there they were still waiting for Keegan. Skip had the top of a file cabinet set up as a bar, with four or five bottles and some mix and a bucket of ice cubes. A Styrofoam ice chest on the floor was full of cold beer. I asked if there was any coffee left. Kasabian said there was probably some in the kitchen, and he came back with an insulated plastic pitcher full of coffee and a mug and some cream and sugar. I poured myself black coffee, and I didn't put any booze in it for the time being.

I took a sip of the coffee and there was a knock on the door out front. Skip answered it and came back with Billie. "The late Billie Keegan," Bobby said, and Kasabian fixed him a drink of the same twelve-year-old Irish Billie drank at Armstrong's.

There was a lot of banter, joking back and forth. Then it all died down at once, and before it could start up again I stood up and said, "Something I wanted to talk to all of you about."

"Life insurance," Bobby Ruslander said. "I mean, have you guys thought about it? I mean, like, really *thought* about it?"

221

I said, "Skip and I were talking last night, and we came up with something. The two guys with the wigs and beards, we realized we'd seen them before. A couple of weeks ago, they were the ones who stuck up Morrissey's after-hours."

"They wore handkerchief masks," Bobby said. "And last night they wore wigs and beards *and* masks, so how could you tell?"

"It was them," Skip said. "Believe it. Two shots into the ceiling? Remember?"

"I don't know what you're talking about," Bobby said.

Billie said, "Bobby and I only saw 'em Monday night from a distance, and you didn't see 'em at all, did you, John? No, of course not, you were around the block. And were you at Morrissey's the night of the holdup? I don't recall seeing you there."

Kasabian said he never went to Morrissey's.

"So the three of us got no opinion," Billie went on. "If you say it was the same two guys, I say fine. Is that it? Because unless I missed something, we still don't know who they are."

"Yes we do."

Everybody looked at me.

I said, "I got very cocky last night, telling Skip here that we had them, that once we knew they pulled both jobs it was only a question of zeroing in on them. I think that was mostly some Wild Turkey talking, but there was a certain amount of truth in it, and today I got lucky. I know who they are. Skip and I were right last night, the same pair did pull both jobs, and I know who they are."

"So where do we go from here?" Bobby wanted to know. "What do we do now?"

"That comes later," I said. "First I'd like to tell you who they are."

"Let's hear."

"Their names are Gary Atwood and Lee David Cutler," I

said. "Skip calls them Frank and Jesse, as in the James brothers, and he may have been picking up on a family resemblance. Atwood and Cutler are cousins. Atwood lives in the East Village, way over in Alphabet City on Ninth Street between B and C. Cutler lives with his girlfriend. She's a schoolteacher and she lives in Washington Heights. Her name is Rita Donegian."

"An Armenian," Keegan said. "She must be a cousin of yours, John. The plot thickens."

"How'd you find them?" Kasabian wondered. "Have they done this before? Have they got records?"

"I don't think they have records," I said. "That's something I haven't checked yet because it didn't seem important. They probably have Equity cards."

"Huh?"

"Membership cards in Actors Equity," I said. "They're actors."

Skip said, "You're kidding."

"No."

"I'll be a son of a bitch. It fits. It fucking fits."

"You see it?"

"Of course I see it," he said. "That's why the accents. That's why they seemed Irish when they hit Morrissey's. They didn't make a sound, they didn't *do* anything Irish, but it felt Irish because they were acting." He turned and glared at Bobby Ruslander. "Actors," he said. "I been robbed by fucking *actors*."

"You were robbed by two actors," Bobby said. "Not by the entire profession."

"Actors," Skip said. "John, we paid fifty thousand dollars to a couple of actors."

"They had real bullets in their guns," Keegan reminded him.

"Actors," Skip said. "We shoulda paid off in stage money."

I poured out more coffee from the insulated pitcher. I said, "I don't know what made me think of it. The thought was just there. But once I had it, I could see a lot of places it could have come from. One was a general impression, there was something off about them, some sense that we were getting a performance. And there was the very different performance at Morrissey's compared to the one staged for us Monday night. Once we knew it was the same two men both times, the difference in their manner became noteworthy."

"I don't see how that makes them actors," Bobby said. "It just makes them phonies."

"There were other things," I said. "They moved like people who were professionally conscious of movement. Skip, you commented that they could have been dancers, that their movements might have been choreographed. And there was a line one of them said, and it was so out of character it could only be *in* character—in character for the person if not for the role he was playing."

Skip said, "Which line was that? Was I there to hear it?"

"In the church basement. When you and the one in the yellow wig moved the extra furniture out of the way."

"I remember. What did he say?"

"Something about not knowing whether the union would approve."

"Yeah, I remember him saying it. It was an odd line but I didn't pay attention."

"Neither did I, but it registered. And his voice was different when he delivered it, too."

He closed his eyes, thinking back. "You're right," he said.

Bobby said, "How does that make him an actor? All it makes him is a union member."

"The stagehands have a very strong union," I said, "and they make sure actors don't move scenery or do other similar jobs that would properly employ a stagehand. It was very much an actor's line and the delivery fit with that interpretation."

"How'd you get on to them in particular?" Kasabian asked. "Once you got that they were actors, you were still a long way from knowing their names and addresses."

"Ears," Skip said.

Everybody looked at him.

"He drew their ears," he said, pointing to me. "In his notebook. The ears are the hardest part of the body to disguise. Don't look at me, I got it from the horse's mouth. He made drawings of their ears."

"And did what?" Bobby demanded. "Advertised an open audition and looked at everybody's ears?"

"You could go through albums," Skip said. "Look at actors' publicity pictures, looking for the right pair of ears."

"When they take your picture for your passport," Billie Keegan said, "it has to show both your ears."

"Or what?"

"Or they won't give you a passport."

"Poor Van Gogh," Skip said. "The Man Without a Country."

"How did you find them?" Kasabian still wanted to know. "It couldn't have been ears."

"No, of course not," I said.

"The license number," Billie said. "Has everyone forgotten the license number?"

"The license number turned up on the hot-car sheet," I told him. "Once I got the idea that they were actors, I took another look at the church. I knew they hadn't just picked that particular church basement at random and broken into it. They had access to it, probably with a key. According to the pastor, there were a lot of community groups with access, and probably a great many keys in circulation. One of the groups he mentioned in passing was an amateur theater group that had used the basement room for auditions and rehearsals."

"Aha," someone said.

"I called the church, got the name of someone connected with the theater group. I managed to reach that person and explained that I was trying to contact an actor who had worked with the group within the past several months. I gave a physical description that would have fit either of the two men. Remember, aside from a two-inch difference in height, they were very similar in physical type."

"And did you get a name?"

"I got a couple of names. One of them was Lee David Cutler."

"And a bell rang," Skip said.

"What bell?" Kasabian said. "That was the first the name came up, wasn't it? Or am I missing something?"

"No, you're right," I told him. "At this point Cutler was just one of several names in my notebook. What I had to do was tie one of those names to the other crime."

"What other crime? Oh, Morrissey's. How? He's the one saloonkeeper doesn't hire out-of-work actors as waiters and bartenders. He's got his own family to work with."

I said, "What's on the ground floor, Skip?"

"Oh," he said.

Billie Keegan said, "That Irish theater. The Donkey Repertory Company or whatever they call it."

"I went there this afternoon," I said. "They were in final rehearsals for a new play, but I managed to drop Tim Pat's name and get a few minutes of one young woman's time. They have display posters in the lobby, individual promotional pictures of each cast member. Head shots, I think they're called. She showed me posters for the various casts of the plays they've staged over the past year. They do short runs, you know, so they've put on quite a few shows."

"And?"

"Lee David Cutler was in *Donnybrook*, a Brian Friel play that ran the last week of May and the first week of June. I recognized his picture before I saw the name under it. And I recognized his cousin's picture, too. The family resemblance is even stronger when they're not wearing disguises. In fact it's unmistakable. Maybe that helped them get the parts, since they're not regular members of the rep company. But they played two brothers, so the resemblance was a definite asset."

"Lee David Cutler," Skip said. "And what was the other one's name? Something Atwood."

"Gary Atwood."

"Actors."

"Right."

He tapped a cigarette on the back of his hand, put it in his mouth, lit it. "Actors. They were in the play on the ground floor and decided to move up in the world, is that it? Being there gave them the idea to hit Morrissey's."

"Probably." I took a slug of coffee. The Wild Turkey bottle was right there on the file cabinet, and my eyes were drawn to it, but right now I didn't want anything to take the edge off my perceptions. I was glad I wasn't drinking, and just as glad that everyone else was.

I said, "They must have had a drink upstairs once or twice in the course of the run of the play. Maybe they heard about the locked wall cupboard, maybe they saw Tim Pat put money into it or take some out of it. One way or another, it must have occurred to them that the place would be easy pickings."

"If you live to spend it."

"Maybe they didn't know enough to be afraid of the Morrisseys. That's possible. They probably started planning the job as a lark, making a play out of it, casting themselves as members of some other Irish faction, silent gunmen out of some old play about the Troubles. Then they got carried away with the possibilities of it, went out and got some guns and staged their play."

"Just like that."

I shrugged. "Or maybe they've pulled stickups before. There's no reason to assume Morrissey's was their debut."

"I suppose it beats walking people's dogs and working office temp," Bobby said. "The hell, an actor's got to make a living. Maybe I ought to get myself a mask and a gun."

"You tend bar sometimes," Skip said. "It's the same idea and you don't need props for it."

"How'd they get on to us?" Kasabian asked. "Did they start hanging out here while they were working at the Irish theater?"

"Maybe."

"But that wouldn't explain how they knew about the books," he said. "Skip, did they ever work for us? Atwood and Cutler? Do we know those names?"

"I don't think so."

"I don't either," I said. "They may have known the place, but it's not important. They almost certainly didn't work here because they didn't know Skip by sight."

"That could have been part of the act," Skip suggested.

"Possibly. As I said, it doesn't really matter. They had an inside man who stole the books and arranged for them to ransom them."

"An inside man?"

I nodded. "That's what we figured from the beginning, remember? That's why you hired me, Skip. Partly to see that the exchange went off without a hitch and partly to find out after the fact who it was that set you up."

"Right."

"Well, that's how they got the books, and that's how they got on to you in the first place. For all I know they never set foot inside Miss Kitty's. They didn't have to. They had it all set up for them."

"By an inside man."

"That's right."

"And you know who the inside man was?"

"Yes," I said. "I know."

The room got very quiet. I walked around the desk and took the bottle of Wild Turkey from the top of the file cabinet. I poured a couple of ounces into a rocks glass and put the bottle back. I held the glass without tasting the whiskey. I didn't want the drink so much as I wanted to stretch the moment and let the tension build.

I said, "The inside man had a role to play afterward, too. He had to let Atwood and Cutler know that we got their license number."

Bobby said, "I thought the car was stolen."

"The car was reported stolen. That's how it got on the hot-car sheet. Stolen between five and seven P.M. Monday from an address on Ocean Parkway."

"So?"

"That was the report, and at the time I let it go at that. This afternoon I did what I probably should have done off the bat, and I got the name of the car's owner. It was Rita Donegian."

"Atwood's girlfriend," Skip said.

"Cutler's. Not that it makes a difference."

"I'm confused," Kasabian said. "He stole his girl-friend's car? I don't get it."

"Everyone picks on the Armenians," Keegan said.

I said, "They took her car. Atwood and Cutler took Rita Donegian's car. Afterward they got a call from their accomplice telling them that the plate had been spotted. So they called in then and reported it as having been stolen, and they said it had been taken thus and so many hours earlier, and from an address way out on Ocean Parkway. When I dug a little deeper this afternoon I managed to establish that the report of the theft hadn't been called in until close to midnight.

"I've got things a little out of sequence. The hot-car sheet didn't carry the name of the Mercury's owner as Rita Donegian. It was an Irish name, Flaherty or Farley, I forget, and the address was the one on Ocean Parkway. There was a phone number, but it turned out to be wrong, and I couldn't pick up any listing for the Flaherty or Farley name at that address. So I checked Motor Vehicles, working from the plate number, and the car's owner turned out to be Rita Donegian with an address on Cabrini Boulevard, which is way up in Washington Heights and a long ways from Ocean Parkway or any other part of Brooklyn."

I drank some of the Wild Turkey.

"I called Rita Donegian," I said. "I represented myself as a cop checking the hot-car sheet automatically, making sure what cars have been recovered and what ones are still missing. Oh, yes, she said, they got the car back right away. She didn't think it was really stolen after all; her husband had a few drinks and forgot where he parked it, then found it a couple blocks away after she'd gone and reported it stolen. I said we must have made a clerical error, we had the car listed as stolen in Brooklyn and here she was in upper Manhattan. No, she said, they were visiting her husband's brother in Brooklyn. I said we had an error in the name, too, that it was Flaherty, whatever the hell it was. No, she said, that was no error, that was the brother's name. Then she got a little rattled and explained it was her husband's brother-in-law, actually, that her husband's sister had married a man named Flaherty."

"A poor Armenian girl," Keegan said, "gone to ruination with the Irish. Think of it, Johnny."

Skip said, "Was any of what she said true?"

"I asked her if she was Rita Donegian and if she was the

owner of a Mercury Marquis with the license number LJK-914. She said yes to both of those questions. That was the last time she told me the truth. She told a whole string of lies, and she knew she was covering for them or she'd never have been so inventive. She hasn't got a husband. She might refer to Cutler as her husband but she was calling him Mr. Donegian, and the only Mr. Donegian is her father. I didn't want to push too hard because I didn't want her to get the idea that my call was anything beyond simple routine."

Skip said, "Somebody called them *after* the payoff. To tell them we had the plate number."

"That's right."

"So who knew? The five of us and who else? Keegan, did you get waxed and tell a roomful of people how you were the hero and wrote down the plate number? Is that what happened?"

"I went to confession," Billie said, "and I told Father O'Houlihan."

"I'm serious, goddammit."

"I never did trust the shifty-eyed bastard," Billie said.

Gently, John Kasabian said, "Skip, I don't think anybody told anybody. I think that's what Matt's leading up to. It was one of us, wasn't it, Matt?"

Skip said, "One of us? One of us *here?*"

"Wasn't it, Matt?"

"That's right," I said. "It was Bobby."

23

The silence stretched, with everybody looking at Bobby. Then Skip let out a fierce laugh that caromed wildly around the room.

"Matt, you fuck," he said. "You had me going there. You just about had me buying it."

"It's true, Skip."

"Because I'm an actor, Matt?" Bobby grinned at me. "You figure all actors know each other, the way Billie figured Kasabian would have to know the schoolteacher. For Christ's sake, there's probably more actors in this town than there are Armenians."

"Two much-maligned groups," Keegan intoned. "Actors and Armenians, both of them much given to starving."

"I never heard of these guys," Bobby said. "Atwood and Cutler? Are those their names? I never heard of either of them."

I said, "It won't wash, Bobby. You were in classes with Gary Atwood at the New York Academy of Dramatic Arts. You were in a showcase at the Galinda Theater on Second Avenue last year, and that was one of Lee David Cutler's credits."

232

"You're talking about that Strindberg thing? Six performances to a roomful of empty seats and not even the director knew what the play was supposed to be about? Oh, that was Cutler, the thin guy who played Berndt? Is that who you mean?"

I didn't say anything.

"The Lee threw me. Everybody called him Dave. I suppose I remember him but—"

"Bobby, you son of a bitch, you're lying!"

He turned, looked at Skip. He said, "Am I, Arthur? Is that what you think?"

"It's what I fucking know. I know you, I know you all my life. I know when you're lying."

"The Human Polygraph." He sighed. "Happens you're right."

"I don't believe it."

"Well, make up your mind, Arthur. You're a hard man to agree with. Either I'm lying or I'm not. Which way do you want it?"

"You robbed me. You stole the books, you sold me down the fucking river. How could you do it? You little fuck, how could you do it?"

Skip was standing up. Bobby was still sitting in his chair, an empty glass in his hand. Keegan and John Kasabian were on either side of Bobby, but they drew a little ways away from him during this exchange, as if to give them room.

I was standing to Skip's right, and I was watching Bobby. He took his time with the question, as if it deserved careful consideration.

"Well, hell," he said finally. "Why would anybody do it? I wanted the money."

"How much did they give you?"

"Not all that much, tell you the truth."

"How much?"

"I wanted, you know, a third. They laughed. I wanted ten, they said five, we wound up at seven grand." He spread his hands. "I'm a lousy negotiator. I'm an actor, I'm not a businessman. What do I know about haggling?"

"You screwed me for seven thousand dollars."

"Listen, I wish it was more. Believe me."

"Don't joke with me, you cocksucker."

"Then don't feed me straight lines, you asshole."

Skip closed his eyes. The sweat was beading up on his forehead and tendons showed in his neck. His hands knotted into fists, relaxed, knotted up again. He was breathing through his mouth like a fighter between rounds.

He said, "Why'd you need the money?"

"Well, see, my kid sister needs this operation, and—"

"Bobby, don't clown with me. I'll fucking kill you, I swear it."

"Yeah? I needed the money, believe it. I was gonna need the operation. I was gonna get my legs broken."

"What the hell are you talking about?"

"I'm talking about I borrowed five thousand dollars and put it into a cocaine deal and it fell in the shit, and I had to pay back the five because I didn't borrow it from Chase Manhattan. I haven't got that good of a friend there. I borrowed it from a guy out in Woodside who told me my legs were all the collateral I'd need."

"What the hell were you doing in a coke deal?"

"Trying to make a dollar for a change. Trying to get out from under."

"You make it sound like the American Dream."

"It was a fucking nightmare. The deal went in the toilet, I still owed the money, I had to come up with a hundred a week just to keep paying the vig. You know how it works. You pay a hundred a week forever and you still owe the five grand, and I can't cover my expenses to begin with, never mind finding another hundred a week. I was running behind, and there's interest on the interest, and the seven grand I got from Cutler and Atwood, it's fucking *gone*, man. I paid the shy six grand to get him off my back forever, I paid some other debts I owed, I got a couple hundred dollars in my wallet. That's what's left." He shrugged. "Easy come, easy go. Right?"

Skip put a cigarette in his mouth and fumbled with his lighter. He dropped it, and when he reached to pick it up he accidentally kicked it under the desk. Kasabian put a hand on his shoulder to steady him, then lit a match and gave him a light. Billie Keegan got down on the floor and looked around until he found the lighter.

Skip said, "You know what you cost me?"

"I cost you twenty grand. I cost John thirty."

"You cost us each twenty-five. I owe Johnny five, he knows he'll get it."

"Whatever you say."

"You cost us fifty thousand fucking dollars so you could wind up with seven. What am I talking about? You cost us fifty thousand dollars so you could wind up even."

"I said I got no head for business."

"You got no head at all, Bobby. You needed money, you could have sold your friends to Tim Pat Morrissey for ten grand. That's the reward he was offering, that's three thousand more than they gave you."

"I wasn't gonna rat 'em out."

"No, of course not. But you'd sell me'n John down shit creek, wouldn't you?"

Bobby shrugged.

Skip dropped his cigarette on the floor, stepped on it. "You needed money," he said, "why didn't you come and ask me for it? Will you just tell me that? You coulda come to me before you went to the shy. Or the shy's pushing you, you need money to cover, you could of come to me then."

"I didn't want to ask you for the money."

"You didn't want to ask me for it. It's okay to steal it from me, but you didn't want to ask me for it."

Bobby drew back his head. "Yeah, that's right, Arrrr-thur. I didn't want to ask you for it."

"Did I ever refuse you?"

"No."

"Did I ever make you crawl?"

"Yeah."

"When?"

"All the time. Let the actor play bartender for a while. Let's put the actor behind the stick, hope he don't give away the whole store. It's a big joke, my acting. I'm your little windup toy, your fucking pet actor."

"You don't think I take your acting seriously?"

"Of course you don't."

"I can't believe I'm hearing this. That piece of shit you were in on Second Avenue, fucking Strindberg, how many people did I bring to see that? There was twenty-five people in the house and I brought twenty of them."

"To see your pet actor. 'That piece of shit you were in.' That's taking my acting seriously, Skippy baby. That's real support."

"I don't fucking believe this," Skip said. "You hate me." He looked around the room. "He hates me."

Bobby just looked at him.

"You did this to screw me. That's all."

"I did it for the money."

"I woulda given you the fucking money!"

"I didn't want to take it from you."

"You didn't want to take it from me. Where do you think you did take it from, you cocksucker? You think it came from God? You think it rained outta the sky?"

"I figure I earned it."

"You what?"

Bobby shrugged. "Like I said. I figure I earned it. I worked for it. I was with you, I don't know how many times, from the day I took the books. I was along for the ride Monday night, on the scene, everything. And you never had the least suspicion. That's not the worst job of acting anybody ever did."

"Just an acting job."

"You could look at it that way."

"Judas was pretty good, too. He got an Oscar nomination but he couldn't be present at the awards ceremony."

"You make a funny-looking Jesus, Arthur. You're just not right for the part."

Skip stared hard at him. "I don't get it," he said. "You're not even ashamed of yourself."

"Would that make you happy? A little show of shame?"

"You think it's okay, right? Putting your best friend through hell, costing him a lot of money? Stealing from him?"

"You never stole, right, Arthur?"

"What are you talking about?"

"How'd you come up with twenty grand, Arthur? What did you do, save your lunch money?"

"We skimmed it. That's not much of a secret. You mean I stole from the government? Show me anybody with a cash business who doesn't."

"And how did you get the money to open the joint? How did you and John get started? Did you skim that, too? Tips you didn't declare?"

"So?"

"Bullshit! You worked behind the stick at Jack Balkin's joint and you stole with both hands. You did everything but take the empties to the grocery store for the deposit. You stole so much offa Jack it's a wonder he didn't have to close the place."

"He made money."

"Yeah, and so did you. You stole, and Johnny stole where he was working, and lo and behold, the two of you got enough to open a place of your own. Talk about the

American Dream, that's the American Dream. Steal from the boss until you can afford to open up in competition with him."

Skip said something inaudible.

"What's that? I can't hear you, Arthur."

"I said bartenders steal. It's expected."

"Makes it honest, right?"

"I didn't screw Balkin. I made money for him. You can twist it all you want, Bobby, you can't make me into what you are."

"No, you're a fucking saint, Arthur."

"Jesus," Skip said. "I don't know what to do. I don't know what I'm going to do."

"I do. You're not gonna do anything."

"I'm not?"

Bobby shook his head. "What are you gonna do? You gonna get the gun from behind the bar, come back and shoot me with it? You're not gonna do that."

"I ought to."

"Yeah, but it's not gonna happen. You want to hit me? You're not even mad anymore, Arthur. You think you oughta be mad but you don't feel it. You don't feel anything."

"I—"

"Listen, I'm beat," Bobby said. "I'm gonna make it an early night if nobody objects. Listen, guys, I'll pay it back one of these days. The whole fifty thousand. When I'm a star, you know? I'm good for it."

"Bobby—"

"I'll see you," he said.

After the three of us had walked Skip around the corner and said goodnight to him, after John Kasabian had flagged a cab and headed uptown, I stood on the corner with Billie

Keegan and told him I'd made a mistake, that I shouldn't have told Skip what I'd learned.

"No," he said. "You had to."

"Now he knows his best friend hates his guts." I turned, looked up at the Parc Vendome. "He lives on a high floor," I said. "I hope he doesn't decide to go out a window."

"He's not the type."

"I guess not."

"You had to tell him," Billie Keegan said. "What are you gonna do, let him go on thinking Bobby's his friend? That kind of ignorance isn't bliss. What you did, you lanced a boil for him. Right now it hurts like a bastard but it'll heal. You leave it, it just gets worse."

"I suppose."

"Count on it. If Bobby got by with this he'd do something else. He'd keep on until Skip knew about it, because it's not enough to screw Skip, Bobby's gotta rub his nose in it while he's at it. You see what I mean?"

"Yeah."

"Am I right?"

"Probably. Billie? I want to hear that song."

"Huh?"

"The sacred ginmill, cuts the brain in sections. The one you played for me."

"'Last Call.'"

"You don't mind?"

"Hey, come on up. We'll have a couple."

We didn't really drink much. I went with him to his apartment and he played the song five, six times for me. We talked a little, but mostly we just listened to the record. When I left he told me again that I'd done the right thing in exposing Bobby Ruslander. I still wasn't sure he was right.

24

I slept late the next day. That night I went out to Sunnyside Gardens in Queens with Danny Boy Bell and two uptown friends of his. There was a middleweight on the card, a Bedford-Stuyvesant kid Danny Boy's friends had an interest in. He won his fight handily, but I didn't think he showed a whole lot.

The following day was Friday, and I was having a late lunch in Armstrong's when Skip came in and had a beer with me. He'd just come from the gym and he was thirsty.

"Jesus, I was strong today," he said. "All the anger goes right into the muscles. I could have lifted the roof off the place. Matt? Did I patronize him?"

"What do you mean?"

"All that shit about I made him my pet actor. Was that true?"

"I think he was just looking for a way to justify what he did."

"I don't know," he said. "Maybe I do what he said. Remember you got a hair up your ass when I paid your bar tab?"

"So?"

"Maybe I did that with him. But on a bigger scale." He lit a cigarette, coughed hard. Recovering, he said, "Fuck it, the man's a scumbag. That's all. I'm just gonna forget about it."

"What else can you do?"

"I wish I knew. He'll pay me back when he's rich and famous, I liked that part. Is there any way we can get the money back from those other two fucks? We know who they are."

"What can you threaten them with?"

"I don't know. Nothing, I guess. The other night you gathered everybody together for a war council, but that was just setting the stage, wasn't it? To have everybody on hand when you put it all on Bobby."

"It seemed like a good idea."

"Yeah. But as far as having a war council, or whatever you want to call it, and figuring out a way to sandbag those actors and get the money back—"

"I can't see it."

"No, neither can I. What am I gonna do, stick up the stickup men? Not really my style. And the thing is, it's only money. I mean that's really all it is. I had this money in the bank, where I wasn't really getting anything out of it, and now I haven't got it, and what difference does it make in my life? You know what I mean?"

"I think so."

"I just wish I could let go of it," he said, "because I go around and around and around with it in my mind. I just wish I could leave it alone."

I had my sons with me that weekend. It was going to be our last weekend together before they went off to camp. I picked them up at the train station Saturday morning and put them back on the train Sunday night. We saw a movie, I remember, and I think we spent Sunday morning exploring down around Wall Street and the Fulton Fish Market, but that may have been a different weekend. It's hard to distinguish them in memory.

I spent Sunday evening in the Village and didn't get back to my hotel until almost dawn. The telephone woke me out of a frustrating dream, an exercise in acrophobic frustration; I kept trying to descend from a perilous catwalk and kept not reaching the ground.

I picked up the phone. A gruff voice said, "Well, it's not the way I figured it would go, but at least we don't have to worry about losing it in court."

"Who is this?"

"Jack Diebold. What's the matter with you? You sound like you're half asleep."

"I'm up now," I said. "What were you talking about?"

"You haven't seen a paper?"

"I was sleeping. What did—"

"You know what time it is? It's almost noon. You're keeping pimp's hours, you son of a bitch."

"Jesus," I said.

"Go get yourself a newspaper," he said. "I'll call you in an hour."

The *News* gave it the front page. KILL SUSPECT HANGS SELF IN CELL, with the story on page three.

Miguelito Cruz had torn his clothing into strips, knotted the strips together, stood his iron bedstead on its side, climbed onto it, looped his homemade rope around an overhead pipe, and jumped off the upended bedstead and into the next world.

Jack Diebold never did call me back, but that evening's six o'clock TV news had the rest of the story. Informed of his friend's death, Angel Herrera had recanted his original story and admitted that he and Cruz had conceived and executed the Tillary burglary on their own. It had been Miguelito who heard noises upstairs and picked up a kitchen knife on his way to investigate. He'd stabbed the woman to death while Herrera watched in horror. Miguelito always had a short temper, Herrera said, but they were friends, even cousins, and they had concocted their story to protect Miguelito. But now that Miguelito was dead, Herrera could admit what had really happened.

The funny thing was that I felt like going out to Sunset Park. I was done with the case, everyone was done with the case, but I felt as though I ought to be working my way through the Fourth Avenue bars, buying rum drinks for ladies and eating bags of plantain chips.

Of course I didn't go there. I never really considered it. I just had the feeling that it was something I ought to do.

That night I was in Armstrong's. I wasn't drinking particularly hard or fast, but I was working at it, and then somewhere around ten-thirty or eleven the door opened and I knew who it was before I turned around. Tommy Tillary, all dressed up and freshly barbered, was making his first appearance in Armstrong's since his wife got herself killed.

"Hey, look who's back," he sang out, and grinned that big grin. People rushed over to shake his hand. Billie was behind the stick, and he'd no sooner set up one on the house for our hero than Tommy insisted on buying a round for the bar. It was an expensive gesture, there must have been thirty or forty people in there, but I don't think he cared if there were three or four hundred.

I stayed where I was, letting the others mob him, but he worked his way over to me and got an arm around my shoulders. "This is the man," he announced. "Best fucking detective ever wore out a pair of shoes. This man's money," he told Billie, "is no good at all tonight. He can't buy a drink, he can't buy a cup of coffee, and if you went and put in pay toilets since I was last here, he can't use his own dime."

"The john's still free," Billie said, "but don't go giving Jimmy any ideas."

"Oh, don't tell me he didn't already think of it," Tommy said. "Matt, my boy, I love you. I was in a tight spot, the world was lookin' to fall in on me, and you came through for me."

What the hell had I done? I hadn't hanged Miguelito Cruz or coaxed a confession out of Angel Herrera. I hadn't even set eyes on either man. But I had taken his money, and now it looked as though I had to let him buy my drinks.

I don't know how long we stayed there. Curiously, my own drinking slowed even as Tommy's picked up speed. I wondered why he hadn't brought Carolyn; I didn't figure he'd care much about appearances now that the case was closed forever. And I wondered if she would walk in. It was, after all, her neighborhood bar, and she'd been known to come to it all by herself.

After a while Tommy was hustling me out of Armstrong's, so maybe I wasn't the only one who realized that Carolyn might turn up. "This is celebration time," he told me. "We don't want to hang around one place until we grow roots. We want to get out and bounce a little."

He had the Riviera, and I just went along for the ride. We hit a few places. There was a noisy Greek place on the East Side where the waiters all looked like mob hit men. There were a couple of trendy singles joints, including the one Jack Balkin owned, where Skip had reportedly stolen enough money to open Miss Kitty's. There was, finally, a dark beery cave down in the Village; I realized after a while that it reminded me of the Norwegian bar in Sunset Park, the Fjord. I knew the Village bars fairly well in those days, but this place was new to me, and I was never able to find it again. Maybe it wasn't in the Village, maybe it was somewhere in Chelsea. He was doing the driving and I wasn't paying too much attention to the geography.

Wherever the place was, it was quiet for a change and conversation became possible. I found myself asking him what I'd done that deserved such lavish praise. One man had killed himself and another had confessed, and what part had I played in either incident?

"The stuff you came up with," he said.

"What stuff? I should have brought back fingernail parings, you could have had someone work voodoo on them."

"About Cruz and the fairies."

"He was up for murder. He didn't hang himself because he was afraid they'd nail him for fag-bashing when he was a juvenile offender."

Tommy took a sip of scotch. He said, "Couple days ago, black guy comes up to Cruz in the chow line. Huge spade, built like the Seagram's Building. 'Wait'll you gets up to Green Haven,' he tells him. 'Every blood there's gwine have you for a girlfriend. Doctor gwine have to cut you a brand-new asshole, time you gets outta there.'"

I didn't say anything.

"Kaplan," he said. "Talked to somebody who talked to somebody, and that did it. Cruz took a good look at the idea of playin' Drop the Soap for half the jigs in captivity, and the next thing you know the murderous little bastard was dancing on air. And good riddance to him."

I couldn't seem to catch my breath. I worked on it while Tommy went to the bar for another round. I hadn't touched the one in front of me but I let him buy for both of us.

When he got back I said, "Herrera."

"Changed his story. Made a full confession."

"And pinned the killing on Cruz."

"Why not? Cruz wasn't around to complain. Cruz probably did it, but who knows which one it really was, and for that matter who cares? The thing is you gave us the lever."

"For Cruz," I said. "To get him to kill himself."

"And for Herrera. Those kids of his back in Puerto Rico. Drew spoke to Herrera's lawyer and Herrera's lawyer spoke to Herrera, and the message was, look, you're going up for burglary whatever you do, and probably for murder, but if you tell the right story you'll draw shorter time than if you don't, and on top of that, that nice Mr. Tillary's gonna let bygones be bygones and every month there's a nice check for your wife and kiddies back home in Santurce."

At the bar, a couple of old men were reliving the Louis-Schmeling fight. The second one, the one where Louis deliberately punished the German champion. One of the old boys was throwing roundhouse punches in the air, demonstrating.

I said, "Who killed your wife?"

"One or the other of them. If I had to bet I'd say Cruz. He had those beady little eyes, you looked at him up close and got that he was a killer."

"When did you look at him close?"

"When they were over to the house. The first time, when they cleaned the basement and the attic. I told you they hauled stuff for me?"

"You told me."

"Not the second time," he said, "when they cleaned me out altogether."

He smiled broadly, but I kept looking at him until the smile turned uncertain. "That was Herrera who helped around the house," I said. "You never met Cruz."

"Cruz came along, gave him a hand."

"You never mentioned that before."

"I must of, Matt. Or I left it out. What difference does it make, anyway?"

"Cruz wasn't much for manual labor," I said. "He wouldn't come along to haul trash. When did you ever get a look at his eyes?"

"Jesus Christ. Maybe it was seeing a picture in the paper, maybe I just have a sense of him as if I saw his eyes. Leave it alone, will you? Whatever kind of eyes he had, they're not seeing anything anymore."

"Who killed her, Tommy?"

"Hey, didn't I say let it alone?"

"Answer the question."

"I already answered it."

"You killed her, didn't you?"

"What are you, crazy? And keep your voice down, for Christ's sake. There's people can hear you."

"You killed your wife."

"Cruz killed her and Herrera swore to it. Isn't that enough for you? And your fucking cop friend's been all over my alibi, pickin' at it like a monkey hunting lice. There's no way I coulda killed her."

"Sure there is."

"Huh?"

A chair covered in needlepoint, a view of Owl's Head Park. The smell of dust, and layered over it the smell of a spray of little white flowers.

"Lily-of-the-valley," I said.

"Huh?"

"That's how you did it."

"What are you talking about?"

"The third floor, the room her aunt used to live in. I smelled her perfume up there. I thought I was just carrying the scent in my nostrils from being in her bedroom earlier, but that wasn't it. She was up there, and it was traces of her perfume I was smelling. That's why the room held me, I sensed her presence there, the room was trying to tell me something but I couldn't get it."

"I don't know what you're talking about. You know what you are, Matt? You're a little drunk is all. You'll wake up tomorrow and—"

"You left the office at the end of the day, rushed home to Bay Ridge, and stowed her on the third floor. What did you do, drug her? You probably slipped her a mickey, maybe left her tied up in the room on the third floor. Tied her up, gagged her, left her unconscious. Then you got your ass back to Manhattan and went out to dinner with Carolyn."

"I'm not listening to this shit."

"Herrera and Cruz showed up around midnight, just the way you arranged it. They thought they were knocking off an empty house. Your wife was gagged and tucked away on the third floor and they had no reason to go up there. You probably locked the door there anyway just to make sure. They pulled their burglary and went home, figuring it was the safest and easiest illegal buck they ever turned."

I picked up my glass. Then I remembered he had bought the drink, and I started to put it down. I decided that was ridiculous. Just as money knows no owner, whiskey never remembers who paid for it.

I took a drink.

I said, "Then a couple hours after that you jumped in your car and raced back to Bay Ridge again. Maybe you slipped something into your girlfriend's drink to keep her out of it. All you had to do was find an hour, hour and a half, and there's room enough in your alibi to find ninety spare minutes. The drive wouldn't take you long, not at that hour. Nobody would see you drive in. You just had to go up to the third floor, carry your wife down a flight, stab her to death, get rid of the knife, and drive back into the city. That's how you did it, Tommy. Isn't it?"

"You're full of shit, you know that?"

"Tell me you didn't kill her."

"I already told you."

"Tell me again."

"I didn't kill her, Matt. I didn't kill anybody."

"Again."

"What's the matter with you? I didn't kill her. Jesus, you're the one helped prove it, and now you're trying to twist and turn it back on me. I swear to Christ I didn't kill her."

"I don't believe you."

A man at the bar was talking about Rocky Marciano. There was the best fighter ever lived, he said. He wasn't pretty, he wasn't fancy, but it was a funny thing, he was always on his feet at the end of the fight and the other guy wasn't.

"Oh, Jesus," Tommy said.

He closed his eyes, put his head in his hands. He sighed and looked up and said, "You know, it's a funny thing with me. Over the phone I'm as good a salesman as Marciano was a fighter. I'm the best you could ever imagine. I swear I could sell sand to the Arabs, I could sell ice in the winter, but face-to-face I'm just no good at all. Wasn't for phones, I'd have trouble making a living selling. Why do you figure that is?"

"You tell me."

"I swear I don't know. I used to think it was my face, around the eyes and mouth, *I* don't know. Over the phone's a cinch. I'm talkin' to a stranger, I don't know who he is or what he looks like, and he's not lookin' at me, and there's nothing to it. Face-to-face, somebody I know, whole different story." He looked at me, his eyes not quite meeting mine. "If we were doin' this over the phone, you'd buy what I'm telling you."

"It's possible."

"It's fucking certain. Word for word, you'd buy the package. Matt, suppose for the sake of argument I said I killed her. It was an accident, it was an impulse, we were both upset over the burglary, I was half in the bag, and—"

"You planned the whole thing, Tommy. It was all set up and worked out."

"The whole story you told, the way you worked it all out, there's not a thing you can prove."

I didn't say anything.

"And you helped me, don't forget that part of it."

"I won't."

"And I wouldn'ta gone away for it anyway, with or without you, Matt. It wouldn'ta got to court, and if it did I'da beat it in court. All you saved is a hassle. And you know something?"

"What?"

"All we got tonight is the booze talking, your booze and my booze, two bottles of whiskey talkin' to each other. That's all. Morning comes, we can forget everything was said here tonight. I didn't kill anybody, you didn't say I did, everything's cool, we're still buddies. Right? Right?"

I just looked at him.

25

That was Monday night. I don't remember exactly when I talked to Jack Diebold, but it must have been Tuesday or Wednesday. I tried him at the squad room and wound up reaching him at home. We sparred a bit, and then I said, "You know, I thought of a way he could have done it."

"Where have you been? We got one dead and one confessed to it, it's history now."

"I know," I said, "but listen to this." And I explained, just as an exercise in applied logic, how Tommy Tillary could have murdered his wife. I had to go over it a couple of times before he got a handle on it, and even then he wasn't crazy about it.

"I don't know," he said. "It sounds pretty complicated. You've got her stuck there in the attic for what, eight, ten hours? That's a long time with no one keeping an eye on her. Suppose she comes to, works herself free? Then he's got his ass in the crack, doesn't he?"

"Not for murder. She can press charges for tying her up, but when's the last time a husband went to jail for that?"

"Yeah, he's not really at risk until he kills her, and by

251

then she's dead. I see what you mean. Even so, Matt, it's pretty farfetched, don't you think?"

"Well, I was just thinking of a way it could have happened."

"They never happen that way in real life."

"I guess not."

"And if they did you couldn't go anywheres with it. Look what you went through explaining it to me, and I'm in the business. You want to try it on a jury, with some prick lawyer interrupting every thirty seconds with an objection? What a jury likes, a jury likes somebody with greasy hair and olive skin and a knife in one hand and blood on his shirt, that's what a jury likes."

"Yeah."

"And anyhow, the whole thing's history. You know what I got now? I got that family in Borough Park. You read about it?"

"The Orthodox Jews?"

"Three Orthodox Jews, mother father son, the father's got the beard, the kid's got the earlocks, all sitting at the dinner table, all shot in the back of the head. That's what I got. Far as Tommy Tillary, I don't care right now if he killed Cock Robin and both Kennedys."

"Well, it was just an idea," I said.

"And it's a cute one, I'll grant you that. But it's not very realistic, and even if it was, who's got time for it? You know?"

I figured it was time for a drunk. My two cases were closed, albeit unsatisfactorily. My sons were on their way to camp. My rent was paid, my bar tabs were all settled, and I had a few dollars in the bank. I had, it seemed to me, every reason in the world to check out for a week or so and stay drunk.

But my body seemed to know there was more to come,

and while I did not by any means stay sober, neither did I find myself launched upon the bender to which I felt roundly entitled. And, a day or two later, I was nursing a cup of bourbon-flavored coffee at my table in Armstrong's when Skip Devoe came in.

He gave me a nod from the doorway. Then he went to the bar and had a quick drink, knocking it back while he stood there. And then he came back to my table and pulled out a chair and dropped down into it.

"Here," he said, and put a brown manila envelope on the table between us. A small envelope, the kind they give you in banks.

I said, "What's this?"

"For you."

I opened it. It was full of money. I took out a sheaf of bills and fanned them.

"For Christ's sake," he said, "don't do that, you want everybody following you home? Put it in your pocket, count it when you get home."

"What is it?"

"Your share. Put it away, will you?"

"My share of what?"

He sighed, impatient with me. He had a cigarette going and he dragged angrily on it, turning his head to avoid blowing the smoke in my face. "Your share of ten grand," he said. "You get half. Half of ten grand is five grand, and five grand is what's in the envelope, and whyntcha do us both a favor and put it the hell away?"

"What's this my share of, Skip?"

"The reward."

"What reward?"

His eyes challenged me. "Well, I could get something back, couldn't I? No way I owed those cocksuckers anything. Right?"

"I don't know what you're talking about."

"Atwood and Cutler," he said. "I turned 'em in to Tim Pat Morrissey. For the reward."

I looked at him.

"I couldn't go to them, ask for the money back. I couldn't get a dime from fuckin' Ruslander, he already paid it all out. I went over and sat down with Tim Pat, asked him did he and his brothers still want to pay out that reward. His eyes lit up like fucking stars. I gave him names and addresses and I thought he was gonna kiss me."

I put the brown envelope on the table between us. I pushed it toward him and he pushed it back. I said, "This doesn't belong to me, Skip."

"Yes it does. I already told Tim Pat half of it was yours, that you did all the work. Take it."

"I don't want it. I already got paid for what I did. The information was yours. You bought it. If you sold it to Tim Pat, you get the reward."

He drew on his cigarette. "I already gave half of it to Kasabian. The five grand I owed him. He didn't want to take it either. I told him, listen, you take this and we're square. He took it. And this here is yours."

"I don't want it."

"It's money. What the hell's the matter with it?"

I didn't say anything.

"Look," he said, "just take it, will you? You don't want to keep it, don't keep it. Burn it, throw it out, give it away, I don't give a shit what you do with it. Because I cannot keep it. I can't. You understand?"

"Why not?"

"Oh, shit," he said. "Oh, fucking shit. I don't know why I did it."

"What are you talking about?"

"And I'd do it again. That's what's crazy. It's eating me up, but if I had to do it all over again, I'd fucking do it."

"Do what?"

He looked at me. "I gave Tim Pat three names," he said, "and three addresses."

He took his cigarette between thumb and forefinger, stared at it. "I never want to see you do this," he said, and dropped the butt into my cup of coffee. Then he said, "Oh, Jesus, what am I doing? You had half a cup of coffee left there. I was thinking it was my cup and I didn't even have a cup. What's the matter with me? I'm sorry, I'll get you another cup of coffee."

"Forget the coffee."

"It was just reflex, I wasn't thinking, I—"

"Skip, forget the coffee. Sit down."

"You sure you don't want—"

"Forget the coffee."

"Yeah, right," he said. He took out another cigarette and tapped it against the back of his wrist.

I said, "You gave Tim Pat three names."

"Yeah."

"Atwood and Cutler and—"

"And Bobby," he said. "I sold him Bobby Ruslander."

He put the cigarette in his mouth, took out his lighter and lit it. His eyes half-lidded against the smoke, he said, "I ratted him out, Matt. My best friend, except it turns out he's not my friend, and now I went and ratted him out. I told Tim Pat how Bobby was the inside man, he set it up." He looked at me. "You think I'm a bastard?"

"I don't think anything."

"It was something I had to do."

"All right."

"But you can see I can't keep the money."

"Yeah, I guess I can see that."

"He could get out from under, you know. He's pretty good at squirming off the hook. The other night, Christ, he walked outta the office at my joint like he owned the place. The Actor, let's see him act his way outta this, huh?"

I didn't say anything.

"It could happen. He could pull it off."

"Could be."

He wiped his eyes with the back of his hand. "I loved the man," he said. "I thought, I thought he loved me." He took a deep breath, let it out. "From here on in," he said, "I don't love nobody." He stood up. "I figure he's got a sporting chance, anyway. Maybe he'll get out of it."

"Maybe."

But he didn't. None of them did. By the weekend they had all turned up in the newspapers, Gary Michael Atwood, Lee David Cutler, Robert Joel Ruslander, all three found in different parts of the city, their heads covered with black hoods, their hands secured with wire behind their backs, each shot once in the back of the head with a .25-caliber automatic. Rita Donegian was found with Cutler, similarly hooded and wired and shot. I guess she got in the way.

When I read about it I still had the money in the brown bank envelope. I still hadn't decided what to do with it. I don't know that I ever quite came to a conscious decision, but the following day I tithed five hundred dollars to the poor box at Saint Paul's. I had, after all, a lot of candles to light. And some of the money went to Anita, and some went in the bank, and somewhere along the line it stopped being blood money and became, well, just money.

I figured that was the end of it. But I kept figuring that, and I kept being wrong.

The call came in the middle of the night. I'd been asleep for a couple of hours but the phone woke me and I groped for it. It took me a minute to recognize the voice on the other end.

It was Carolyn Cheatham.

"I had to call you," she said, "on account of you're a

bourbon drinker and a gentleman. I owed it to you to call you."

"What's the matter?"

"Our mutual friend ditched me," she said, "and he got me fired out of Tannahill & Co. so he won't have to look at me around the office. Once he didn't need me he just went and cut the string, and do you know he did it over the *phone?*"

"Carolyn—"

"It's all in the note," she said. "I'm leaving a note."

"Look, don't do anything yet," I said. I was out of bed, fumbling for my clothes. "I'll be right over. We'll sit down and talk about it."

"You can't stop me, Matthew."

"I won't try to stop you. We'll talk a little, and then you can do whatever you want to do."

The phone clicked in my ear.

I threw my clothes on, rushed over there, hoping it would be pills, something that took its time. I broke a small pane of glass in the downstairs door and let myself in, then used an old credit card to slip the bolt of her spring lock. If she had engaged the dead-bolt lock, I would have had to kick it in, but she hadn't, and that made it easier.

I smelled the cordite before I had the door open. Inside, the room reeked of it. She was sprawled on the couch, her head hanging to one side. The gun was still in her hand, limp at her side, and there was a black-rimmed hole in her temple.

There was a note, too, one page torn from a spiral notebook and anchored to the coffee table with an empty bottle of Maker's Mark bourbon. There was an empty glass next to the empty bottle. The booze showed in her handwriting, and in the sullen phrasing of the suicide note.

I read the note. I stood there for a few minutes, not for very long, and then I got a dish towel from the kitchen and wiped the bottle and the glass. I took another matching glass, rinsed it out and wiped it, and put it in the dish strainer on the counter.

I stuffed the note in my pocket. I took the little gun from her fingers, checked routinely for a pulse, then wrapped a sofa pillow around the gun to muffle its report.

I fired one round into the soft tissue below the rib cage, another into her open mouth.

I dropped the gun into a pocket and got out of there.

They found the gun in Tommy Tillary's house on Colonial Road, stuffed between the cushions of the living-room sofa. The outside of the gun had been wiped clean of prints, but they found an identifiable print inside, on the clip, and it turned out to be Tommy's.

Ballistics got a perfect match. Bullets can shatter when they hit bone, but the shot into her abdomen didn't hit any bones and it was recovered intact.

After the story made the papers, I picked up the phone and called Drew Kaplan. "I don't understand it," I said. "He was free and clear, why the hell did he go and kill the girl?"

"Ask him yourself," Kaplan said. He did not sound happy. "You want my opinion, he's a lunatic. I honestly didn't think he was. I figured maybe he killed his wife, maybe he didn't, not my job to try him, right? But I didn't figure the son of a bitch for a homicidal maniac."

"There's no question he killed the girl?"

"No question that I can see. The gun's pretty strong evidence. Talk about finding somebody with the smoking pistol in his hand, here it was in Tommy's couch. The idiot."

"Funny he kept it."

"Maybe he had other people he wanted to shoot. Go figure a crazy man. No, the gun's damning evidence, and there was a phone tip, some man called in the shooting, reported a man running out of the building and gave a description that fitted Tommy better than his clothes. In fact his clothes were in the description. Had him wearing that red blazer of his, tacky thing makes him look like an usher at the old Brooklyn Paramount."

"It sounds tough to square."

"Well, somebody else'll have to try to do it," Kaplan said. "I told him it wouldn't be appropriate for me to defend him this time. What it amounts to, I wash my hands of him."

I thought of all this when I read that Angel Herrera got out just the other day. He did all ten years of a five-to-ten because he was at least as good at getting into trouble inside the walls as he had been outside.

Somebody killed Tommy Tillary with a homemade knife after he'd served two years and three months of a man-slaughter stretch. I wondered at the time if that was Herrera getting even, and I don't suppose I'll ever know. Maybe the checks stopped going to Santurce and Herrera took it the wrong way. Or maybe Tommy made the wrong remark to some other hard case, and did it face-to-face instead of over the phone.

So many things have changed, so many people are gone.

Antares & Spiro's, the Greek bar on the corner, is gone. It's a Korean fruit store now. Polly's Cage is now Cafe 57, changed from sleazy to chic, with the red flocked wallpaper and the neon parrot long gone. The Red Flame is gone, and the Blue Jay. There's a steak house called Desmond's where McGovern's used to be. Miss Kitty's closed about a year and a half after they bought their books back. John and Skip sold the lease and got out. The new owners opened a gay club called Kid Gloves, and two years later it was out and something else was in.

The gym where I watched Skip do lat-machine pulldowns went out of business within the year. A modern-dance studio took over the premises, and then a couple of years ago the whole building came down and a new one went up. Of the two side-by-side French restaurants, the one where I had dinner with Fran is gone, and the latest tenant is a fancy Indian restaurant. The other French place is still there, and I still haven't eaten there.

So many changes.

Jack Diebold is dead. A heart attack. He was dead six months before I even heard about it, but then we didn't have much contact after the Tillary incident.

John Kasabian left the city after he and Skip sold Miss Kitty's. He opened up a similar joint out in the Hamptons, and I heard he got married.

Morrissey's closed late in '77. Tim Pat skipped bail on a federal gunrunning charge and his brothers disappeared. The ground-floor theater is still running, oddly enough.

Skip is dead. He sort of hung around after Miss Kitty's closed, spending more and more of his time by himself in his apartment. Then one day he got an attack of acute pancreatitis and died on the table at Roosevelt.

Billie Keegan left Armstrong's in early '76, if I remember it right. Left Armstrong's and left New York, too. The last I heard he was off the drink entirely, living north of San Francisco and making candles or silk flowers or something equally unlikely. And I ran into Dennis a month or so ago in a bookstore on lower Fifth Avenue, full of odd volumes on yoga and spiritualism and holistic healing.

Eddie Koehler retired from the NYPD a couple of years back. I got cards from him the first two Christmases, mailed from a little fishing village in the Florida panhandle, I didn't hear from him last year, which probably only means that he's dropped me from his list, which is what happens to people who don't send cards in return.

Jesus, where did ten years go? I've got one son in college now, and another in the service. I couldn't tell you the last time we went to a ball game together, let alone a museum.

Anita's remarried. She still lives in Syosset, but I don't send money there anymore.

So many changes, eating away at the world like water dripping on a rock. For God's sake, last summer the sacred ginmill closed, if you want to call it that. The lease on Armstrong's came up for renewal and Jimmy walked away from it, and now there's yet another goddamned Chinese restaurant where the old joint used to be. He reopened a block farther west, at the corner of Fifty-seventh and Tenth, but that's a little out of my way these days.

In more ways than one. Because I don't drink anymore, one day at a time, and thus have no business in ginmills, be they sacred or profane. I spend less of my time lighting candles and more in church basements, drinking my coffee without bourbon, and out of styrofoam cups.

So when I look ten years into the past I can say that I would very likely have handled things differently now, but everything is different now. Everything. All changed, changed utterly. I live in the same hotel, I walk the same streets, I go to a fight or a ball game the same as ever, but ten years ago I was always drinking and now I don't drink at all. I don't regret a single one of the drinks I took, and I hope to God I never take another.

Because that, you see, is the less-traveled road on which I find myself these days, and it has made all the difference. Oh, yes. All the difference.

ABOUT THE AUTHOR

Lawrence Block's writing has won him the Nero Wolfe, Shamus, and Edgar Allan Poe awards, along with an increasing body of enthusiastic readers. His most recent novel about Matthew Scudder, *Eight Million Ways to Die*, was filmed, starring Jeff Bridges. Block is a member of the board of directors of the Mystery Writers of America and a past president of the Private Eye Writers of America. "Write for Your Life," his intensive seminar for writers, has revolutionized the teaching of writing. A New Yorker for many years, Lawrence Block now lives on the Florida Gulf Coast.